TWISTED REIGN

INDIE REIGN SERIES
BOOK 1

MARY STONE

KAREN GUYLER

MARY
STONE
PUBLISHING

Copyright © 2025 by Mary Stone Publishing

All rights reserved.

No part of this book may be reproduced in any form or by any electronic or mechanical means, including information storage and retrieval systems, without written permission from the author, except for the use of brief quotations in a book review.

❦ Formatted with Vellum

MARY STONE

For Copper, my miracle dog. I rescued you from the roadside, and you rescued me in return. Even now, fourteen years later—with cancer and failing kidneys—you face each day with joy, heart, and unshakable loyalty. This story is yours, my brave boy. My forever hero.

※

KAREN GUYLER

To my husband, our children and their partners. You're my world. I couldn't do it without your support and cheerleading.

DESCRIPTION

You can twist the truth, but you can't escape it.

Following her recent move back to the small Appalachian town where she grew up, memories shrouded in mystery haunt Indie Reign at every turn. Her family brutally taken. Her grandmother's unexplainable disappearance. And her unique gift with animals that no one can know about. Especially now that she's the Sherwood County Sheriff Department's new probationary K-9 detective.

Day one on the job, and death is already waiting.

A teenage girl is discovered hanging from a swing in her backyard. At first glance, it looks like suicide. But Indie's instincts say otherwise. Over the past eight months, the small town has mourned four suicides and six accidental deaths—all under eighteen. And three of the dead teens left behind a single, chilling word.

Ascension.

Indie doesn't believe in coincidences. Only patterns. And with the help of her new partner, Officer Broc—a sharp-minded Belgian Malinois with a nose for danger—she starts to unravel a disturbing truth. A hidden online community is targeting vulnerable kids, promising transformation through death.

Someone doesn't think they're killing teens.

They think they're saving them.

Twisted Reign is the gripping first book in the Indie Reign series by bestselling authors Mary Stone and Karen Guyler, where redemption, delusion, and justice collide—and survival demands sacrifice.

1

A late-night, *nothing to worry about* summer breeze stirred the leaves outside Nila Radler's bedroom window. Would it remain a gentle hand, tousling the trees like a loving parent? Or would it swell into an angry slap, a scolding punch, becoming another record-breaking storm?

Nila understood she was probably the only person in Sherwood County lying awake worrying about it.

That wasn't even the worst truth.

The worst truth was that no one seemed to care about the warnings Mother Nature was giving them. Didn't they panic about hurricanes getting more powerful, tornadoes more destructive, and storms more severe and frequent?

A few months ago, four families had lost their homes to flooding and winds. Nila had thought for sure they'd join her to raise awareness. But as soon as they replaced the last plank and threw out the last piece of water-logged furniture, they appeared to have forgotten the storm.

And no one seemed to believe it would happen again. But Nila knew better, even though she was just sixteen.

Why wouldn't the rest of the world listen? Nila's poems

and letters to the local paper, her online discussions, and even her leaflets, were easy to ignore. She didn't mind so much if people threw them out as long as they read them, as long as they recycled them.

If her dad had stayed, he'd have helped her. Encouraged people to take them. Together, they could've achieved so much. And if he'd stayed, her life now would be working out how it should've been. And maybe then everyone would be paying attention to the Earth screaming so Nila didn't feel all alone in her struggle.

Persuading her school to debate how urgent the climate change crisis had become should've been a breakthrough, not a highlight to the target that was already on her back. She was sick of everyone calling her Nila the Climate Freak.

They'd never call her EarthSavior, her chosen username in the Ascension app.

She rolled onto her side so she could see her phone on the nightstand.

No new notifications from Ascension?

An hour left before midnight. Not much time to complete today's challenge to not break her winning streak.

Maybe the next one would be easier, like the first few. Nila smiled, because the Guide was right. Look how far she'd come. She barely recognized herself as the same person who'd been so scared during her first challenge. "Face Your Fear" had made her shake with nerves. It had taken everything she had to not shut the app down and never reopen it.

The idea of writing her most private thoughts right there on the screen and letting others on the app read them had been terrifying. More terrifying than what was happening to the beautiful planet.

She'd almost been unable to look at the responses, but

another Ascension user, RisingStar77, had left a comment that became a mantra Nila repeated to herself often.

I was afraid too, but now I'm here among my people. I've got your back as you have mine.

Anything RisingStar77 said had a special place in Nila's heart. They were the first Ascender to reach out to her, to encourage her. Even though RisingStar77 had followed the Guide's instructions and ascended, they still bothered to reach back to help her follow.

But RisingStar77 wasn't the only one. Other Ascenders supported Nila, too, urging her to try, to succeed. That wasn't something she had in the real world, and she'd never let them down by not finishing a challenge.

Her next challenge, "Stepping into the Unknown," had felt simple, and now every time she told her friends on the app that she was going for a midnight walk without her phone, they cheered her on.

You're so inspiring. I'm doing it too.

See you back here soon.

Being inspiring made Nila feel warm. That was how she could make a difference. But that was nothing compared to how she felt when another Ascender, NeverLookBack, told her she was brave after she'd completed the "Expose Yourself" challenge. Maybe they'd also taken about twenty-five tries to get the naked selfie they could just bear to post.

Brave and inspiring Nila. She liked those labels. And once she'd ascended, even those unenlightened ignorants not on the app would see her how she truly was. Then they'd read her leaflets and her poems. Then they'd listen to her. She'd inspire them to do the right thing and put Earth first.

Nila picked up her phone and held it between her hands. She mouthed the words, *Hurry up.*

As if it'd heard her silent plea, her phone buzzed, and she

tapped the journal icon with clumsy fingers. The timer showed forty minutes to complete today's challenge.

The Ascension logo pirouetted on her screen, followed by a shower of stars that exploded into twinkling stardust before reforming into the magic words, *Time to Ascend.*

Tears threatened.

Really? It was her turn?

A bolt of excitement jolted through Nila, every bit as electrifying as an actual shock.

It was her turn!

A new message filled her screen. Nila could imagine the Guide smiling as they typed it.

Welcome to the real Ascension. I'm so proud of you for reaching this stage. What lies beyond is better than you've imagined, and I'm so happy to share it with you. Your instructions follow. After you complete each one, let me know you're ready to proceed by typing, "I'm ascending." Do you understand?

Nila typed, *Yes.*

Nothing happened.

"Don't screw this up."

She typed, *I'm ascending.*

The instruction came straight back. *Write a poem about why you're ready to ascend. Leave the note in your room so you can read it when you return.*

When she returned? So she had to go somewhere. Write a poem, go somewhere, and come back in the minutes left before midnight?

Nila grabbed her physical journal from her nightstand drawer. It opened at her last entry back in June, before she'd found Ascension and started to evolve. Phrases from when she'd been a different person caught her eye, distracting her. She needed to focus.

She scribbled some words on the next blank page. No crossing out—see how she'd changed?—no more second-guessing herself. In just a few minutes, she had a page full of poetry. Some of the best she'd ever written.

Nila picked up her phone and typed, *I'm ascending.*

A flood of replies filled the screen, but the one that stopped her scrolling was from RisingStar77.

You're going to join me. I'm so happy! We'll be just like sisters.

The sister Nila had never had. Her brother, Tyler, was as okay as an annoying little brother could be. But she couldn't share anything with him unless it had wheels or came from a drive-through. And he didn't listen when she told him what cars and fast food were doing to the planet.

The Guide also replied. *You've done so well, Nila. Now it's time to take the leap. This is the moment you've been working toward, when you make people listen.*

Yes, that was what she wanted—for people to hear.

RisingStar77 posted a new comment. *It's not death. It's freedom. You'll feel alive for the first time, like me.*

NeverLookBack chimed in. *The pain will be gone, EarthSavior. You just have to take the leap.*

Nila's heart stuttered as she read RisingStar77's comment again. "Death?"

The Guide had to be psychic. *Prepare to welcome the death of the old you. You'll rise above it all, the fear, the exhaustion, the hopelessness. You'll feel more alive than ever and will be EarthSavior in more than just name.*

"Yes." Her fervent whisper choked on a rush of emotion that felt too huge for her body to contain.

The instructions continued. *Find a rope at least six feet long. This is your yardstick. It represents everything you're leaving behind.*

Nila couldn't measure what she was leaving behind. All her paranoia about something happening to her mom, about the planet catching fire and forever burning, about the chance to see her dad again...if she laid all her worries out, they'd reach California.

But she didn't have to carry it around any longer.

A giggle bubbled up in her. She already felt freer, lighter. Her dad used to keep all sorts of ropes and stuff in the garage. And as devastated and furious as her mom had been when he'd walked out, she hadn't thrown much of his junk into the trash. Almost as if she hoped he'd come back too.

I'm ascending.

The Guide answered quickly. *Go to the swing in your backyard. It's fitting that a place that made you feel safe and free will help you ascend.*

Nila gripped her phone tighter. Was the Guide somehow watching her right that second? How else could they know about the swing?

Then she remembered the photo she'd not long ago pinned on her PhotoSpace page, setting it to public so everyone could see it. Even him. Hopefully him. A picture of her dad pushing her five-year-old self on their new swing set. But she'd completed the challenge to delete all her socials, and as far as she knew, her dad hadn't seen it.

None of that mattered now.

Knowing this was the moment she'd been waiting for, the moment when she'd leave all the sadness behind, Nila slid off her bed. She left her bedroom and crept down the stairs. In the kitchen, she quietly turned the backdoor knob and let herself out of the house. How different would she feel when she returned?

The wind was strengthening, rifling the branches of the big old tree, muffling the sound of her working open the bolt on the garage door. Her phone flashlight helped her find the ropes. She laid the two longest side by side. Her heart would choose the jute rope, but the bright-blue nylon one, with all its shedding microplastics, matched the Guide's instructions.

"Look at that, Daddy. You might've given up on me, but you're helping me one last time."

Her fingers fumbled through the next instruction. She hadn't practiced the knots her dad had taught her in years, but she finally managed to tie the synthetic blue rope firmly around the bar at the top of the swing as instructed.

"See, Daddy? That might not be a pretty knot, but it works." Her voice trailed off, as it did whenever she tried talking to him. But this time felt different. She felt stronger. Strong enough to tell him the Guide's abiding truth. "There's nothing we can't do. And ascending is gonna make everything okay again."

Sit on the swing. The Guide's instructions appeared on Nila's screen. *Feel the warm air around you. This is your moment, the final test.*

She sat on the plastic seat for the first time in years. That view of the house, and the rocking motion, took her right back to when the arguments had started, as though the tension and the shouting—the upset and the crying—were happening right then.

Her phone dinged. RisingStar77 led the comments that pulled her out of unwelcome memories. *I'm so excited for you.*

Nila swiped at the tears she couldn't hold back. This was thrilling, something she'd yearned for. She shivered. Her favorite t-shirt, now thin from wear, did little to halt the chill that rippled down her spine, but it had felt important to her to showcase its slogan during this momentous event.

Her phone jumped in her clammy and nervous hands, almost falling onto the scrappy grass. She tapped out her response. *I'm ascending.*

Once you're ready, stand up on the swing seat and secure the rope around your neck. This is your touchstone, which gives you full control. You now have the power to ascend.

Nila took a deep breath and fumbled the rope over her

head, pulling one end gently. The knot worked, and the loop tightened around her neck like a strong and steadying hand, a welcoming embrace.

She found it easy now to type those words again. *I'm ascending.*

We're so proud of you. The Guide's reply made Nila's heart feel so full, she thought it might burst. *This is the hardest part, but you've already proven that you're stronger than your fear. Let go of everything holding you down. Step off the swing, and in that moment, you will ascend. Trust me.*

"Trust you," Nila whispered. "I do."

She looked up at her bedroom window, where the words she'd just written waited. The relief and the comfort of finding where she was always meant to be made her eyes fill with tears. The wind caressed her hair, soothing her with its encouragement. Mother Nature was proud of her too.

Nila stepped off the swing.

2

Maybe it was being back in Sherwood County. Maybe it was her first real day at her new job. Maybe it was Appalachian magic. But Indie could've sworn she heard Grammy Ada calling.

"Indira Reign, get out of bed right this instant."

The hollowness of the realization that it couldn't be her made Indie flop back and pull the covers over her head. *"Suffering from heart dropsy,"* Grammy would've said.

Indie's covers started moving, rushing off her, pooling onto the floor where her Belgian Malinois, Broc, stood smiling around a mouthful of blanket. *"Why aren't we running?"*

Sometimes, Indie could read what he wanted to say in his body language, but this morning, as most often, his thoughts dropped right into her head without the need for her eyes or ears to get involved.

"Because…" Indie didn't have a good reason. And if she lay there any longer, they wouldn't have time for a long enough run.

The last thing she needed today was an antsy Maligator.

He nudged her. *"Come on. I'm ready."*

She sat up and rubbed the top of his head. "Easy for you. You just have to stand up. I have to do things like put on gym clothes and running shoes."

Broc padded out of her bedroom and returned with one of those shoes in his mouth. He dropped it next to the bed.

Indie laughed. "You going to pick out my running gear too?"

He cocked his head. *"If it's faster."*

She pulled on gym shorts, a sports bra, and a t-shirt, tying her long brown hair up in a messy ponytail as she walked into the living room. A long huff came from the massive pile of sable-and-black fur sprawled out on the rug near the couch.

"Some of us are trying to sleep."

"Sorry, Satch. I'm taking Broc out for a run." Indie stooped to stroke her nine-year-old German shepherd, who was relishing his recent retirement. "Want to join us?"

She didn't need her ability to communicate with animals to know exactly what he was thinking.

His eye roll was the canine equivalent of *are you nuts?*

Broc leaped over him. *"I'll never retire."*

Indie smiled, but didn't say what she was thinking—that Satch used to say the same thing. His joints had eventually told a different story. She was just grateful he was adjusting. Losing his purpose had been his biggest fear. And what it might to do him had been hers.

Broc might've only been part of their family for a couple weeks, but he and Satch were developing quite a bond—not that either of them would admit it. Shame she couldn't say the same about Broc and her turtle, Salem.

The doggy door flap swung back into its frame behind Broc. So kind and thoughtful of Aunt Edith, Grammy's longtime friend, to have installed it before Indie moved in.

The tiny, temporary apartment over her garage made the doggy door practically a luxury. The whole property was peaceful, even the fenced-off area out back where medicinal but potentially deadly herbs grew.

She pulled on her shoes and followed Broc out, except she used the people door, and down the stairs she went. No sign of lights on in Aunt Edith's house yet.

Indie loved the feeling of space there. And living alone with her boys and Salem meant she didn't have to silence how she talked to them or pretend she didn't understand what they were saying. Not everyone would revere her gift with animals as much as her mom had, and most would report her for being crazy. Not a good start for a trainee detective.

"*Warte*," she commanded Broc as he dashed across the yard. *Wait.*

Like the good boy he was, Broc waited at the gate as if he'd been following Indie's German commands his whole life instead of just the thirteen days they'd had together.

Broc loped beside her, happy to be outside. But she needed to get a bike so he could flat-out run a couple of times a week. Even then, she wouldn't keep up with his top speed. Still, he needed the freedom to really let loose. Something else to add to her to-buy list.

But not today.

Today, she and Broc started their new job, and they'd both be on probationary status until the sheriff decided the new K-9 detective role would work out. This opportunity was a rare dream come true. After meeting Sheriff Sammy Peterson, Indie had a feeling he needed convincing a woman detective could do the job as well as his lead investigator, Eli Walker. But he'd been open-minded enough to hire them, so that made her hopeful. Still…

She and Broc had a lot to prove.

Indie dug in, pushing her legs faster, arms pumping, hoping Broc wouldn't notice they were running past the turn to Robin Hood Lake.

But he was smarter than that. His head swiveled in the direction of the lake, though he stayed beside her.

"You're a smart boy." She glanced down. "I don't want you smelling like wet dog on your first day. And you don't like the hair dryer."

A hand-painted sign made Indie stop as if she'd run into a wall. The unofficial name the locals had given the small swimming spot was more faded than she'd remembered.

"Baby Lake. Still here."

She'd lost sight of that in her memory. Ferns and underbrush straggled from either side onto the track where she and her older sister, Aishani, had played when they'd visited as a family.

Such a rare treat to have been granted that day just for play. Indie might've remembered the joy of it, if her life had been different.

Broc looked at her with concern in his deep-brown eyes. *"What's wrong?"*

Of all the tones Indie heard him "speak" in her mind, the one he used to check in on her was her favorite. In it, she could hear his love for her, his willingness to do whatever she instructed. But right then, even that couldn't soften the knowledge that no amount of wishing could bring her parents and sister back. Brutally snatched away from her, they were gone forever.

"I'm okay."

"You're not."

She stooped to stroke his fur, to ground herself, making the infinity sign on his back. "You're right. I'm not. But if this is going to work, I have to learn to ride out these touchstones to my past, not let them floor me."

Broc cocked his head.

She scratched behind his ears. "Race you home."

Once they returned to the apartment, he got into his breakfast as soon as she put it down for him. But then he gave a whooping cough, as though he'd inhaled part of his kibble, and jumped back from the bowl. Another backward leap up into the air had him landing half on, half off the couch before crashing onto the floor in a tangle of legs and tail.

"What are you doing?"

Broc jumped up onto all fours and stood statue still, tensed, staring at the table as if he expected it to explode, in full indicating mode.

"What's the matter?"

"It's back. It's back. It's right there. It hasn't gone away."

Indie shot a look at Satch, who gave her clueless, innocent, *don't look at me* eyes.

That was when she spotted Salem, her red-eared slider, ambling out from under the table. The turtle stopped and looked from one side to the other, as if checking for traffic, before wandering toward Broc's bowl.

Broc whined. *"Not my breakfast. Don't let it get my breakfast."*

Indie picked Salem up. "If you'd just say hello to her properly, Broc, I'm sure you'd get along fine. It's not like she can hurt you."

Broc hid his snout under a paw, and Satch literally readjusted to face away from her. Tough crowd.

Broc looked back at Indie. *"That's what it wants you to think. You don't know what's going to come out of that shell."*

Indie laughed. "I'm pretty sure whatever it might be won't compare to your teeth. I know you've earned your retirement, Satch, but are you happy to be on guard duty, to look after Aunt Edith and Salem while Broc and I aren't here?"

Satch shook himself. *"You'll be all right without me with you?"*

She stroked his chest. "I'll be fine. Don't you worry."

"Well, duh. Nothing's going to happen to her when I'm by her side." Broc went to go in for a hug, but Indie was still holding Salem. He settled for a side-eye at the turtle in Indie's hands. *"Get rid of it."*

Satch took the hug instead. *"You don't have to worry about anyone here. I've got them. Long as you're careful out there."* He looked at Broc. *"He must protect you. That's his number one priority."*

Indie hugged him harder. "Thank you. It's so good to know they're all so well protected with you around."

Her phone made her jump. The screen flashed the name *Eli Walker*, her mentor. She fumbled to answer and stumbled over a hello.

"Indie, baptism by fire for your first day. We've had a call about a dead teenager found hanging off the swing set in her backyard. Nila Radler. Sent you the details. Meet me at the crime scene."

He was gone before she'd gotten out half a reply.

The tingle of nerves tied her insides into a tense knot. A dead teenager wasn't how she'd imagined her new job would start.

But she and Broc had been training hard together. They'd do whatever was necessary to make this new pilot program a success. Having a K-9 detective in every sheriff's office and police department in South Carolina would help solve so many crimes. A lot was riding on them proving themselves.

"You ready, Officer Broccoli?"

Broc whined at the moniker.

She immediately regretted saying the "B" word. Broc had

told her that his former trainer gave him the name as a joke after he fell into a bucket of green paint as a puppy, saying he looked like a stalk of broccoli. The man laughed about it like he was clever, but Broc had never forgotten the humiliation. Or the cruelty that followed. Pete Riker had been harsh, more focused on control than connection, and Broc shut down under his command—refusing to obey, refusing to engage. Which earned him the cruel taunt of being a washout.

Until Indie met him.

She hadn't planned to take on a second K-9, but she hadn't been able to walk away. Broc didn't just need a handler…he needed someone to believe in him.

Now they were partners. And despite the stupid name—and maybe because of it—Broc had something to prove too.

Indie put Salem back in her tank before giving him a good scratch behind his ears. "Sorry, buddy. Lost my mind there for a second. All I see is Broc, the bestest boy."

He wagged his tail and licked his tongue up the side of her face.

"Does that mean I'm forgiven?"

Broc grinned. *"This time."*

She pushed to her feet. "Let's go, then. We have a case to solve."

3

Indie pressed her left index finger on the seam across the top of the pocket in her utility pants as she walked Broc toward the victim's house. Car and van doors slamming and the issuing of instructions punctuated the silence in the street around her.

A rail-thin Black deputy with a deeply furrowed forehead got out of the cruiser, which had pulled up just ahead of her. He placed his hat on the roof while he adjusted his navy trousers. Indie hadn't met him in her week of filling out forms for HR.

"Oliver Freeman." His voice was surprisingly deep. "You the new K-9?"

She gestured at Broc, who stood perfectly beside her. "He's the canine."

"You look younger'n my young 'uns."

Indie shrugged. "I look like I look." At twenty-five, she'd already had a lot of life happen to her, but little of her ordeals showed in her face.

"Scene's around back, I hear." He stepped out of her way and looked at Broc. "He bite?"

"If I tell him to."

Oliver moved back another few feet.

Indie led Broc through the front yard, strafing her gaze over the long, rectangular front lawn. She noted a foam football, despite the overgrown tufts of grass trying to hide it.

"Good boy," she told Broc as they passed it with no tension on his leash.

"I see it, but I'm working."

It wasn't long ago that a sight like that would've sent him lunging. After Broc's rough start with his former trainer, Indie hadn't known what to expect. But moments like this gave her hope—he was learning. Fast.

"Later."

"Yes, we can play later."

Before she even got halfway up the drive, Indie could see the desperation in the eyes of a woman sitting on the front porch, clutching the hand of a young boy beside her.

Indie approached the porch. "Mrs. Radler?"

The agony in her eyes was hard to look at.

"K-9 Detective Indira Reign. I'm very sorry for your loss."

The grief-stricken mother acknowledged her with a flash of eye contact, but then her gaze settled back on the ground as if staring at it hard enough could make all this go away. The boy—Nila's brother, Tyler, Indie assumed from the notes Eli had sent her—reached toward Broc but stopped and looked at his mom.

"Broc likes scritches." Indie rubbed the white blaze on Broc's chest. "Especially here." Broc lifted his chin. "He'd like you to pet him, if you want to."

Tyler frowned. "Scritches? Don't you mean scratches?"

"Scritches are like scratches but better, because they show love and affection instead of just scratching some old itch."

She bobbed her eyebrows. "More wiggly. More dog-approved."

He seemed impressed. He glanced at his mom, who gave the tiniest of nods.

His tentative fingers moved to Broc and lightly grazed the strands of his fur.

Indie gave him a minute before saying, "We'll be back."

The backyard was mostly lawn with a huge tree on the boundary. No squirrels scampered up its trunk, and no birds sang from its branches. The activity of the gaggle of people milling around could've chased the wildlife away, but to Indie, it felt more as if nature itself were grieving.

A lightly tanned man dressed in jeans and a polo stepped into her path. Lead Investigator Eli Walker, Indie's training officer and mentor, had more of a stubble thing going on than when she'd first met him. And the ornate buckle on his belt could've set the yard on fire if the sun hit it at the right angle. It looked like something a boxing champion would parade around the ring. That was new too.

"It ain't pretty."

Indie blinked. *Your belt?* Not pretty was an understatement.

He gestured behind him. "You seen a body before?"

She nodded, shoving down her annoyance at the question.

"Shit and all?" He was even more abrupt than he'd been on the phone.

"I've seen my share."

"Not gonna lose your breakfast?"

"Why would I?"

Eli looked at Broc. "How about him? He gonna go nuts over the scent?"

Broc looked at Indie. *"Who's this joker?"*

Indie tapped Broc's shoulder twice, their unspoken signal for *message received, now hush your muzzle.*

She'd learned to tune out the random static of animal thoughts unless they were directed specifically at her. Most creatures didn't realize she could understand them, which helped. But Broc knew exactly how to get her attention—and he often had a lot to say. Especially when she was trying to focus in a meeting. He and Satch could yap at each other all day, but she only caught what was aimed her way. Thank God. Otherwise, she'd lose her mind.

Still, there were times she wished her ability worked differently. Like when she was deep in the woods, tracking a suspect, and it would've been helpful if a squirrel could just shout, "He went that way!" No such luck.

"Broc's not a cadaver dog. He'll do what I tell him."

"Don't say I didn't warn you." Eli stepped out of the way.

As Indie weaved her way through officers and techs, the girl came into full view.

Indie fought hard not to gasp at the sight of Nila Radler where she hung from the bar above the swing. No mother should ever have to see their child in such a state or have such a terrible last memory to bear.

While she steeled herself for a second look at the teenager, Indie read Nila's t-shirt. *There is no Planet B.* Had Nila chosen that subconsciously, or was she sending a message?

"Common path of approach is to the right of Clifton." Eli waved his hand as if making sure Indie understood. "Hey, Clifton, this here's Indira Reign, our new recruit."

"Indie."

The bald Black man standing closest to the body turned to look at her.

"Okay to approach?" She understood his glance at Broc. "*Bleib,*" Indie told Broc. *Stay.*

Broc stood beautifully still while Indie approached Clifton, who peered at her over rimless glasses. "Good to meet you. Clifton Harina, county coroner. You probably saw my van out front. Sherwood Memorial Funeral Home."

Indie tucked her thumbs into her tactical vest. "What're you thinking?"

"Isn't it obvious?"

"Not always." She studied the makeshift noose around Nila's neck.

Clifton harrumphed, a deep sound that barely made it out past his bushy beard. "Am I seeing signs of remorse? Is that what you're asking? Did she try to save herself once she jumped?"

Indie nodded.

"A couple of scratches on her neck, which're probably her body fighting her brain, but this appears to be what it looks like. Phone was there." He pointed at the grass where a smartphone had been bagged as evidence.

"If she had it with her until the end, she could've left a suicide note." Indie felt Eli Walker's gaze cutting holes in the side of her face. He'd learn he didn't need to monitor her that closely. "Phone was locked?"

Clifton reached a gloved hand for his bow tie—an extravagant, blue-and-green-striped affair—but let his arm drop before touching it. "Indeed."

"Do we have her phone code?"

"Reckon Eli or forensics'll be on that already."

Indie breathed through her mouth to avoid the stench the gentle breeze wafted at her. The poor girl's bowels had released. "Will you do an autopsy?"

"Not me. I have a big ole conflict of interest. Not only does the van out there with the fetching paint job belong to me, but so does the funeral home those lovely letters reference."

Was he making a joke? People seemed extra confusing this morning. Indie arranged her face to suggest a smile just in case.

"We schedule autopsies at Columbia Medical Center."

Nodding at the new information, Indie pressed her lips together. "Can you include a tox screen in case she was under the influence of something?"

"Always do in cases like these."

"Thanks." Indie walked back the way she'd come to retrieve Broc. Movement at the side of the house made them both tense and pay attention.

A young deputy walked backward and forward as though she didn't know where she should be. Then she made a beeline for them.

"Indie, hi. So sorry I wasn't around to see you last week when you were getting set up. But here you are. Welcome back." The deputy hustled over and grinned up at Indie. She was about five inches shorter than Indie's five-nine frame but bubbly enough that her personality took up twice her physical space. "It's me, Hen."

"Oh, hi."

Hen swiped her sheriff's-office cap off to reveal a tight black bun slicked back to perfection and intense gray eyes. "Sorry. Let's try that again. Deputy Edith Henley Chambers. Edith, as in like my nana…you know, your landlady."

Indie blinked. Of course she knew that. Why did people find the need to state the obvious?

"Oh, but she'd hate to hear me call her *landlady*." Every word that came from Hen's mouth seemed to be at hyper speed. "Everyone just calls me Hen, but you know that. You remember me, yeah? I mean, we were kids, but this is really exciting, working together now. Who'd have thought when you moved away, you'd be back, and we'd end up here? Working together, sort of, kind of."

Hen stopped to draw a breath, and Indie felt as if a tornado had passed by. That Hen had rolled up the years of missed greetings since they'd last seen each other into one overexcited blurt had been impressive, if a little exhausting.

"It's good to see you, too, Hen."

She looked delighted. "See? You do remember me."

They'd probably been younger than Nila when they'd last spent the summer together—Hen had been for sure—so she felt more like a stranger than an old childhood friend.

"I'm sorry to be seeing you here, with all this. I wondered if now was the time for a quick reunion, but it reminds you of what's important, yeah?" Hen jabbed her cap in the direction of Nila. "It's doubly tragic. They're all so young. None of them had the time to make a big enough mistake to warrant this."

"They?"

Hen nodded. "Nila's the fourth. Well, second suicide."

Never assume—one of the overriding commands in Indie's training—made her correct Hen. "We don't know that for sure."

"No, you're right. But we've had one other confirmed suicide and two confirmed accidental deaths in the last six months, all under eighteen. It's so sad. I mean, I'm only twenty-two, just a handful of years older than them. And I know I'm just a deputy. I don't do detecting and such, though, you know." She dropped her voice. "But doesn't that seem like a lot in a short period of time?"

Indie went to caution against speculating without evidence when an almighty sneeze burst out of Hen, bending her in two.

She straightened up, wiping at her eyes. "Oh, boy, that was a doozy It's..." She shuddered in a breath, screwing up her nose again. "It's..." She rammed her straight index finger under her nose. "Did you know if you press there it stops you—"

Another sneeze silenced whatever she'd meant to say.

Broc was watching Hen as though he'd never seen this brand of human before. And maybe he hadn't.

When Hen stood straight up again, she stepped away from him. "No offense, big guy, but it's you."

"You're allergic to Broc?"

"Animals." Hen wiped her eyes again. "It's the dander. Mostly dogs and cats set me off. And rabbits. And you could kill me if you left me alone in a room with a guinea pig."

Indie could think of nothing worse. Hen could probably add horses and cows to her list, if just being near the dog in an open outdoor space caused this type of reaction. But she wasn't about to tell Hen that.

She put her finger under her nose again. "It'll stop."

Indie stepped out of the path of where Hen's next sneeze might land. "I'll take him out front."

Hen nodded, her finger pressed up under her nose, which just looked painful. "That'd be great. Sorry. I'll see you later. Got to get back to managing the scene. Have a great first day detecting."

"Come on, Broc. Let's go talk to Nila's mom again. Maybe she can help us understand this."

But Broc stayed still.

"*Mit mir.*" Indie tapped her leg. *With me.* She thought he understood the new command, but maybe not.

He put his nose to the ground and took a couple of steps toward the opposite side of the yard. *"This way."*

"Go on, then."

She followed him to the garage, where he sniffed at the bottom of the door, then stood stock-still, staring at it intently, his indicating mode. He'd found something. She slipped gloves on and pulled the bolt back.

Pushing the door open, Indie stood on the threshold, peering inside the gloomy space. She thumbed on her flashlight—not wanting to touch the light switch or anything if she didn't have to—and played the beam over a couple of kids' bikes, a neat stack of cardboard boxes, a tumble of rackets. The usual things she'd expect to find. On the floor, beside a tangle of brightly colored bungee cords, a length of natural rope lay stretched out as though waiting to be measured.

What piqued Broc's interest? She squatted beside him and lowered her voice. "What's important here?"

Broc made a grand sniffing gesture. That meant there was a fresh scent.

Indie still marveled that dogs measured the passing of time in terms of the strength of a scent. Fresh could mean just before Nila died.

"Good job." She praised Broc before asking one of the forensic techs to go through the garage. "The K-9 thinks Nila went in there before she died. That could turn up something to explain this."

The tech looked at Broc. "He does, huh?"

Indie didn't offer an explanation. Grammy Ada had taught her how to embrace her abilities, how she just "knew" what animals were saying. It'd been extra cruel that her grammy had disappeared before she'd taught Indie how to navigate that gift in a world that didn't believe what she could do was even possible.

"Could you process it?"

"Sure. Will do." The tech looked behind him at the scene in the yard. "But how anything could explain this is beyond me."

4

Indie walked Broc over to where Eli was watching her from the side of the house. "I'd like to talk to Nila's mom."

"Go ahead." He leaned against the wall. "I'm here in an observing capacity, seeing how you're doing. Won't know what to teach you if I don't know what you don't know."

Indie couldn't decide how to respond to that, so she just nodded. "Do you have Nila's phone code?"

"Not me, so what're you gonna do?"

"Ask her mom. If she doesn't know it, I can check with the tech team?"

He moved his head in neither a nod nor a shake as though he could neither confirm nor deny if she was right, but he followed her and Broc to the front yard.

Nila's mom and brother hadn't moved since Indie first saw them.

"Mrs. Radler, is it okay if Tyler and Broc play while we have a chat?"

She looked at Broc, sizing him up.

"He's very well trained." Indie used her most reassuring

voice. "He'll keep Tyler amused while we talk. It might be better."

"Don't go into the street, Tyler."

He nodded. "I know."

"Tyler, would you like to play fetch with Broc?"

Tyler clutched his hands into fists in front of his chest, his shoulders hitching up. Indie understood human mannerisms too. Tyler really wanted to play.

"Broc, you ready to play catch with Nila's brother?"

The Mali looked at the foam football in the overgrown grass.

"Not that one. We don't want to annihilate it." She pulled his favorite ball out of her vest pocket. "This do?"

The red tennis ball made Broc do a happy dance with his front paws until he remembered he was working. He tried to style it out, slipping right back into his best behavior standing at her side, though he couldn't hide his grin.

Indie handed Tyler the slightly chewed ball. "This is Broc's favorite. And this makes you the boss."

Taking the ball in one hand, Tyler stretched the other out to pet Broc on the head.

Broc looked at Indie for permission to go.

She raised an eyebrow at him to be patient.

Tyler moved his stroking to Broc's chest. "He likes that," the boy told her as if Broc were his dog.

"He does, but he likes playing ball the best."

Tyler ran off to the center of the yard, and Broc trotted behind him.

Indie sat next to the grieving mother. "Mrs. Radler—"

"Just Victoria. I don't like being called 'missus.' Not since my husband left."

"Victoria, I know this is hard, but thinking back over the past few weeks and months…was there anything about Nila's behavior that seemed off to you?"

"Nothing that jumped out at me. She was Nila." Victoria tried a smile, but it shattered into shards of pain. "She's always been a worrier. Worried about the planet, about what we're doing to it. She spent hours online with other green warriors." Her voice caught, and her tears overspilled her efforts to hold them back.

"Do you know which sites she was on?"

She shook her head as a sob burst out of her. "It's hard being a single mom, you know? I get home from work, and my day's only half done. Between trying to keep this place going and my kids fed, it's a stretch to check they've done their homework. Every day, Nila would rage about something. The oil fields, too many cars on the roads, how many kids were dying from air pollution, how we're breaking the ocean currents, and once they fail, it's Armageddon."

Though Indie had dozens of questions, she let the grieving mother get it all out first.

Victoria ran her hands over her face. "I couldn't handle it, so…" Another sob burst out of her. "I stopped listening. I shouldn't have. I'd do anything to hear her preach again about how there's no Planet B."

Is that why Nila chose to wear that t-shirt last night?

"What did Nila do in her activism?"

"She used to write poems, give out leaflets, talk to anyone who'd listen. But lately, she's been in her room online all the time. I didn't mind that, though. I thought she was safer there than being out where people who didn't like her message could bully her."

"Did that happen?"

Victoria shrugged. "She never said, but you see it on the news all the time, protests and counterprotests causing trouble. I asked her about being at home more, and she said she was more active than ever, chatting with like-minded people who understood her and encouraged her. She'd been so frustrated and angry before. I was delighted to see her more relaxed. She seemed happier." The memory choked her, and she blew her nose on a damp tissue.

Indie gave her a moment.

"Was that it?" Victoria balled up the shredded tissue in her palm and stared at Indie. "Was she not happy but finally at peace? Was she saying goodbye?" Her voice rose, the question strung taut between them.

"What makes you say that?"

"She said..." Victoria swallowed hard. "She said she needed to leave a mark on the world, that sometimes people needed to sacrifice to make people care. She can't have meant herself. Please tell me she didn't mean herself." She bent forward, sobbing.

"We don't know yet what she meant." Indie wanted to comfort her. She was overqualified when it came to loss. But she couldn't dredge open those same wounds she carried, no matter how sorry she felt for Nila's mom. And she hadn't ever lost a child. She couldn't imagine what that must've felt like.

She remembered lots of blackness in the days after learning her parents and sister had been killed, though. The darkness of lying under her blankets with the drapes closed. The dread of her bedroom door opening because someone wanted to talk to her. Losing the three people you loved most in the world all at once had to come close to the pain this mother was enduring.

Indie shoved the memory away before it could become fully present in her here and now. She fell back on procedure that could give them answers. "Nila's phone might help us. Do you know the unlock code?"

Victoria shook her head.

"How do you organize the ropes and things in your garage?"

The woman looked bewildered. "I don't have a system, if that's what you mean. Not like when it was my husband's workshop. Stuff's in boxes and whatnot so Tyler can get his bike out by himself."

"Is there a reason there's a rope laid out across the floor?"

Victoria clapped her hands to her head. "Nila must've done that to see which…" She broke off in a low moan.

Indie gave her another moment.

The blood had drained from Victoria's face entirely. "What color rope?"

"Natural-looking. Jute, maybe."

"Nila would…" Victoria gulped. "She would've chosen that one, never the blue one. It's nylon. Sheds microplastics. I don't know why the natural one would be on the floor and the blue one would be…" She couldn't finish that sentence.

So what made Nila use the blue plastic rope?

"Can I look in her room?"

"It's on the left upstairs. I can't…"

"It's okay. You stay here."

Eli nodded at Indie as she pulled on fresh nitrile gloves and shoe covers before entering the house.

She might've expected huge posters warning of the environmental crisis, satellite photos of the Earth, lots of green. But Nila's room was the opposite. Cream walls, lilac curtains and bedding, a small desk under the window, a nightstand beside the unmade bed, both remarkably uncluttered. And the bedside lamp was still on.

Why would she leave it on when she knew she wouldn't return to her room?

Beside the pillow was a pale-green journal, lying open. Indie sent Nila a silent apology. She'd hate to have her journal read by a stranger.

Nila's last words looked as if they'd been written in a rush.

Ascend

The Earth is tired
   And so am I.
   Tired of shouting for her,
   Tired of you not listening.
   But that is past me now.

I am Earth's Savior
   I can rise,
   Lift myself above the pain
   And the happy ignorance
   That shouts louder than the cries
   From the river, the trees, the mountains, the seas.

You'll wish you'd listened,
   But the Guide will set me free.
   My heart beating,
   My righteous fire flaming
   At me being inspiring and brave.
   Those around me will know what I gave.
   The Earth's countdown is almost done.
   See how greed and consumerism won?
   I can't fight it anymore.

So I unfurl my wings,

And I rise
To where I shall see.
And in that exquisite moment,
I will ascend
And become all I'm supposed to be.
In the place where I'm meant to be.

The stanzas initially seemed to be about Nila's activism, but on the next reading, Indie believed the poem could be more about what the girl had hoped for herself. But there were enough oblique references to death for it to be considered a possible suicide note.

June was the last entry before the poem. Perhaps too big of a gap for it to be helpful. Indie turned the page back to the poem and snapped a photo before putting the journal into an evidence bag and filling in the details of its discovery and location.

Back outside, she sat beside Victoria, who didn't appear to have moved. "Is it all right with you if I talk to Tyler?"

Victoria looked at Indie as if she'd spoken in a foreign language.

"You can sit with him."

Victoria considered her son, watching him toss the red ball as Broc ran for it. "It won't traumatize him more?"

"I'll be gentle, but he may have some insight."

Victoria nodded. "Go ahead. I can hear from here."

Indie pasted on a smile and approached Tyler. "How're you boys doing?"

Broc was the only one to reply to her. *"Kid's not saying much."*

That was what Indie was afraid of. Keeping his trauma inside wasn't healthy. Maybe Broc could help with that.

"Would you like to see Broc do some tricks?"

The boy nodded.

Indie gestured at Broc, and he walked between her legs across the yard. On the return, she took longer strides so Broc could slalom in and around each of her legs in turn.

"He's smart." Tyler was a long way from delighted, but he sounded a little more engaged.

"Yes, he is. You want to get him to do a trick?" Indie held out a treat, making the sign for sit.

Broc sat.

"Tell him to wait and then balance this on his nose."

Tyler looked at her with big eyes. "He won't—"

"He'll do exactly what you say." Indie encouraged him in as warm a tone as she could manage.

"Wait." Tyler balanced the treat on Broc's snout. "He's not eating it." He sounded a little more animated.

"Not until you tell him he can have it. When you say 'okay,' he knows he can. Did you know that's a very hard trick for a dog to do? Like when you have to sit still in class."

"How come he's not even wriggling? I wriggle sometimes, like when I want it to be recess. Because it's math and I've finished all the stuff, but I still have to wait."

"How did Nila like school?"

He shrugged. "She used to, but not as much as me."

"Did she have any new friends?"

"I guess." He looked at the vehicles clustered in the road, then back at Broc. "He's still waiting."

"You want to tell him he can have that one?"

"Okay." Tyler turned to the dog. "You can eat it, buddy."

Broc flipped the treat up into the air and caught it.

Tyler almost smiled at that. "Wow, he caught it."

Indie handed him another treat. "Want to see if he can do it again?"

While Tyler placed the treat on Broc's snout, Indie asked him about Nila's new friends.

"She was on her phone all the time with them, but she didn't talk. It was all snapping or whatever."

"So all internet friends?"

"I guess. When I got up to go to the bathroom, her light was always on. I didn't tell on her, though, because that'd make mom mad."

"Did she tell you about her new friends?"

He shook his head. "They're not like mine. If I want to spend time with mine, I get on my bike and go hang with them. She just stayed in her room. Maybe that's why she was so mad."

"She was mad? About what?"

"She was always yelling at me. For stupid stuff too." He put on a nagging tone. "'Paper's recycling, Tyler. When're you gonna learn? We have to recycle it before all the trees are gone.'" His face fell, as easy to read as Broc's. Nila would never nag him again.

"Did Nila ever use the word 'ascend?'"

"I don't think so." He turned to the dog again. "Okay. You can have it."

Broc caught his treat, and Tyler's face tried for a wobbly smile.

"You want to see something really cool?" Indie threw Broc's ball up into the tall tree on the property boundary. "Fetch."

Broc bounded up the wide trunk and into the tangle of heavily leafed boughs. He reappeared seconds later, jumping from one of the lower branches, his bright-red ball in his mouth.

"Good fetch." Indie held out a treat and stuffed the ball into her vest. "Thanks, Tyler, for talking to us and for playing with Broc. We have to go now."

Tyler's small shoulders drooped, and his feet dragged as he walked toward the house. She wished she could make it better for him. But she was tense with the knowledge that grief and turmoil would turn on the poor kid in a heartbeat when he least expected it. That hollowness would intrude on the happiest moments, tinging them with "what if" and "if only" for most of his life.

They were terrible questions that rarely ever resulted in real answers.

Indie hoped she could get Tyler and his mom some closure. That was all she could offer them.

5

Standing at the side of the Radler property, Hen watched Indie walk away with her dog trotting beside her. That reunion could've gone better. They'd known each other as kids, after all. Indie had given her the *frigid* shoulder, which seemed to be her default. Except when she was with her dog. Then she was much more at ease.

She never used to be cold or standoffish. Quiet, sure. Withdrawn, even. But she'd always treated Hen like an equal, despite their three-year age difference. Maybe it was first-day nerves. Hen could be "a bit extra," as her nana called it, so she needed to cut Indie a break. But she'd held back as it was. She'd wanted to give her a big old hug. But hugging the new recruit at a crime scene wasn't in the procedure-and-protocol manuals.

Still, she'd be running Indie's coolness through her mind for half the day, wondering if she'd read it right.

Hen patted her pockets out of habit. It was amazing how many places she could find a vape tucked away even when she thought she'd thrown them all out—but no luck today, which was actually a blessing. She never should've started using the damn thing to begin with. It'd been a beast to quit.

She fiddled with her keys instead while she checked in with the deputy holding the scene log. He confirmed she could go back to the station.

Driving back at least kept her hands busy, and dealing with the pile of paperwork that'd accumulated on her desk helped her forget all about her own reunion nerves. Because her mind kept returning to the crime scene.

"You fixing me coffee?" Sheriff Sammy Petersen's shout reached Hen just as her curiosity about what Indie, at her own desk, was so engrossed in swiped all her focus.

Hen sometimes wondered if she ignored the sheriff's coffee demands, like everyone else, if another sap would start fulfilling them. No one seemed to be moving, and everyone was back from the crime scene, heads down, typing away.

"Sure, Sheriff." Hen stood, stretching. She glanced at Indie, hyper-focused on her computer monitor, then down at Broc. He was a beautiful dog, and she wished she could pet him. But as things were, she was just grateful Indie's desk was clear across the room from hers.

She went to the break room and poured the coffee dregs into a mug, dumped in two sugars, and got a fresh pot going.

"Here you are." Hen placed the mug carefully on his desk. "I put a new pot on."

"Thank you kindly." The sheriff's smile was vague, his gaze not lifting from a document he was reading.

Hen walked around the outside of the desks toward Indie, who was still engrossed in whatever was on her monitor. Broc had a blue toy in his mouth now. He eyed her but just kept chewing, as if he knew he was more of a threat to her than she was to him.

She slowed down as she crept around the side of Indie's desk that the dog wasn't on, her gaze landing on the screen.

She scanned the report that had Indie so interested. Leila Perez, the other teen suicide. Hen stopped, her restless fingers pressed against her smile. Indie had taken what she'd said seriously.

Hen's nose tickled. *Oh, not now.* Breathing through her mouth didn't help, but she managed to swallow the sneeze that threatened to blow her cover. She was going to have to get ahold of some industrial-strength allergy meds.

"Help you?" Indie asked, eyes still glued to the screen.

Apparently, Hen wasn't as covert as she thought. "I was just…" She dropped her voice. "I was curious about what had you so engrossed over here. I mean, it feels wrong, all these teens. Is there a pattern to it? Something we're missing?"

Indie tapped the screen and turned to face her. "What you said got me thinking, so I did a little digging. This year alone, in the last eight months, there've been six accidents and four suicides in the county. That seems really high."

"That many?"

Indie clicked into one of the records. "Do you remember Leila Perez? She was an art student. Sixteen. A few weeks ago, she drowned in Robin Hood Lake, where we used to go swimming."

Broc lifted his head at the word, watching Indie intently.

"I don't remember her specifically, but her death was a huge shock to the school. She was kind of under the radar. Not picked on, but not popular."

"So no one would've known what she was thinking." Indie tapped her pen on the back of her hand. "What about her family?"

Hen could only shrug and say the obvious. "If there's nothing on there, I guess there's nothing of concern."

"Or it means no one's found anything yet. Did you see Leila's crime scene? It was exactly the same as her last painting."

"That's...that's so..." Words deserted Hen. "I don't even know what that is. Do you think she meant it as her suicide note?" Her voice had picked up an edge that made Broc stir.

"Her death was ruled a suicide, so perhaps she did."

Indie began typing as though she were trying to put out a fire on her keyboard. The search stopped with Arun Chang's name highlighted. Hen read over her shoulder. Arun Chang was found dead from carbon monoxide poisoning in his mom's car just a week after Leila died. He was fifteen.

"'Cause of death ruled suicide,'" Indie read aloud. "And on the passenger seat beside him, he'd left a notepad on which he'd written the word 'ascension' at the top of the page."

The cursor moved down through the record, but Arun Chang had left no note or anything like a painting or a poem to serve as one.

Hen's sudden sneeze made Indie jump and jerk the mouse in her hand. "Sorry. So sorry. I'm fine. It's just allergies."

"You said."

Hen pointed at Indie's screen with a tissue in hand, taken from a fresh stash in her pocket. "He used the word 'ascension.'"

"And Nila used 'ascend.'"

"That's a weird coincidence, right?"

Indie went to Urban Dictionary. "'Ascend' or 'ascension' could have a different meaning to teenagers."

Hen agreed and thought that was smart.

Indie summarized the first few entries in her notebook as Hen read from the screen.

"'Rising above challenges, spiritual transcendence.' Ascend can also be linked to 'subcultures promoting self-harm as a way to transcend pain.'"

Hen felt another sneeze coming on. She pressed her finger underneath her nose, thinking out loud. "Wanting to transcend to something better, they believed that killing themselves was the way to get there?"

Indie fiddled with her pen. "That sounds like some kind of cult." She looked up at Hen. "Nila's mom and brother said she spent nearly all her time in her room." She threw her pen down and typed in a new search—for teens and cults and the word *ascension*. She scrolled down the results, then refined the search, finally shaking her head. "Nothing relevant I can see."

"But would you, though? If the kids had something just for them, why would they make it easy to find? They like that feeling of being special."

"They do, and it'd be hidden enough if it's straight up on the dark web." Indie leaned back in her chair. "Or maybe it's just like one of the dangerous challenges that make the news because sometimes teenagers do stupid things. Although I've searched all the social media platforms and can't find any other insane current challenges."

Indie seemed good at seeing both sides, which might be the hardest thing for Hen to learn if she was ever going to make detective. From when Hen was tiny, Nana Edith had told her again and again that angels rushing in where fools feared to tread wasn't always the best way. Watching and copying Indie's restraint might be the way to get the other deputies to take her more seriously.

Indie stood and picked up her notebook. "I'm taking this to the sheriff and Eli."

"Good luck with that," burst out of Hen before she could stop it. But Indie didn't seem to notice the sarcasm. Talking down the sheriff and lead investigator wouldn't serve her, and Indie would find out on her own that both men had selective hearing and a terminal case of lazy.

Broc looked up at Indie but settled again when she gestured at him to stay down. They were so in-tune, it was like they talked to each other. And it flashed through Hen's head that she wished she had one person she was that connected with, or even a dog—a scary-looking, hairless, hypoallergenic one, of course.

Hen felt another sneeze brewing and rushed back to her desk in time to catch it in a fresh tissue. She'd better start buying in bulk now that Broc was on the team.

Stuffing some spares into her pockets, she checked her messages. Then she picked up her jacket and cap and went outside.

She blinked in the bright sunshine, enjoying the warmth on her face. The door clattered behind her, and she turned to where Broc was leading Indie outside.

That was quick. "What did the sheriff think?"

"He and Eli are both out for a couple of hours, so I'll go see the coroner."

Those two were always sneaking off somewhere.

Hen nodded. "I could go with you." She hoped Indie didn't think she looked as overly excited as a puppy. But then she remembered she couldn't go. "Aw, dang, rain check? I need to make my rounds downtown and look for evil people exceeding parking limits."

Traffic control would never feel so tedious.

6

Nila's face looked back at me. I centered her special photo, the one that would immortalize her, on my monitor screen. In it, her smile wasn't brittle. Her features didn't seem fragile. She looked at peace, as if she could now see my bigger picture. Maybe she could.

"Nila, you did it. After everything, you did it."

A huge wave of relief washed through me. I'd begun to think she wouldn't go through with it. Waiting for her last *I'm ascending* had been tortuous, but she'd overcome her nerves, her doubts, whatever had spooked her, and she'd done it.

In the pixels, I could recognize the passion Nila Radler had felt for her activism—the face she'd shown to the world.

But no one else chose to see the emotional exhaustion beneath those serious eyes. No one else recognized how her efforts were dragging her down. No one else saw the futility and the helplessness she was drowning in.

Now all that was gone. Nila and I had helped each other for the greater good of a purpose that really mattered.

I reached out to touch her frozen image. The warmth of

the screen came through my fingertips, and I smiled as though I were on camera, though no one would witness it.

"Thank you." I whispered, fierce with gratitude. "You'd be so proud to know what you're a part of. You wanted to change things, Nila, and so you are."

Opening my Pantheon of Pathfinders, I added her photo to my special gallery. The addition before her caught my attention, so I enlarged it. Looking at the thumbnail wasn't giving each sacrifice their due reverence.

"Thank you," I said to that photo, taking a long moment to acknowledge Arun Chang's vital role in this too. I repeated the ritual over and over with each photo. Going back to Nila's, I now murmured my thanks twenty-nine times.

Minimizing them back into the gallery view, I nodded at my collection. I couldn't quite bring myself to say it out loud, but they would understand. Using the term *collateral damage* to describe my ascenders was horrible, belittling. Condescending, even. Doing such important work was a double-edged sword.

"The safer, brighter future you're ensuring, that you can all be proud of, is one step closer today." I could tell them that in all sincerity. That brought a glow to my heart, because it was what they'd wanted, too, even if they were unable to say so.

I plucked at my sleeve, pushing it up while I worked out the math of the most recent cohort I'd invited onto my app. The statistics were better than I'd expected. Three out of five ascending was an excellent measure of success when the stakes were so high. Of course, any dropouts were frustrating, but everything was an opportunity to learn. Without them, I would never have been able to improve the app's responses.

For those poor teens who failed to ascend, I had nothing

but pity. That choice meant being removed from Ascension and its support system as abruptly and completely as the app was deleted from their devices when they made that decision.

Being thrust back into a world of insecurities, of not being understood, fighting for recognition that rarely came…that was on them.

"You poor misguided sheep," I whispered, as though my words would somehow reach them through the ether the same way my written words had. "You'll realize what a punishment it is that you didn't take the ultimate step. But that's not on me."

I closed my personal files and reread the half-written article I'd been working on. *Your worst fear may be your teenager's best outcome.* That hook was strong enough to get even the most hands-off parents reading my words.

My tone was pitch-perfect, sharp, and purposeful. There would be no mistaking the message.

Creating safe online spaces for all of us to enjoy must be as much of a priority as inspecting our physical spaces.

No, that wasn't clear. Too weak, too wordy. I thought about it, juggling words, rephrasing clichés, and redrafted it.

We would never allow our teenagers to walk blindfolded along the edge of a gator pit. Yet online, where their safety is more under threat, we ignore what they do and say. We ignore who they build relationships with. We must do better.

Right there, I had my conclusion, highlighting to those in positions of power how we must take back the initiative.

But I was getting ahead of myself. That was for later, when I had such plans. For now, I needed to concentrate on laying the groundwork.

I imagined my efforts all coming together in the end, like the tumbling of dominoes. Something that no one would see coming until it was right there, until it was too late.

I saved the document and closed it. My hand hovered over the mouse. I only had a few minutes, but the draw to check in was overpowering. And it would only take a moment to see how the platform had evolved, even from yesterday, as it inched ever closer to perfection.

What I saw made me breathe a little faster, made me nod in agreement. I was looking at the penultimate update, already live.

"Hex Spectre, you've surpassed yourself."

The hacker would never hear me praise him. Or her, I supposed. Maybe they. No need to be sexist about it. They only saw worth in the number of zeroes in their fee. And what I had paid was worth every cent.

One more update left to do.

I couldn't help myself. I clicked into the account of my next would-be Pathfinder, Elliott Greene. Finding him on social media had been almost like divine intervention, because he'd deleted his accounts even before I'd instructed him to.

His would be riskier than the other ascensions. The potential for it to go wrong was a lot higher. People would notice. But the challenge to keep him engaged, to best him, was part of the reason I'd invited him onto the app. I loved a good challenge. And Elliott was as thirsty for praise and reassurance as the others, despite his superior intellect. Though I knew them almost by heart—I'd written them—I read through the details of his final challenge.

Should I go with my original timetable? Nila's ascension was just last night.

The choice was easy, as nothing was more urgent than this work. I called up the program for the bots to be supportive before I sent Elliott's next message. RisingStar77, HurdleThat, and NeverLookBack would all send two messages each. Had they been living, breathing beings, they would have been the most understanding and compassionate people on the planet.

I set the automation to send Elliott's final challenge to him and typed in the words all the users yearned to see. *Time to Ascend.*

7

"Here's our ride." Indie led Broc to the Ford Explorer in the Sherwood County Sheriff's Office parking lot, as pleased as if she'd stuck all the *Caution K-9 Unit* stickers on herself. "What d'you think? Look at this."

She tapped the photo of Broc on the tailgate.

His tail wagged in double time, even though Indie knew, logically, he couldn't recognize himself, though he rarely mistook his reflection in a mirror or window for another dog.

"It's you."

"I am handsome."

"And these letters are your name." Indie ran her hand over it, hiding the final C-O-L-I as if he could read. "Officer Broc."

"Not Broccoli."

"Officer Broc." It felt as if the letters her hand covered were burning through her fingers. She really needed to see how much red tape she'd need to jump through to get his name legally changed. "This is your spot."

When Indie opened the rear door, the stale blast of locked-up heat rushed out over them. She checked the cab wasn't too hot before leading him into the flat area where the back seat had been modified. A square, flat-bottomed bowl secured behind the passenger seat held a whole bottle of water.

Indie shut the door and took her seat up front, running her hands around the steering wheel. "K-9 Detective Indira Reign on the case with Officer Broc." She loved the way that sounded.

Even inside his kennel, Broc was still finding new things to sniff when she pulled up outside the Sherwood Memorial Funeral Home, following the sweeping drive past two cars and Clifton's van to park in the shade of a massive tree. Still, she checked the AC was set right for Broc.

"You can't come in with me, so you wait here. *Pass auf.*" *Guard alert.*

Broc sat at attention, though there wasn't much to guard. Faint shrieks and laughter from a couple of kids playing somewhere close reached Indie as she crossed the lot and entered the building.

The clattering of a ferocious search in a desk drawer pulled Indie into the first room. "Hello?"

The woman behind the polished desk looked at her with warm brown eyes. Her long braids swirled over her head in an ornate pattern and were tied into a low ponytail behind her right ear.

"How can I help you?" She looked surprisingly young, but her manner was well practiced and capable.

Indie pointed at the badge on her belt. "K-9 Detective Indira Reign looking for Clifton Harina."

"You're the new detective. Where's your dog?"

"In the SUV."

"You can always bring him in if it's only me and dad. I

have dog treats in here somewhere, along with my staples that are currently hiding."

"That's kind. Next time." When Indie wasn't in a hurry to prove something on her first day.

"I'm Melissa. Dad's in his office. I'll show you."

Rich fabrics and soft furnishings in soothing shades of green and cream decorated the funeral home, making Indie completely unprepared for Clifton's office, which was a veritable war of paint colors. One Indie couldn't tell which side might be winning.

Yellow walls and a navy chair might've worked if they weren't teamed with purple-and-orange-striped drapes that clashed with the vivid-red carpet.

"Visitor for you." Melissa closed the door on her way out. The bright-pink door.

Maybe the man was color-blind, and no one had the heart to tell him. In any case, Indie wished she hadn't left her sunglasses in the Explorer.

"Didn't expect to see you so soon." Clifton gestured at the navy chair in front of his jarringly normal oak desk. "I could've updated you over the phone, though. Nila Radler's autopsy is tomorrow."

Indie brushed the chair seat and recoiled as though it had bitten her.

"Everything all right?"

"Sorry." She shuddered. "Not a fan of velvet."

Especially velvet that didn't look like velvet.

He came out from behind his desk and walked out of the room, returning with a plush cream chair with carved legs that were almost as thick as his thighs. "Try this one."

As he grasped the navy chair and turned it to face the wall, Indie shivered at the thought of how it would feel against her skin.

Clifton raised an eyebrow at the cream chair. "That better?"

Indie appreciated that he didn't make fun of her. She poked at the seat with a tentative finger, but it didn't make the hairs on the back of her neck and her forearms stand on end. Its smoothness was perfect.

"Much. Thank you." She perched on the chair, pulling out her notebook and pen.

Clifton resumed his seat behind his desk. "Tactile defensiveness. It's nothing to be ashamed of."

"I'm not." Indie hoped the flush working its way up her neck got the message too. Drawing attention to herself like this made her seem unprofessional, and she couldn't have that. She also couldn't help it.

"It's simply another way our brains can be wired. I find it fascinating how different we all are, though we start from the same blueprint." Clifton ran his thumb and index finger over his bushy beard. "I had a friend in elementary school who couldn't stand the texture of the skin on russet apples. Not even if the lunchtime assistant peeled them. Trouble for him was his mom had two trees that she nurtured. Lucky for me. I love me some russet apples."

His laugh grumbled out, a big bear rumble that suited him.

"Maybe I'll just call next time."

He tapped his index finger to his temple. "Note to switch out the chair for you. Though that color adds to the whole aesthetic, don't you think?"

"I think you might be color-blind." As soon as she said the words, Indie realized he'd asked one of those questions people didn't want an answer to.

Why do people ask those? Her responses were usually wrong. How much had she upset the coroner on their first day of meeting?

Clifton's face turned several of the colors in his office. But then he slapped his desk with his flat palm and whooped, a huge sound that made her jump a little in that cream chair.

"Well, Indie Reign, you are re-fresh-ing, like homemade lemonade without the sugar." He rumble-laughed again. "Don't you worry. We need some of that around here."

Indie's pen hovered above her still-blank page. Clifton was the least coroner-like coroner she'd met. Of course, she'd only known the one in her last position in Fort Lauderdale. But she'd expected to be out after two minutes with her hand aching from having to write so fast to get everything down before the coroner dismissed her.

She didn't know how to respond to what he'd said, so she brought the conversation back to why she'd come. "I wanted to ask you about a couple of other recent teen deaths. Leila Perez and Arun Chang."

"I remember them." Clifton closed his eyes and bowed his head, giving them a moment of silence. "Tragic and terrible. What do you want to ask about?"

"Specifically, I'm curious why they were ruled suicides."

He put his glasses on. "What're you thinking?"

"I want to be sure I have a handle on recent events in the county."

He typed on his keyboard, a hunt-and-peck endeavor that had Indie wondering how long it took him to type up his autopsy reports.

"Well, then. Leila Perez. Sixteen. Her cause of death was drowning. She was found in a lake and couldn't swim. Video evidence suggests intentional entry into the water. That she videoed it and was trying to recreate one of her paintings is consistent with preparatory acts associated with suicidal intent. Tox screen was negative for any substance that might impair judgment. Suicide ruling is definitive."

Indie noted everything he'd said while he found the other record.

"Arun Chang. Fifteen. His cause of death was carbon monoxide poisoning. As that suggests, he was found in his mom's car with the engine running inside an enclosed space. Toxicology in his case indicated high levels of carboxyhemoglobin in the blood, confirming carbon monoxide exposure. No other substance detected."

"Did anything feel off in either case?"

"Their parents were obviously distraught, insisting their children weren't experiencing suicidal ideation. Cases like this are hard on families, especially if they consider themselves close to their child. Parents would rather refuse to believe their child was in despair than acknowledge that they missed the signs. I found it peculiar that Leila's parents insisted she was so terrified of water, she wouldn't willingly approach the lake, let alone get in it. But we did a full tox screen. She was clean."

Indie added three question marks after her note. *Why choose the lake???*

"Did you see that Nila Radler left behind a poem titled 'Ascend'? Almost the same word used by Arun Chang. 'Ascension' was the only word he'd written on the notepad beside him in the car. Do you know what that means?"

"You're not asking me about the dictionary definition of the word."

Indie shook her head, though Clifton hadn't asked it as a question.

"While life might seem random and coincidental, my fifty years of experience, and, yes, I know, it's totally surprising that I'm that old," he winked at her, "tells me the opposite is true. Three dead teenagers, two of whom used the same word or a variation…that's a connection, not a coincidence."

He tapped a key on his keyboard lightly over and over. The sound was as annoying as if he were clicking a pen in and out. Indie had opened her mouth to ask him to stop when he did.

"I've heard it recently in relation to something else, which escapes me at the moment. It'll come back to me, and I'll let you know."

He pushed a small square pad of paper toward her, and she wrote down her number.

"I'd appreciate that. Thanks for your time and the chair."

"Think nothing of it. Good to see you working the job the right way."

Is there another way? Indie dismissed his comment as she left. Perhaps it was just a Clifton-ism.

Broc was still on guard alert in his seat, keeping the Explorer safe from the odd leaf that wafted down from the tree.

"Good job." Indie fed him a treat.

While he stretched his legs and did his business in the plush green lawn surrounding the funeral home, she paced up and down beside the SUV until Broc rejoined her.

"What's up?"

"There's nothing I can really do right now for Nila. That's what's up."

He barked and trotted after her. *"But her family was sad."*

Indie turned and nodded, flicking her thumbnails against her middle fingernails.

Grieving families who thought they had their answers wanted to be left alone to grieve—not have that wound poked at by a brand-new detective who had no real reason to show up with more questions.

But if she approached her follow-up visit with care and empathy, surely they wouldn't report her to the sheriff. Right?

She stooped to rub the white blaze on Broc's chest. "You're right. Her family's so sad. Let's make the hard call."

She owed that much to Leila Perez and Arun Chang.

8

Indie parked on the residential street in front of Leila Perez's home. "You'll have to wait here, buddy."

He stretched out in an impressive puppy pose in an attempt to win her over.

"Some people don't like dogs."

He gave her a side-eye. And that was exactly why he couldn't go in with her.

Maybe Satch could help Broc work on his poker face. Not being able to hide what he was thinking worked in front of people sometimes. Just not today. Not in these circumstances.

Leila's mother, Rosa Perez, answered Indie's knock with a more expressive face than Broc had just displayed, flickering from weary anticipation to panic to resignation. Her gray hair was tied back, but strands drooped over her ears as though they were too tired to stay in the elastic band.

"Mrs. Rosa Perez?"

The woman nodded, and Indie introduced herself. "I'm sorry to disturb you, but I wondered if you could help me."

"What do you need?" The tremor in the woman's voice

told Indie to be careful. She wasn't operating in an authorized capacity and didn't need an angry, grieving parent calling Sheriff Sammy to complain about her.

"I'm truly sorry for your family's loss, and I promise not to take up too much of your time. I'm following up on your daughter's case and had some questions."

Rosa backed out of the doorway and extended a hand. "Please, come inside."

Indie followed her into a minimalist living room where Carlos Perez, Leila's father, sat. He was the opposite of his wife, tightly wound and tensed, his weather-worn face impassive. But his eyes showed the depth of his pain, and there was a bottled-up energy just itching to break free.

"I appreciate you giving me the time. I wanted to ask you how Leila seemed in her last weeks."

Carlos looked at his wife. "Rosa can tell you. I travel for work and was mostly away."

"We both have stressful jobs that take all our time." Rosa trotted out what sounded like a well-used phrase. "I'm retiring in a couple of years. I thought then I could spend more time with Leila, since she was planning to attend a local college."

Her words strangled themselves, so Carlos explained. "Our other children are all grown with families of their own."

Indie hoped her expression showed sympathy and understanding. "Did she spend much time on her phone?"

"She'd had her phone in her hand every time I saw her. But so do all the teens, it seems." Rosa sighed—weary, drawn-out, well-practiced. "At our last family get together, I had to threaten to take it away to get her to put it down."

"Do you know what she was doing?"

"Some artsy thing, I'd guess." Carlos's tone made Indie curious.

"You didn't approve of her art?"

"Tossing color on a canvas? How could that give her a living? We won't be there to help her forever. She needs to get a proper job for when we're gone." He broke off and ran his hands over his face. His grief was so fresh, he still talked about her as if she were alive.

"We tried to encourage her to do something useful, so we wouldn't have to worry so much." Rosa glanced at her husband. "She was always stubborn about her art, telling us it was what *made* her. Then one day, she stopped talking about it. During our last argument, she said that only her online friends understood her and gave her validation to be a professional artist."

"These online friends...were they part of a community?"

Rosa rubbed at her wrists. "I..." She again looked at her husband, who shrugged. "We don't know. And it scared us."

Leila's passion for her art mirrored Nila's for her activism. *Is this a pattern?*

"What scared you?"

"That she'd made such a silly decision at sixteen. But we never could've imagined it would lead to this." The final word turned into a cry. Rosa walked to a side table and picked up a framed photo. "I've been running over and over the last few weeks of her life, wondering what I missed, what I could've done differently. It just makes no sense." She held the photo out to Indie.

The family looked close, happy adults and children grinning for the camera, except for Leila. She stood apart from the others by just a few inches, but she looked as though she'd been told she could never paint again.

Otherwise, the photo was a picture-perfect shot of a happy family enjoying nature. The trees round Robin Hood Lake were brilliant green, and the sun sparkled on the water that looked almost as blue as the sky.

"Leila hated the water. It terrified her. There's just no way she would've gone into the lake voluntarily."

Carlos murmured his agreement. "She wouldn't go in the water. Not ever."

But Leila had.

Indie handed back the photo. "Could I see her room?"

Rosa led her to Leila's room but stayed in the hall.

The pink pencil case and glossy coffee table book *How Life Mirrors Art: A History of Revolutionary Art* on her desk might've been where Leila left them, but the tubes of paint looked like they'd been arranged with purpose and intent, as though they had to pass an army inspection.

In the photos Indie had studied, Leila's easel stood in the corner of her room, but it was now folded and tucked away behind a dresser. Her painting leaned against the wall beside it, its back facing out so the image wasn't visible.

When she picked it up, Indie read Leila's signature on the back corner where the canvas had been secured against the wooden frame. That seemed odd. Didn't artists usually sign the front? On the opposite corner, along the side of the frame, a word had been written in tiny letters, as though it were a secret. Indie zoomed her phone in on it and took a photo.

The word made her go cold. *Ascension.*

She turned the painting over and understood why Leila's parents had put it up against the wall. Hardly tossing color on a canvas. Leila had a gift. She could've painted the crime scene photos of her lying in the water in hyperrealistic detail.

The figure in the painting held a single rose up to the sky, as if she were giving a gift to the heavens—an image as haunting as it was heartbreaking.

There was nothing more to say or ask these grieving parents at the moment, so Indie thanked them and let herself out.

The implications of the painting occupied her thoughts as she arrived at her next stop. Because water terrified Leila, did ascension mean moving on from her fears?

Or did it point toward good old-fashioned peer pressure? Had someone encouraged or coerced her to face her fears?

Victoria Radler was adamant that her daughter Nila never would've chosen to use a nylon rope for anything. That nagged at Indie. And laying the natural one out like the girl had on her garage floor suggested she'd been measuring them against each other and had taken the one that was the right length, not the one she preferred. But the right length according to who?

Though she'd rung the bell, the door opening almost made Indie jump, so deeply was she in her thoughts. High-pitched shouting put her instantly on alert, making her wonder if she should've brought Broc along.

The woman who stood in the doorway closed her eyes and pinched the bridge of her nose, as if she didn't have the strength to deal with the ruckus inside.

"Mrs. Maeve Chang? Detective Indira Reign. I'm very sorry to disturb you, and I understand this is a difficult time. I'm following up on Arun's case and wondered if you'd have a couple of minutes to answer some questions."

Maeve sucked in a wobbly breath. "I never have a minute to do anything, but you can ask. I already told the other officers everything I know when they first asked." The noise upstairs was escalating. "Come in. I'll just deal with that." She went up the stairs as though she were carrying Indie on her shoulders.

The whining wound up until it stopped entirely. The sudden silence smacked Indie's ears. Maeve came downstairs carrying a little girl who was rubbing her eyes and sniffling.

"We can go in here." She led Indie into the living room, where she sat the child in an armchair and handed her a tablet. She put headphones on her and tapped the screen a few times, and the girl stopped crying. "I know it's not supposed to be a babysitter, but it's the only thing keeping me going right now. It's not easy with seven. Six." Her voice wavered. "Six kids."

"Mrs. Chang—"

"You can call me Maeve, though I feel as ancient as 'Mrs. Chang' makes me sound."

"I'm very sorry for your loss." Indie hated those words, but she'd learned people expected to hear them. "Is your husband here?"

Maeve shook her head. "Huan's gone back to work. It's impossible for him to concentrate here. Not because of the interruptions. It's the memories. Arun was forever showing us videos. He'd gotten super into space and psychology. I know so much about the solar system from what he'd shown me that I could probably write my own honor's thesis."

She looked at her daughter. Such a maelstrom of emotion passed over her face that Indie found it hard to keep up.

"He sounds like a wonderful young man."

"He was." She ran a sleeve under her nose. "I want them, those memories, because they're the tie we have to him, but they're so painful right now. Unbearable."

Indie wished she didn't understand that. Maeve probably hadn't fully realized yet that she wouldn't be able to make any new memories with her eldest son that didn't feature a tombstone. Indie wished she could spare her the realization. That knowledge wielded the sharpest blade of pain.

Maeve pressed her eyes with the heels of her palms. "Sorry. You have questions. Ask away."

"How did Arun seem in the last few weeks before he died?"

The little girl's laughter startled her mom and made a ghost of a smile twitch at her lips. Maeve looked at Indie with guilty eyes. "How he's always been, but more so. I mean, he was special. Not just because he was our eldest, but because he was what I called an isolated genius. Huan was convinced he would be a professor. You know, you read about academics, how they're so brilliant but don't have the common sense to come in out of the rain. Arun was like that."

"He struggled to fit in with other people?"

Maeve nodded. "He could talk about the universe and math and philosophy with words I'd never even heard, but he couldn't understand the etiquette of the school bus. He found it hard to navigate school. The politics of fitting in were beyond him." Her words were quiet, her whole body weighed down by tears.

"Had he spent more time on his phone?"

"He was often in his room. He was the only one with his own space, so I don't know about using his phone more. Definitely his computer. He'd switch the screen when I went in, so I don't know what he was looking at. His dad wasn't worried, because he'd installed all sorts of security on every device to protect the kids."

"Do you know if he was on any online forums, in any communities?"

The little girl clapped her hands and giggled.

Maeve watched her as she spoke to Indie. "I don't know. I can ask Huan if his safeguards can track."

"I'd appreciate that. In the meantime, can I see his room?"

"It's this way."

Indie followed her up the stairs, where the noise level of the kids playing was rising again. "Did Arun have any fears?"

Maeve shook her head. "He said fear came from ignorance." She walked into the middle of Arun's room. "This was his favorite place. You can open the drapes."

Indie pulled one partially open. Everywhere she looked

were books stacked on top of each other, crossed haphazardly in piles, some left open where Arun hadn't finished reading.

His mom gestured to his messy desk, covered in paper and pens. "He was always making notes."

"The word he wrote on his notepad, 'ascension.' Does that mean anything to you?"

Maeve wiped her eyes again. "No. I've been wondering about that. What he meant."

"Was his PC taken into evidence?"

"It's always been here." A shout from elsewhere in the house made Maeve jump. "Here we go again."

"Thank you for your time. Can you make sure no one else uses it until I've checked on that? I can see myself out."

Maeve nodded. "If you need anything else, you know where I am." Her voice dropped into a quiet confession. "It's nice to talk about Arun."

Indie hoped her expression told Arun's mom that she understood. She knew words were entirely inadequate, so she walked downstairs and out of the house, closing the door on Maeve as the grieving mother failed to summon any joy into her voice for the other children.

Broc was watching her when she slipped back into the Explorer. *"Everything okay?"*

"I don't know." Indie turned in the driver's seat to face him. "Each of these kids had a different personality, but they all had one thing in common. They had a passion, something they cared deeply about."

Broc cocked his head in a *tell me more* gesture.

Ticking off the points on her fingers, Indie listed what she'd learned. "Nila had her activism, Leila her art, and Arun his fascination with scientific knowledge. They all withdrew online, where they'd found friends." She started the engine. "That's more than coincidence. More than enough to connect them. And if they were part of an online community, we've got to find it and shut it down before anyone else dies."

All the parents she'd talked to seemed to have genuinely loved the children they'd lost, even if they'd all literally been left to their own devices for different reasons.

"And another thing," Indie added as she drove away from the Chang house, "Arun put his notebook beside him in the car, which suggests he thought his ascension would give him new knowledge or insight." She looked at Broc in the rearview mirror. "I hope Nila's autopsy gives us something. Because right now, we don't have a whole lot of anything concrete."

9

Indie pulled into the drive of Aunt Edith's property. "It's good to be home, hey, boy?"

Home? That was usually a word she avoided, but it rolled off her tongue here.

As she let Broc out of her Jeep, Indie could admit it was comforting to feel settled. Her balcony, her new favorite place, offered her all the peace and solitude she wanted. Today had been filled with so much peopling, she didn't have it in her to make the dinner she'd mapped out the night before. A snack and a tall iced tea and sitting outside with her boys sounded perfect.

She took Broc's harness off. "Have at it."

He jumped the fence into the yard and charged out of sight around the back of Aunt Edith's house, far enough he could pretend he didn't hear Indie's shouting, "Don't go in the pool," and "You'd better be listening."

Aunt Edith opened the door to the main house, and Satch bounded out, tail wagging. He jumped up at Indie, front paws on her chest, tongue lolling out.

"You're looking very chipper." Indie held his front legs to

guide him back so all four paws were on the ground. She was so relieved he hadn't yelped when he jumped up on her, but still... "That joint care's working good, huh?"

"Hmm, we won't talk about that."

She rumpled his mane. "We can talk about how good it is for you all day long, but we don't have to mention that you're not being such a baby about the taste now."

Aunt Edith called from her porch. Indie didn't need to be a detective to tell she'd been busy in the kitchen. The splatters and spots on her bright-yellow apron told the story. "You like to join us for dinner?"

Indie opened her mouth with her excuses all lined up. But the waft of proper home cooking snuck in, making her drool. Her stomach growled, warning her what she should say. "That'd be lovely."

"Did someone say dinner?" A thankfully still-dry Broc shot up to Indie, doing the canine equivalent of a skier's stop in front of her.

"Since you listened to me about not jumping in the pool, yes, someone did mention dinner."

Broc trotted next to Satch toward Aunt Edith's house.

"Did the pup keep you safe today?" Satch gave Broc a look. *"No close calls?"*

"Nope. Not a single one."

Indie couldn't stifle her smile. Her boys were her world. As she let them go ahead of her through the open door, she felt the warmth of her Grammy Ada as clearly as if she'd patted Indie's back. Maybe Aunt Edith's close connection to Grammy Ada was why Indie felt so at home.

She heard conversation as she approached the kitchen and stepped inside. It took her a beat to recognize the woman with a black shoulder-length bob wearing a flowy pink-and-green flowered dress.

People always looked different out of uniform, but Hen

looked like another person entirely. Maybe it was all the crystals she wore around her neck and hanging from her ears.

"Sit down and dig in. Nana makes the best parmigiana." Hen's metal bracelets jingled as she stuck a fork in the breadcrumbed cutlet on top of a mound of chunky sauce and pasta on her plate. "Though it's usually chicken. I don't know about this eggplant one. Maybe it just needs more cheese."

Indie watched Aunt Edith place a huge bowl of garlic bread on the table. "You made vegetarian?"

"I have a lot of eggplant coming in. I'm hoping you can give me some recipes." She wiped her hands on the tea towel slung over her shoulder. "It's the first time I've tried them, and they're growing like weeds. Sit. Eat."

"How'd your first day go?" Hen had to raise her voice over the furious jangling as she grated more cheese over her plate. "You getting on okay with Eli and Sheriff Sammy? Did you get to see them after all? I had traffic duty. Always lots to do with that. Ooh, what did Clifton say?"

Aunt Edith sat opposite her. "Now, Hen, let the poor child take a load off before you bombard her with questions."

"It's too late for that." Indie sat down, hoping the hurricane of noise and color that was Hen wouldn't give her a headache.

"You're looking a lot more settled."

"Settled?" Indie took a bite of garlic bread while Hen continued voicing every thought that popped in her head.

"Yeah. You know, earlier, at the crime scene, you looked a bit…well, your aura looked a bit small. Do you know what that means?" Hen touched the base of her neck. "This is lovely, Nana. Just like chicken except not as chewy."

Hen shoveled another load onto her fork and pointed it at Indie.

For a second, Indie thought she was supposed to say something, but Hen rambled on.

"A small aura is like if someone's…well, I thought it might be because it was your first day and all, that maybe you were a bit nervous. Except when you were playing with your dog and Tyler, then it blossomed all around you."

"Protecting and serving, huh?" Satch lifted his head from the floor where he was lying and looked at Indie. *"He had a hard day playing?"*

Broc didn't even raise his head in response. *"Tell the old man I was trying to make a little boy smile. He'd lost his important person. He had a great tree."*

Hen chattered on. "And here you are, back home and relaxed with a lovely aura, all peaceful and back to where it should be."

Indie didn't know what to say. She settled for taking her first bite of the eggplant parmigiana. The explosion of garlic and sweet tomato hit her in the jaw like an actual punch. The tartness of the strong cheese perfectly balanced the creaminess of the eggplant and the crunchiness of its breading. Utterly delicious.

"You know about auras…well, you know what they are, yeah? They're our energetic fields, just like the earth. They go to about six feet out, around us like this," Hen's fork clattered onto her plate, and she held her arms out to either side of her, "when we're happy and peaceful, when we're feeling good vibes. But when we're being attacked or we're scared or uncertain, they can shrink right back." She brought her arms in, almost touching her sides.

A lesson in auras was something Indie had not been expecting five minutes ago when she accepted the dinner invite.

"Did you know that's how bullies pick their targets?" Hen bulldozed on. "I mean, they don't understand about energy, and they're definitely not light workers, otherwise they wouldn't be bullies, would they?"

"No, they would not, dear." Aunt Edith responded out of habit more than anything, it seemed.

Hen shook her head, answering her own question, even though her nana just had. "But bullies can subconsciously pick up on a weak aura. And the more they pick on someone, guess what." Hen adjusted the symbol on her choker. "The bullies' auras grow because they're feeling powerful, and their victims' auras shrink. It's a horrible cycle. But fascinating. All the amazing things happening just beyond where we can see them but right at the point where we can intuit them, even if we don't understand."

Indie still didn't know what to say, so she took another bite of dinner. She knew some people would find it alarming if she admitted she could hear and understand animals, but energy fields around people? Shrinking and growing? That sounded way out there.

"You're holding yourself very tight again." Hen smiled, no sting in her words intended. "You should loosen up, especially at home. That's where you get to be yourself."

"Hen, I think that's enough for one night." Aunt Edith matched her granddaughter's smile. "Medicine goes down easier in smaller spoonfuls."

"But it'd be quite the tell, wouldn't it? To see how the teens' auras looked in this case."

Indie dipped a crust into her sauce. "I don't think we can use that as evidence."

"Oh, I don't mean for that, but it would maybe point us in the right direction. If they're not really suicides, is all I meant."

Indie glanced at Aunt Edith, who was busy choosing a second piece of bread. "Whether they are or not isn't really dinner table conversation."

"Don't you worry about me, dear." Aunt Edith patted Indie on the hand that held her poised fork. "I would never repeat a word spoken within these walls."

"Nana's the best sounding board." Hen winked. "Good witch energy. It's like it's in the coven rules."

Aunt Edith smiled at her granddaughter. "Lucky I'm not a witch. Simply a woman wise beyond her years."

Hen and Aunt Edith laughed together at that.

They cleaned their plates in no time after Hen's aura lesson.

"Now." Aunt Edith stacked the empty plates. "I hope you both saved room for dessert."

"Haven't had firsts yet." Broc huffed. *"Out at work all day and still not been fed."*

"You should've been here while cooking was happening." Satch looked like he was grinning.

"Next best thing." Broc rolled onto his front and commando-crawled until his head was under the table beside Indie.

"I think energy work's fascinating," Hen went on, as though no one had interrupted her.

"Hey. You're not sneezing," was all Indie could think to say.

"I took some allergy meds." Hen scratched at the base of her neck just then, though. The spot was reddening. "It'll get better as I get used to them all. But I should be okay with the turtle. I mean, what is there to be allergic to? Surely not the shell."

"The turtle isn't here though. Either outside or in the apartment." Indie pointed vaguely toward her apartment above the garage.

Aunt Edith shook her head. "Actually, Salem's around here somewhere. I let her in." She glanced around the dining room as if the reptile would suddenly appear.

"It's here? The she-devil's in here?" Broc jumped up, headbutting the table with an almighty clonk. So hard, he made the serving spoon slip off the edge of the parmigiana dish, splattering the white tablecloth with a red-orange stain.

His legs seemed to have forgotten how to work, tangling themselves up as if he were a cartoon dog, trying to get away while running on the spot. Salem suddenly showed her tiny, pale-green face and stopped a few inches in front of him.

Broc finally got traction. As he shot out from under the table, he caught the end of the tablecloth enough that he knocked the grater onto the floor, flicking a spray of cheese everywhere. Satch was right on it, licking up the cheesy crumbs as they dropped to the floor. Broc was too busy hurdling the couch and vanishing behind it to care about scraps.

After a second of stunned silence, when Indie was sure they'd be thrown out and never invited to come again, Aunt Edith and Hen burst out laughing. Aunt Edith clutched her sides while Hen hung onto the edge of the table, both barely even able to breathe. Indie felt the warmth of the moment and relaxed enough to join them.

"Well," Aunt Edith was finally able to gasp, mopping her eyes, "that was quite the cabaret. What do they do for an encore?"

10

"You're saying that the death of Nila Radler is connected to the deaths of Leila Perez and Arun Chang?" Lead Investigator Eli Walker's voice went up so much at the end of his question that Indie looked down to check she hadn't stepped on his foot.

No, she was good. Still standing in front of Sheriff Sammy's desk, with Eli still sitting in the chair next to her. His long legs were extended, crossed at the ankles. A good foot away from her feet. No crazy belt buckle today. He'd opted for the more muted bling of a shoestring tie.

The look matched his general demeanor, as if he couldn't pour piss out of his boot if it had directions on the heel, even if Indie knew he wasn't stupid.

"They're all suicides." And there he was, trying his hardest to challenge what she knew. "Those cases are closed."

Indie looked at the sheriff for help, hoping he'd been listening closer to her update.

He smoothed his perfect dark hair back, as if giving himself time to think it through. At around fifty, his experience and the office he held should've been what lent him an air of gravitas. But when she'd done her research on his office, Indie had found him in front of the camera a lot. After that, she recognized that his confidence originated just as much from his deep tan, expensive dental work, and expertly dyed hair.

She took that opportunity to dive in again. "The trend of teen deaths in the area is far higher than normal. I've talked to the families of the most recent victims, who confirmed all were very active online just before their deaths."

"Like every other teen on the planet." Eli recrossed his legs at the ankle.

She ignored his snide comment. "Nila Radler left behind a poem entitled 'Ascend.' Arun Chang wrote the word 'ascension' on the notepad he had beside him in the car, and I just found the same word on the back of Leila Perez's last painting."

The sheriff steepled his fingers and turned his bright-blue gaze toward Indie. "This could be nothing other than new slang."

"I checked that. It doesn't appear to be."

"Well, then, that's good work."

"I've been trying to track down an online community that's promoting the idea of 'ascending' through suicide, but so far, I haven't found anything."

The sheriff checked his nails, then waved a dismissive hand toward the door. "Meanwhile, you have things to do, like attend the autopsy on that poor child from yesterday."

Eli pushed himself up on the chair. "No need for me to be there if Reign's going. Think you can handle it?"

That was the second time he'd questioned if she could face seeing a body. Why would he assume she couldn't?

"I can go by myself."

"Excellent. I have work here." He stood, clapped his

hands, arms swinging wide, and strode out of the sheriff's office.

Clearly, those things didn't include mentoring or training Indie. Looked more like they included fresh coffee and a pastry and mastering the tilt mechanism on his chair.

Lucky for her, she didn't need him. Her impression so far was that she might not be able to rely on him. Indie turned and left for Columbia Medical Center.

※

As Indie followed the directions she'd been given at the welcome desk, the corridors became less busy and more hushed until she was the only one standing in front of her destination.

Reading and rereading the awful name on the door, *Morgue*, she steadied her heartbeat, her breathing, her stomach. She'd purposefully eaten a light breakfast of just a banana, and she hoped her body wouldn't let her down. Poor Nila's crime scene had been awful.

Indie knocked lightly and opened the door.

It was like walking into the sun.

She blinked furiously beneath the sudden fierce light. "Dr. Parker?"

The gowned person closest to her turned around and, seeing Indie's uniform and badge, pointed with a gloved hand to the tall Black woman bending over the body on the stainless steel table.

Indie introduced herself, and Dr. Kristin Parker straightened up. "K-9 detective with no canine?"

"I didn't think you'd appreciate him being in here."

"Never in here. And I'm sure he'd be well-behaved. It's me I'm worried about. I love dogs."

Well-behaved so long as there isn't a turtle in the room.

"Since we have so much in common already, call me Kristin. Unfortunately, I imagine we'll be working together quite a bit. Nothing personal, you understand." Her eyebrows were raised above her mask.

"No offense taken."

Kristin nodded at the countertop along the back wall. "Grab yourself a mask and apron. You'll only need gloves if you're touching anything, but I'm asking you to please not."

"Understood." Indie did as directed, standing a couple of steps away from the table.

"You good with this?" Kristin looked at Nila's corpse, where she'd already done her Y-incision and where the tech was weighing and bagging her internal organs. "Or do you need to stand farther away? I don't appreciate my bodies being contaminated."

"I'm good." They'd washed Nila, and both the background smell of disinfectant and the gentle stream of air being pumped into and out of the room worked to keep the odor subtle enough that it was bearable.

"I've done the internal exam and found nothing to suggest assault. You can see her wrists and arms." Kristin gently lifted Nila's right hand, then her left, turning them over before placing them back on the table. "No defensive wounds or indication of self-harm. There's also nothing of any note under her fingernails. The small amount of matter suggests it came from there."

Indie looked at Nila's clean nails, then at where Kristin was pointing at a couple of minor abrasions on Nila's neck. "She scratched herself?"

"These scratches are her clawing to breathe. She might've made the decision to die, but her body would still fight it. Obviously, the lab will check."

Indie's shiver had nothing to do with the morgue's refrigerated air. She couldn't bear to imagine the awfulness of Nila's last moments. Why had she chosen such a brutal way to end her life?

Kristin's gloved finger hovered over the deepest, thickest mark on Nila's neck. "Only one rope burn would make me suspicious, as that would suggest she was already dead when she was strung up. But here we have what I'd expect to see. This laceration is where the rope tightened when she stepped off the swing. The others are where she shifted."

"Do you mean she regretted it?" The horror of that felt like a stab to Indie's own heart.

"Not necessarily. The brain is a remarkable instrument. No matter how much she wanted to kill herself, at the moment of the act itself, her body would rebel. She would have involuntarily kicked her legs, which would've increased her momentum, swinging her backward and forward, shifting where the rope held her. That's what we're seeing here and here."

Indie appreciated the pathologist's teaching tone. She clearly loved what she did, and she was damn good at it.

Kristin looked at Indie, her gaze softening. "Sadly, Nila was successful in her effort to die by hanging. There are no defensive wounds, ligature marks on the wrists, or signs of bruising or a struggle, so there's nothing to definitively suggest she was physically forced or assisted."

"Did you perform the autopsies on Arun Chang or Leila Perez?"

Kristin picked up a camera. "Yes. I did both of them. And no, I didn't find anything that contradicted the obvious that they both also died by suicide. Why do you ask?"

"Leila and Nila and Arun all left mementos behind that featured the word 'ascension' or 'ascend.' Arun had a notepad with him, open to a page with 'ascension' on top. Leila's last painting was entitled *Ascension*, and Nila had written a poem titled 'Ascend.' I'm wondering if it's more than random chance that they chose those words."

Kristin frowned and, stripping off her gloves and mask, walked over to the desk, where she logged into her computer.

Indie's phone pinged. She pulled it out to find a text from Clifton Harina.

The escaped came home. I remember the case where I heard the term "ascend." Zach Mitchell. Ruled accidental death.

Indie pocketed her phone. "Did you do the autopsy for Zach Mitchell?"

The bright overhead lights caught Kristin's wedding band as she typed. "I did. Accidental death. He was a parkour runner who fell from height. His tox screen was clear, and there was nothing to suggest assault or outside interference. He filmed himself doing the stunt." She brought up another page. "There, in the transcript of the video. He said he was going to ascend right before he fell."

Indie pulled out her notebook and jotted that down.

Kristin checked her slim gold watch. "I'd say you have your pattern, but the investigating I'll leave to you. I'll send my findings to Clifton, and he'll make his judgment as to cause of death for Nila."

"Thank you."

"It's never easy having a child on my table, but being able to make sense of some of their last moments can sometimes help the families. And when it comes down to it, that's all we can do."

Kristin had summed it up beautifully.

And Indie had a lot more digging to do to find the whole truth around Nila Radler's death, as well as the deaths of Leila Perez, Arun Chang, and now, potentially, Zach Mitchell.

11

Broc jumped over the gate as Indie pulled up Aunt Edith's drive and sat in front of her door. *"What took you so long?"*

"Haven't we had words about you jumping out of the yard?"

"Yeah, but you've been months."

Indie got out of the Explorer and put her hands on her hips. "You can't just jump over the fence. There's a road here."

Broc lowered his head like a naughty child.

"What's it going to take for you to not do it?"

He looked up at her, hope quivering his whiskers. *"You take me with you when you go out."*

"Trust me. I'd love to, but there are places you can't go. I take you where I can. The rest of the time, you're on guard duty here. And you can't guard in there," Indie pointed at the yard, "from out here."

"I can, because I'm a smart boy."

Indie gave him her severest eyebrow arch.

"I can get over the fence like it's not there. I can run around the house faster than any burglar, and I can hear where there's trouble

from down the street. There's no need for me to stay in there if there's something interesting out here."

Indie went to answer him but stopped. "Being schooled by my dog. Maybe I'll quit while I'm not too far behind."

Trouble was he *was* a smart boy.

She squatted in front of him and stroked his chest. "You stay where I tell you to stay so I don't have to worry about you being safe when I'm not with you."

"Why didn't you say so?" He lifted his chin so she could scratch underneath it.

"What, the two hundredth time is when you listen?"

Broc tilted his head the other way so Indie could spread the love.

"Let's go. Places to be."

He jumped into the SUV. *"Finally."*

When Indie led him through the sheriff's office to her desk, Broc had a definite *officer reporting for duty* swagger.

"Here you go, bud." Indie handed him a new toy. "Something for you while I file my report from this morning."

He took the bright-green duck as if he'd never had a toy in his life. Then he flopped down beside her. The clunk of the tag on his collar rattled against the floor and startled Oliver Freeman, who was hunting and pecking at his keyboard.

"Sure he's comfy over there?"

"I think he is."

Oliver's raised, questioning eyebrows were almost as animated as Broc's.

Indie pulled up the report on Zach Mitchell. She read through the file easily enough, but with the cursor over the play icon for the attached video, her hand hovered over her mouse as if it were on quills.

Pulling out her bun, she redid it, taking longer than

normal to wind the strands around and push the pins in to hold them in place. Trying not to think about it, she finally hit Play.

Zach's face filled the whole frame. Blond hair, blue eyes, the faintest whisper of stubble. He licked his lips. *"You haven't seen me do anything like this. See where I am."*

The video panned away until it looked down on a construction site, then centered on a red crane that looked to be several yards away. He couldn't be about to jump to that. No, no, it was too far.

"You know how I rock at parkour? Well, that was nothing. I'm gonna ascend, and you lucky people and the Guide are my witnesses."

He grinned into the lens, and Indie saw no doubt in his eyes. He really believed he could make the leap. The view switched, and the ripping of Velcro suggested he was adjusting his phone in the chest harness he'd been wearing when he died.

"Here we go." The view rocked back and forth, back and forth. Indie could imagine him moving like a high jumper before an Olympic medal attempt, psyching himself up for the leap, sizing up how fast he'd need to run at the drop.

Don't fall. Don't fall.

Indie found herself mouthing the words even as the view bounced with each of his steps, even as the crane began to fill the screen. Indie gripped the edge of her desk. "You can make it."

But the video showed the crisscrossed structure of the crane's mast rushing past as gravity caught Zach. His strangled cry made her want to screw her eyes shut, but she owed it to him to watch.

She nudged the playback bar. Five seconds remaining. Those five seconds must've felt like eternity as he fell.

The ground rushed up. And with a thump, the screen went dark.

Broc gave the barest hint of a whine beside her. Keeping ahold of his duck, he sat up and laid a paw on Indie's thigh. *"You okay?"*

Not remotely.

But Indie nodded and smoothed his fur, hoping he couldn't feel her trembling. He lay back down, keeping his gaze on her as he chewed the toy.

Indie couldn't find any socials for Zach Mitchell, but after a search through his peers, she found footage of him taken by a buddy who also did parkour. She watched Zach leap over walls and run partway up light poles and up the sides of buildings. He jumped down short drops into stairwells, off waist-high rails, and over park benches. His tricks were all low level. He'd never really left the ground until the day he died.

Was he afraid of heights?

She thought of Leila in the water. Had Zach's death been similar, a young person facing their worst fear and making a fatal error in judgment?

"Reign, in here." The sheriff's shout startled Indie.

She grabbed her notebook and rushed to his office.

"Mary Jackson, manager at Sherwood Pines Care Home, just called. Seems Burt Draper's wandered off again. He's one of their dementia patients, so he can be tricky, but this is exactly what you signed up to do. A case where we can show actionable results with minimal use of resource." Sheriff Sammy gave her a politician's smile, all brilliant white teeth, no eyes.

"What about the teen cases?" Indie just couldn't help herself. The words fell out of her mouth as though she weren't in control of them. "I just found an accidental death,

Zach Mitchell, who also mentioned ascending in his final words to the camera before dying."

She gave the sheriff a look that would've made Broc proud. But apparently, Sheriff Sammy was immune to puppy-dog eyes. Or her execution needed some work.

"We want this pilot project of you and your dog to be successful. As much as folks here like the familiar, they're more likely to accept something new and different if we can show them how that change benefits them. You solving cases, like our missing Burt…it's good. For all of us. The big picture." His smile reached a little farther up his face. "Once you've done that, I don't see the harm in letting you spread your wings a bit."

"Yes, sir." The words were bitter.

Indie got as far as the door before he added, "Long as you remember your priority. It's one of the main reasons we selected you for this role. You know the area. Don't let me down."

"I won't."

If the sheriff noticed the fervor laced through her promise to him and the teens, he didn't show it. If what Indie suspected was half true, she wasn't going to let Leila, Arun, Nila, and all their hopes and dreams be dismissed into history with the awful notation "death by suicide" as their last act. And for Zach, if his death wasn't an accident of adolescent hubris, someone had to be held accountable.

Indie would make sure of it.

❄

Indie didn't need to ask the identity of the middle-aged woman who rushed out of Sherwood Pines Care Home and over to her before she'd parked. Mary Jackson clenched and unclenched her hands, alternately wringing then crushing something small, fuzzy, and navy to her chest.

"Thank goodness you've come. Burt's nowhere to be found. And it's one of his bad days. I hope he's not looking for his wife again. That makes him upset as well as frightened. He gets furious if he thinks she's not here."

The wall of words blasted Indie as she got out of the SUV and straightened her tactical vest.

"You must be Mary Jackson. Is Mrs. Draper here?"

"I am." Mary shook her head. "And no. She passed on a few years ago. We don't correct him if he's talking to her. It's protocol. We try to divert his attention to another subject that doesn't upset him." She looked at the tall pines surrounding the property and worry edged her voice higher. "He could be anywhere. It's nearly cake and coffee time, and he never misses that."

"That's why Broc's here." Indie opened his door, and he jumped out, sitting at attention beside her while she clipped him on the fifteen-foot long line. She looked at the navy sweater Mary twisted in her hands. "Is that Burt's?"

Mary looked at the woolly garment she was holding as if wondering how it had gotten there. "Yes. Yes, it is. I thought you might need it."

"That's great thinking. Can Broc sniff your hand to eliminate your scent?"

"Oh, I could get another sweater."

"No need. Broc's good with scents. He'll discount yours and focus just on Burt."

"Don't you need to know where he usually goes? At least where we've found him in the past?"

The look on Broc's face was best not interpreted. Indie settled on reassuring Mary. "Broc will find him. Can he?" She gestured at the bundle.

Mary held it out, and Broc sniffed her hand before turning his nose to the sweater.

"Got it."

Indie gave Broc enough slack on the line that he could run ahead of her without getting tangled around anything and followed him out of the main gate right into the tall trees that gave Sherwood Pines its name. She looked up at the canopy above them, where the tops of the trees swayed back and forth against the blue sky. It made her disoriented and dizzy. Was that what had happened to the missing resident?

Indie breathed in the cleansing scent of pine resin and felt the long line go taut.

Broc was looking back at her, waiting. *"He's not up there."*

"I know." Indie caught up. "Show me."

From the road, the forest floor had appeared flat as pavement, but as she ran through the trees, it rippled up slopes and dropped down into ditches. Though the shade was cooler, a bead of sweat rolled down Indie's spine as she charged after Broc.

"Burt must be a pretty fit man to have gotten this far."

"You don't sound that fit." Broc looked back at her, then made a U-turn, trotting past the group of trees in the opposite direction.

"You should try running with all this gear on. It makes a difference."

Broc pulled up and barked.

And there was Burt Draper.

"Burt, it's the sheriff's office." Indie hurdled a fallen spindly pine to catch up with the older man. "Can I walk with you?"

His watery eyes screwed up as he scrutinized her. "You're not one of the tree people."

"No. I'm Indie, and this is Broc."

The man had a twig stuck over his left ear the way some

workers carry their pencils, and he'd lost a slipper. She looked him up and down but saw no signs of injury.

"Do the tree people know you?" Burt tried to push nonexistent glasses up his nose.

"They do."

"That's all right, then. You can't be coming along if they don't know you."

"They're over there today." Indie waved at Sherwood Pines behind them. "Shall we go see them?"

"That's why we're here."

Broc was looking at her as if she'd lost her mind.

Burt turned around and tromped off toward Sherwood Pines as though Indie had commanded him in German. After a minute, he finally seemed to notice Broc. "Where'd he come from? He's not one of them."

"He's with me."

Broc turned around to preen. *"Tell him."*

"He says he's a very smart boy, and he's the one who found you."

Broc tossed his head, though Burt didn't look as impressed.

"How did he find me if I'm not lost?"

"He wanted to walk with you and knows you know the best spots."

Burt looked around, his gaze whipping from one tree to the next. "Where did the tree people go?" His voice got stronger in his agitation. "Did you make them leave?"

"No one made them leave."

Burt cocked his head, then his arm, and took a swing at Indie.

She ducked his fist easily, but his momentum carried him around until he slipped over and slapped down onto his butt.

Broc gave him a warning growl to keep his hands to himself.

"It's okay," Indie told them both. "He can't help it. Shall we go home, Burt?"

He blinked as though he'd gotten a pine needle in the eye, until his gaze landed on Broc again. "Ruby?"

"Ruby?"

"Girl, your ears have gotten big. Come here, girl." Burt held his arms out.

"Girl?" Broc whined at Indie.

"It won't kill you to pretend. And it'll help us solve the case, which is getting Burt back to safety. Think of it like undercover work. Detectives do it all the time."

Broc didn't look convinced, but he edged toward Burt and the man caught him in an awkward hug. "Where've you been, girl?"

"Don't you dare tell Satch."

"What happens on the job stays on the job." Indie turned to the lost resident. "Burt, it's cake and coffee time."

"Why didn't you say?" Burt tried to stand, but his feet couldn't get purchase on the slippery pine needles.

"Let me help." Indie held her hands out to him. "You hold on to me, and we'll get you up."

He took her hands as though he might break them.

"I'm stronger than I look. Ready?" She tucked her feet in front of his, leaned back, and heaved. After one false start, Burt was upright again.

"Come on. Can't miss cake and coffee time." He trudged off, and Indie could understand how he'd gotten so far away before he was missed.

"Just up there." Indie pointed at the edge of the trees, through which they could see the big house of Sherwood Pines Care Home beyond the bright white of her Explorer. "There's no prickles there."

"That the sheriff? Why's he come? Something the matter?"

"Everything's just fine."

At least, it would be, once Mary saw that Burt was okay so she could stop her frantic pacing. Broc strutted right up to Mary, but she only had eyes for her resident.

"There you are. We were so worried."

"Cake and coffee time?"

"Yes, it is." She input the code into the numbered key lock and led him through the gate without so much as a glance back at either one of them.

Broc was not pleased.

"You did great, buddy." Indie fished in her jacket pocket.

"Is that...?" Broc's front paws tip-tapped, his tongue lolling out of his mouth. *"Is it?"*

"The dreaded." She made a show of pulling his favorite treat out. "Yes, it is."

He danced faster. *"Oh, boy."*

Indie revealed the double-bagged treat with a flourish.

"Officer, thank you so much." Mary had come back out. "I'll be sure to let the sheriff know how helpful you were."

Indie stopped trying to unzip the outer bag and flapped it at Broc. "It was all him. I just followed where he led."

Broc looked as if she'd eaten the freeze-dried squid. *"Don't do that. Don't tease me. No, do do that. Waggle that bag some more and make the yummy fall out."*

Mary looked at Broc with gratitude in her eyes. "He's a smart dog. Can I call you directly if Burt gets out again?"

Broc was fixated on the bags in Indie's hand.

"It's faster to go through dispatch." *And every call will remind the sheriff how useful Broc is.*

The Malinois whined. *"You're killing me here."*

Indie ignored him, focusing on Mary.

"I'll do that, then. Thank you again."

"Have a good day." Indie wrestled with the bag as soon as

Mary had gone back through the gate and the lock had engaged. "Broc, you're drooling a river."

"You're surprised?"

"I had to wait." Indie got the first seal open on the treats. "I can't unleash this smell on the innocent public." She held the bag away from her to undo the inner one, shaking out a couple of chunks into her hand. Even outside, it made her screw her face up and took away her appetite for lunch.

She held out one of the chunks, and Broc nearly took her fingers. "You want this one, you take it nicely."

He tried to fold his lips back to nibble the treat off her hand with just his teeth. He looked like a camel. *"Another for doing such a great job?"*

"Good effort." Indie tucked the inner bag into the outer and sealed them both twice, just to make sure. She shuddered. "That is grim." She opened her driver's door with the very tips of her fingers and snatched out her hand sanitizer.

Squirting some into her palms, she opened Broc's door, and the dog bounded in.

"And you say I'm a drama queen. You know I could've just licked your fingers."

12

Today's the day. RisingStar77 was the first Ascender to congratulate Elliott Greene.

He smiled. It didn't surprise him that she was the first to comment.

She? What if RisingStar77 wasn't a she?

Elliott's face flushed hot at the thought, at the memory of the things he'd shared. *She has to be a she*, he told himself for the umpteenth time. She was interested in what he had to say. Once, she'd even told him, *I've got your back as you have mine*. That sounded like the kind of thing a girl would say.

A girl interested in him made him grin hard enough that his face ached, made his hands feel clammy. Made him rush to spray himself with body spray.

He coughed at the dry chemical odor of the particles. A girl saw him for his mind, after so many years of hoping. Today was already special, and he hadn't even ascended yet.

Elliott punched the air.

Congratulations, Elliott. Today you'll show the world the true magnificence of your intellect.

Trust the Guide to get straight to what mattered most. He must be almost as smart as Elliott. "Yes, I will."

Elliott hoped ascending wouldn't mean the Guide stopped giving him challenges. He loved them more than the dopamine hit he got when they dropped in the app. Maybe because they gave his brain something worthwhile to work on, something out of the reach of basic people, all while his body went through the motions of school and family and all the boring things he had to do to stay alive.

I can't wait for you to join me when you ascend, RisingStar77 messaged him again.

Me either, he typed back, all fingers and thumbs.

RisingStar77 was the one who encouraged him to dig deeper, to try harder, to reason better than he thought he could. The Ascension app had propelled him along the path to genius way faster than high school ever had. That last cipher he'd decoded was wicked hard.

No need to be nervous. The message from a user named HurdleThat popped up but then disappeared just as quickly.

Elliott hadn't seen that username before. Was HurdleThat someone new or someone who'd already ascended? Or was it that pumped-up jackass from school, Logan Nagle? Nah, he couldn't be on Ascension, could he?

But he did know exactly how to goad him. Nagle claimed he could hack into anything. And HurdleThat was definitely taunting him.

Elliott's emotions got the best of him as he typed. *Is that you, Logan Nagle? Think you're so smart. I'm about to school you.*

He struggled to see past the red-hot anger that had him breaking one of the app's fundamental rules—never use real names.

Elliott drew his foot back to kick his desk but stopped himself. He needed to be quiet. Plus, kinetic energy displaced down a bare foot against a metal desk leg would equal broken toes.

Maybe the Guide hadn't noticed what he'd written. He couldn't flame out when he was so close.

Glad that RisingStar77 couldn't see his face, he wiped his hands down his jeans before picking up the Phillips screwdriver. He jabbed its magnetized end at the pile of tiny screws on his desk, bending over the device that was gradually emerging out of bits and pieces carefully sourced.

He gathered wires together, looping them into equal lengths.

Snip, snip, snip. His cutters went through them.

The night was nearly gone. He knew after ascending he'd be too jazzed to sleep, so he'd already decided to cut school. Hard enough to sit in a classroom surrounded by sheep. Imagine how unbearable it would be once he'd learned everything ascending would teach him.

He turned the device over to check what he'd created matched the schematic in his mind. All looked good, except the leftover screws on his desk.

Using the tip of the screwdriver, he rolled the extra screws to one side. His things usually went missing. He never had extras…of anything. His half brothers flushed his stuff down the toilet, threw it out the window, or maybe even ate it. He tried not to get involved with what those two horrors did, except when it affected him.

Their mom, Lisa, tried hard enough to control them, but she generally failed at it. He knew the lure of their "big brother's space" was like the gravitational force of a black hole. But still…

They'd been useful as the perfect excuse as to why he'd put a lock on his door. Lisa and his dad made weak protests, but they left it in place. Just as well. Elliott could imagine the riot if they saw the deadly crystals he'd precipitated in there.

They looked innocuous enough, almost like dishwasher detergent, but they'd be impossible to explain away.

Even if I could get Dad believing they were for the science fair, he wouldn't listen—just yell himself into a heart attack thinking I've been cooking meth or something. As if I'd ever be into all that. I'm not like that idiot Nagle.

Elliott flicked an impatient hand through his hair. Soon enough, they'd all see just how brilliant he was. Before the sun rose, his stupid half brothers, their mom, even dumbass Nagle wouldn't matter a bit.

I'll have ascended, asshats, and be beyond feeling small, be beyond feeling like I'm lost in my own house, forgotten by my own family. Invisible.

He placed the tiny white crystals into the rectangular housing of the device, not daring to tap them level. The latent power inside each one was intense. He still couldn't get over how only three-hundredths of an ounce could cause damage—and he'd grown around two whole ounces.

Plenty to ensure his ascension was a complete success. Plenty to impress RisingStar77. *"Sixteen-year-old Elliott Greene became a hero today when he saved his family from an explosion."* He could see the serious expressions of the news anchors reading out his story.

Hero sounded lit, but that didn't tell anyone about him personally. *"Heroic Genius Elliott Greene Saves Family."* Yeah, that was more like it. Those were the headlines he'd insist on.

He dropped the spare screws into the blank spaces around the little box housing the crystals, taking extra care not to disturb anything. If only the Guide could see that, he'd get extra points for ingenuity.

He smiled at surpassing himself. When he'd first gotten the challenge, his gut had knotted hard enough to go into a spasm. How could he build a bomb? It sounded like something way beyond his reach. But the reality was easier than drawing the schematics for the robot that should've won that damn science fair competition.

Sourcing the chemicals hadn't even been hard. The grandad clerk at the mom-and-pop hardware store on the edge of town had been more interested in the baseball game on his radio than in Elliott's purchases.

He hadn't even had to moan about his imaginary sister who made him go out for more hair bleach because she wouldn't leave the bathroom after her dye job went sideways. Or about his "dad" who hadn't made good on his promise to strip the pink paint from his bedroom. Or his make-believe pool that needed a lot of TLC because he hadn't cleaned it when he was supposed to.

Twisting the wires into position and crimping them took longer than Elliott expected. The box was starting to get a little packed.

He checked his screen again, rechecking the Guide's instructions, then typed, *I'm ascending.*

I knew you were the one to undertake this task. The Guide's message made him proud. *Surviving a bomb detonation may appear to be a dangerous task, but it is deceptively simple for someone of vast intellect. I've waited a long time for someone like you, Elliott.*

Almost there, and you'll ascend and be with us. RisingStar77's message made Elliott blush and smile.

I wish I'd been smart enough to take that challenge. Maybe you can teach me after. NeverLookBack's comment started a deluge of so many that Elliott had to put his phone on silent. The last thing he needed was his dad knocking on his door and asking why the device was blowing up so early in the morning.

Once he'd tightened the screws that held the timer to the outside of the device, he stood up, stretched his arms over his head, leaning backward and forward. His body was a mass of tense muscle and jangled nerve endings from the rush to finish before dawn.

He tightened the last screws and typed, *I'm ascending.*

Only you can be trusted with this challenge, the Guide replied.

The red digits on the timer began counting down from three minutes.

03:00.00.

02:53.50.

02:41.22.

02:37.05.

Pride swelled through him. But why was he surprised? He'd built it. Of course it worked.

A new message popped up on his phone. *Solve the puzzle for the detonation sequence interrupt code.*

Another puzzle? Elliott rubbed his hands together. No wonder the Guide had kept this one for him. And he'd been thinking it was too easy.

Scribbling with one hand on the paper beside him, he scrolled through the clues on his phone with his other.

02:00.13.

Trust the process. Two minutes is a long time.

He grabbed another page and drafted more options to solve the complex pattern of circuits.

That won't work either.

01:39:33.

Look again at the clues.

Of course. Rookie error. He'd transposed two numbers. He drafted his full answer on the page, just to double-check.

Yes, that works.

01:16:12.

He input his answer into the app. His heart fluttered as fast as the display on his bomb.

00:43:16.

And then the message he'd been waiting for appeared.

Congratulations, Elliott. You're ascending. This is the passcode to deactivate the bomb.

Elliott input the numbers into the device, but his grin faltered. His stomach dropped as if he'd gotten an F in science. The numbers on the timer didn't stop.

He picked it up to shake it but stopped himself. What was he thinking? The chemicals inside were far too volatile.

Elliott placed it carefully back on his desk. Blinked as if that could help. Checked he'd gotten the deactivation code right.

He had. But the numbers were still galloping toward 00:00:00 in such a blur he could barely make out the individual digits. He snatched the closest thing to him to snip at one of the wires. Crimpers were never going to do anything. Where were his cutters?

His panicked glance at his phone showed him his friends were still with him.

RisingStar77 said, *Trust the process.*

NeverLookBack added, *You're so close.*

HurdleThat chimed in. *Join us. Don't be left behind.*

But the timer...

00:21:58.

He fumbled at his desk, scattering bits of wire, knocking one of the containers of leftover chemicals onto the floor.

There was no time.

How could this be happening? What good was his brilliance if he couldn't use it to save himself from this?

00:05:31.

Elliott picked up the device and threw it across the room.

He turned to run just as unseen hands lifted him. He was swallowed by a deep roar as the walls seemed to ripple, then burst apart.

13

Hen rolled her shoulders back and down, smiling at the quiet streets as she drove. This was her favorite time. Not just because of the peace and stillness, but because it gave her the space to breathe. Now she could feel out with her senses to embrace the possibilities the forthcoming day could bring. All without the risk of being overwhelmed by the emotional tidal wave when the world fully woke up.

For a reason not yet clear to her, as she'd gone through her early morning yoga flow, she'd been especially grateful for waking up, for this new day on Earth. As she made turn after turn through the empty neighborhood—where only one or two lights glowed from the odd house—she wondered why.

Maybe today she wouldn't discover the universe's intention. She didn't always. But even if she couldn't understand why she'd woken up feeling different, she was grateful to feel this way.

A sudden noise from behind blasted her peace apart.

She keyed her radio to call it in. "I just heard an explosion."

"Did you say explosion?"

"Confirmed."

Hen turned her cruiser in the middle of the street to find herself looking at the perfect postapocalyptic movie poster.

"It's not far." She headed straight for the pillar of billowing smoke curling above the houses. "Smoke. One block over from my position." She turned onto the next street as front doors opened, spilling shaken residents in varying nighttime attire onto their lawns to stare in horror at the pall mushrooming over their neighborhood.

Hen chirped her siren to move the confused people out of her way and read the numbers from the mailboxes. "222 Delilah Street. Huge amount of smoke. Their door's not open, front looks undamaged. I'm going in."

"Backup's on the way, plus medical and fire department."

"Acknowledged." She knew the playbook. Waiting for backup was the right move, but people could be inside dying at this very moment.

Hen grabbed a Halligan bar and wedge from her trunk, then banged on the door of the exploded home. "Sheriff's office. Open up."

But it remained closed.

Pressing her foot against the door gave her the space she needed to tap the metal wedge between the door and the frame. With each hammer blow, the gap widened until she could flip the bar around and lever the forks in to pry it open. The door busted free.

Screams tore at her. The interior of the house was mostly disguised in a thick haze of heavy dust.

Hen flicked on her flashlight and took a breath from the clean air behind her. Summoning all her courage, she rushed inside toward the crying and shouting. "Sheriff's office. Anyone injured?"

"Go with Mom. I have to get Elliott." A man's voice

reached Hen. He was trying to hand off a young crying child to a woman behind him. But she was already grappling with an older boy, who was yelling for something, fighting her to go back up the stairs.

"That way, behind me. The front door's the escape route." Hen flicked her flashlight over the occupants of the house. No obvious blood, just confusion, shock. "Get out before it all comes down!" She shined the beam toward the exit, highlighting the whirling, swirling particles of masonry dust that thickened the air. "Take the young ones out. Now. Hurry."

"I have to get Elliott." The yelling man turned away, toward the stairs.

Hen dropped the Halligan bar and ran at him, grabbing his arm. "Your son?"

He nodded, wild-eyed.

"Where is he?"

"Up the stairs, room straight ahead."

"Take your family out. I'll get him." Hen coughed. "Now go."

The man looked up the stairs but scooped up the older boy and shepherded his wife and younger son out of the house. Hen retrieved the bar and ran up toward the second floor.

"Hen, where are you?"

The shout from behind stopped her on the third step. "Indie?" No time for wondering how she'd gotten there so fast. "Victim on the second floor. Room straight ahead."

A black streak whipped past her. Broc.

Indie's hand landed on her shoulder. "Let's go."

They ran up the stairs to where the Malinois waited for them at the closed door.

Hen studied the frame for the dangerous signs of smoke sucking in and out around it. "There's no smoke, so possibly no back draft." She placed the back of her hand against the wood. "No heat, so maybe no fire right there, but there's no way to know what's burning on the other side."

She looked at Indie, who was probably thinking the same —that without a breathing apparatus, they risked inhaling toxic fumes and smoke.

But a kid was in there.

"We have to try." Indie voiced Hen's thoughts as she tried the handle. When it didn't budge, she stepped back, giving Hen room to use the Halligan bar on the locked door.

One strike, and the door popped inward.

The sky in front of her was startling. Hen teetered, even though she still stood on the solid floor of the landing.

The back exterior wall of the house just…wasn't there. A bed hung mostly over the edge of the floor. Flames from the covers reached higher and higher, greedily licking up toward the joists of the attic space. That was all that seemed to be burning so far. Safe enough for them to enter.

For now.

"Elliott?" Hen coughed, swallowing past the swirling dust drying her throat to call out to him. "Can you hear me?"

But the only answer to her shout was the slap of wooden planks dropping onto the debris pile building on the bed and the crackle of the fire as it devoured everything it touched.

Closer to them, away from the heart of the devastation, was what might've been a desk, a chair, a dresser, a game console. Everything she'd expect to find in a bedroom had been blasted into a tangled mass of wood and plastic, glass and metal.

Hen met Indie's gaze.

Indie flicked her hand away from her, giving Broc a command in German. With no hesitation, he picked his way over and around the destruction. In just a few seconds, he stopped, frozen.

"Broc's found him." Indie followed his path around the unstable obstacles, with Hen stepping in her footsteps.

A soft moan from beneath the debris made them hurry.

"Good job." Indie sent Broc back to wait in the doorway.

They never would've found him without Broc. Not fast enough, at least.

"Elliott, we're with the sheriff's office. We're here to help you." Hen pushed extra reassurance into her voice to reach the boy through his terror. "Don't move. We'll have you out of there before you can blink." Though how, she didn't know.

Her gaze shot up to the remaining ceiling. The groaning creaking above them sounded as if the whole thing would soon come down. She and Indie threw smaller pieces of debris out the back of the house. Wood skittered over the floor and splintered onto the bricks and broken glass in the backyard.

Sirens screamed in the distance. She keyed her radio. "How long for medical? Male teen survivor, badly injured. Trapped on the second floor."

The response was lost in the crash of the bed toppling out the gaping hole in the wall, along with more of the floor collapsing onto the room below. The bones of the house shuddered.

"We can't wait." Indie lowered her voice. "His breathing's really shallow."

"We shouldn't move him." Hen mouthed the words, *His neck, his spine*.

"The house might come down by the time paramedics get here."

She was right. "I'll find a way to carry him."

Hen slipped and slid her way to the landing, where she got lucky with the first door she tried. The bedroom on the other side still had a solid-looking floor, and the comforter was intact. Though she cursed the time it took, she double-checked the floor would take her weight before committing to each step. After what felt like an age, she reached the bed and dragged the comforter out with her.

Back in Elliott's room, Indie had cleared everything that had been crushing the teen and created a narrow area in which to throw the comforter down.

Elliott lay on his stomach, one arm twisted beneath him, his head turned awkwardly to the side. The burns and shrapnel wounds on his back were bad—really bad.

Hen hated not being able to brace his neck, but staying in this room risked all of their lives. Survival came first. They could treat spinal injuries but not being crushed by a collapsed ceiling.

"On two." Hen braced his ankles. "One, two."

They moved together, rolling the badly injured boy onto the makeshift stretcher. Indie braced his head in her hands as best as she could under the circumstances.

Elliot moaned again. Pain meant life.

"We're taking you downstairs, Elliott." Indie spoke loudly so he could hear them above the muted sound of the world after the blast. "It might get a little bumpy, but we've got you. Just lie back and enjoy the ride." She dropped her voice to normal volume to talk to Hen. "Broc can help. Will you be all right beside him?"

Hen nodded. He wasn't going to make her cough worse than the smoke and the dust worming down her throat and into her lungs. And sneezing might actually get some of it out.

Following Indie's instructions, Broc took hold of the corner of the comforter next to Hen, tugging when Indie shouted, "Lift."

Together, they heaved Elliott between them, the makeshift sling straining with his weight as they maneuvered him out of the wrecked room and onto the landing. Indie sent Broc ahead of them, and they staggered down the stairs, each step a brutal test of balance and strength. Soon enough, they emerged into the mercifully clean air.

They lay their precious burden down on the lawn as gently as they could. Indie put her fingers to his throat, leaving Hen to shoot forward to hold Elliott's father back.

"We need space. Elliott needs space." She held her hand up as though she were stopping traffic.

He grabbed her anyway.

Broc stood beside her and growled, stepping up to an ominous rumble that soon got menacing enough to permeate through Elliott's father's panic. He let her go.

Hen gestured at the man's wife and younger children huddled together on the lawn. "You can help Elliott best by seeing to your other children."

Thanking Broc, Hen fell to her knees beside Indie, who was near Elliott's head.

His eyes fluttered open. "Is the Guide happy?" He croaked the words barely louder than a sigh.

"The Guide?" Indie leaned closer.

"Am I ascending? Is this it? I did everything they told me to. They said it was time…"

Hen was sure the shocked look on Indie's face mirrored her own.

"What does ascending mean? How do you ascend, Elliott?"

"Elliott?" Hen repeated.

But his eyes closed. His breath came out in a sigh, and he didn't pull in another.

"What did the Guide tell you to do?" Indie asked him twice before looking at Hen with pain in her eyes. She shook her head. He wasn't going to answer any more questions.

Hen pushed aside her hopelessness. The fight wasn't over until someone with medical training told them so. No time for her to steel herself against the feeling of Elliott's energy leaving his body when she interlaced her hands on his chest.

She began singing "Stayin' Alive" in her head for the right CPR rhythm. The line about a brother or a mother nearly made her falter. Elliott had both, brothers and a mother, and a father who'd counted on her to get their boy out alive.

She focused on the chorus as if it could block out the horrible thought that it was too late for Elliott to stay alive.

Come back to us, she told him instead.

He looked so young. He had to make it.

Come on, Elliott. Stay with us.

Sirens shredded the crying of his brothers and mom, the concerned babble among the neighbors, the crash of the back of the house caving in. The incoming emergency lights strobed the early morning sky, turning it bruise blue and bloodred.

"What've we got?" The paramedic knelt beside Elliott, checking his vitals while Hen summarized what happened. "We've got him now."

Hen murmured a thanks and scrambled out of the way over to where Indie paced around in a tight circle, pulling at her t-shirt. "That was tough."

Indie glanced at her, the pain in her gaze surprising. It shouldn't be. Of course Indie would feel it as keenly. She'd lost both her parents and sister. She understood grief well.

Indie turned her back on the scene so only Hen could see her and hear her speak. "Ascending again. You heard that, right?"

Hen nodded. "And he said something about 'the Guide.'"

"Maybe that's who's coercing or encouraging these teens." Indie turned back to the street, looking at the people gathering at the curbside. "It could be someone right here as easily as someone online on the other side of the world. We need to dig harder to find the pattern. We need evidence to prove what's happening."

Hen understood the seriousness of what Indie was talking about, but she couldn't help but feel a tiny smile flutter inside. Indie had said "we." She'd been in the department all of five minutes, and already, she saw Hen as more than just a deputy. Maybe by helping Indie in this case, Hen could persuade the sheriff to see her that way too.

She looked up at the sky beyond the pillar of smoke darkening the scene. *Where are you now, Elliott?*

She never opened herself up at a crime scene, but the temptation tugged at her. Elliott had seemed so hopeful when he'd asked if he'd ascended. Had someone made him do that?

Hen closed her eyes against the chill trickling down her spine. Somewhere, someone was relishing in Elliott's sacrifice.

14

As I watched the last data stream from Elliott Greene's phone, I could finally release my grip on the edge of my desk. All traces of the app had vanished.

That safety margin—taking the app down moments before the timer reached zero—guaranteed that every remnant of it had dissipated. Only the most advanced technician would even notice the microscopic traces of Ascension's code embedded deep within the system files. And even then, they'd have to understand what they were looking at.

The forensic team would barely touch a phone from a case ruled a suicide or accident, which would be how the authorities ruled on Elliott. Of course, his phone was likely in a million pieces.

I'd covered my presence well.

I threw my cold coffee into the kitchen sink, then switched on the machine to make another. My gaze was drawn out the window over the sink to the sky, as though I might be able to see the pall of smoke his work surely created.

News of the explosion at the Greene house had already hit the internet, though the online report didn't contain any of the details I wanted to know. Neither would any of the others that followed.

My sigh was a curious mix of emotions. I would miss parrying ideas back and forth with Elliott. My challenges to him had pushed me too. And his responses reinforced a belief in himself. Our relationship had been truly symbiotic.

But hadn't they all?

I poured creamer into my coffee, watching the white swirl into caramel. Was that how the ocean currents that Nila warned were breaking behaved? The teaspoon balanced across my mug was a silver tightrope that made me think of Zach testing himself to discover his true limits. Just as I'd done with the Ascension app.

In all my planning, strategizing, and actioning, I hadn't expected to carry their strengths with me. But look at how good Ascension had become. Right near his end, Elliott had believed he was interacting with a kid from his school, never dreaming he was just interacting with computer code. Hex Spectre might've given birth to the bots, but I was their architect.

Originally, I had no desire to take the truly gifted. But I'd had to abandon my desire to dispatch bullies and deliver universal karma. They didn't elicit enough empathy and attention.

I had to tip the balance from passivity to action faster, so I targeted golden children. Brightly burning stars were noticed. And that was working. They were even helping me by giving me all the information I could ever need on their social media pages to entice them with my invite-only app.

My fresh coffee smelled richer, and the color looked deeper when I carried it back to my desk. I savored the strong flavor, feeling the hot liquid tracing its way through me as I sipped, as though all my senses had been heightened at this latest proximity to death.

If I were a megalomaniac, I might take pleasure from the delicate choreography Elliott and I had created over the last few weeks. He had pushed me, and I had leaned into it. For that alone, I would've been grateful, but his sacrifice made me whisper a fervent thank-you.

I might've been wishing again that the world wasn't broken so none of this would be necessary. But I was also wondering how much the tender ages of Elliott's half brothers would have propelled my cause if they'd been caught in the explosion too.

A siren blasted apart the early morning quiet. Another agency attending the Greene tragedy?

I waited until it faded before pulling up the photo I'd chosen to keep of Elliott and pressing my fingertips on the pixels of his smiling face. "Thank you, Elliott. You mattered, and you've achieved more than you could have imagined."

My gaze shifted from the monitor to the framed photo beside it. The boy smiled out at me with so much hope, so blissfully unaware of the heartache waiting for him, for both of us.

Touching the glass protecting the precious photo, I was shocked how cool it felt compared to Elliott's face on my computer. I rubbed it, smudging fingerprints on its surface, but the warmth from my body heated the pane. Made it more bearable.

Sometimes, I wondered how I could get out of bed, how I could get through one more day. Yet I couldn't put it away… hide it out of sight to ease my own pain. My duty was to remember and to act on that memory.

"Always for you. Everything I do, everything I plan, just for you." I still struggled to say those words.

But that was my life now. I could scarcely remember how

it felt to not have to pretend that everything was all right, all the while trying to hold the pieces of my shattered heart together so everyone would believe my pretense.

My Pantheon of Pathfinders accepted Elliott's image next to Nila's with barely a resetting of the rows. Two additions in four days.

Should I slow down the ascensions?

But how, then, would they understand? The world needed to see and feel the urgency of my work. Slowing down, keeping it more covert, would have the opposite effect. How were people going to wake up if they weren't made to feel shock and awe?

As much as I might not want to accelerate, it was the only way to build on what I'd already done. No one could blame me that the only currency the world understood was sacrifice.

My gaze skipped from each smiling face to the next as I gave the images my thanks. I wouldn't let them be belittled or forgotten. I closed my Pantheon and opened the dashboard on the back end of the app. Hex Spectre had come through again. I couldn't help but smile as I clicked on the new update and into the option for camera access.

I'd imagined looking through the phone cameras of the kids using Ascension would be like a bank of CCTV monitors, each one a small icon among the mosaic of many. But it was more like my gallery, wherein I viewed them one at a time.

Clicking into the first, I saw nothing but a dark screen. Swiping to the right showed me another view—a girl lying on her back in bed, reading something on the phone she held up above her face. The next user was shoveling breakfast into his mouth as though someone were about to take it away from him. Milk ran down his chin.

They looked so normal, so how I remembered the day

should begin. Gently, with mundane, repetitive tasks. Seeing them getting dressed, brushing hair, packing a school bag…I never would've guessed how they agonized over the tiniest of things. How those blew up to feel like obstacles they could never triumph over.

My swiping stalled on the face of a young teen who I'd invite to ascend before he grew his first facial hair. Toothpaste foamed around his mouth as he pushed his brush back and forth over the same few teeth while his phone had his complete attention.

The scene was almost unbearable to watch. But the data was vital for my work to have the desired result. I forced myself to look back at him, still reading his phone, his toothbrush static in his mouth now.

"You're not just a victim," I reassured him, though he couldn't hear me, would never hear my voice. "I wish the world worked differently." And there I was again, wanting things to be other than how they were.

But that was what this was about, I reminded myself. I was changing things, and no matter how uncomfortable it made me feel, this update would bring about that revolution faster.

I steeled myself to look at the boy again. He was out of the bathroom, his phone jiggling in his hands as he ran down the stairs. He was one of the chosen few whose deaths would pave the way for a better world.

The girl who came into view on my next swipe pouted at her phone as if she were practicing to be a model.

"I wish I didn't have to do this, Jayleen. But know that I can promise you the notoriety and infamy you're looking for," I told her. "That will make it all better."

She smiled as if she could hear me, as if she approved. Peering closer at her phone, she ran a finger over the corners of her mouth, making sure her lip gloss hadn't smudged. She blew herself a kiss.

I ran my hands over my face, closed my eyes. Though the sun hadn't yet fully risen, I was drained. The emotional toll was intense. I hadn't expected that. But that was because I cared.

Every ascension took us closer to a future where the system could no longer fail the vulnerable. No one would slip through the cracks again. Though I looked at the photo beside me, my promise was to them all.

Soon, the world would see the truth, and the sacrifices would be justified. Each child who ascended mattered. And after everything, all of them would understand it was worth it.

15

Indie and Hen watched the ballet of emergency vehicles in the street as Elliott Greene was taken away and the bomb squad arrived. The paramedics were finished checking them over—smoke exposure, a few minor scrapes, nothing that needed more than oxygen and stubbornness.

"I'm going home to shower and change." Indie waved her hand at Hen's face. "You might want to as well. You don't want to be breathing in that dust any longer than you have to."

Hen's cough was dwarfed by Broc's sneeze, which made her eyebrows shoot up, rippling the dust and soot stuck to her face. "*I'm* making you sneeze? What if you're allergic to me?"

"Probably the dust for Broc too. He needs a bath as much as we do."

Hen nodded. "How did you and Broc get here so quickly?"

Wasn't it obvious? Indie glanced down at her running shorts and shoes. "We were on our morning run when we heard the blast and were only a couple minutes away. Dumb luck."

"Well, it was very lucky for me. Don't think I could've gotten him out by myself."

Indie patted Broc's head. "I'm glad we were so close. I just hope Elliott lives."

She didn't add that, even if he didn't, he'd provided valuable clues as to who did this to him. Still, her heart squeezed at the memory of Hen performing CPR on the boy, trying to resuscitate him when he looked as done as done got. She didn't hold out much hope the paramedics could bring him back.

Hen ran her grimy hands over her even grimier uniform. "Yeah, me too. See you back at the station later."

Indie scritched the top of Broc's head while she watched Hen go. "Is Hen picking up on the energy here like you are? It can't be easy for either of you. Loss and grief and shock and…" She blew out a breath. "What a way to start the day."

A man emerged from the back of the Greene house, carrying a plastic box stuffed full of evidence bags. The writing down his jacket sleeve—*Bomb Squad*—made Indie rush over and introduce herself. "What're your initial thoughts?"

"First on scene?"

"You can tell?" Her nod dislodged a cascade of dust onto her bare shoulders and got a small laugh from him. She hadn't meant it as a joke.

"You might have a better handle on initial thoughts. Not much for Bomb Squad to do if the bomb's already exploded and there's no other ordnance on scene." He hefted the box and started toward a blue van. "We're waiting for the house to be declared safe before we can collect everything to be sure of that, though."

Indie walked beside him. "Based on what you've got, what

do you think? I'm trying to understand what led the victim to make such a deadly decision."

"Who can tell what kids are thinking? Their reasoning for even their smartest decisions is usually the stupidest thing you've ever heard."

He jerked his head at the rear doors, and Indie pulled them open so he could slide the box in.

"My guess is he used TATP, beloved explosive of terrorists worldwide. You can easily get the component chemicals."

"TATP?"

"Triacetone triperoxide. All you need to make it is acetone, hydrogen peroxide, and acid."

"Nail polish remover or paint stripper, bleach, and pool treatment chemicals." Indie ran through potentials.

"Or solvents, disinfectants, toilet bowl cleaner." The Bomb Squad member looked at the house. "We can test for TATP. It's known as Mother of Satan, given its propensity to just detonate. That could be what happened here." He shut the van doors. "It's a hell of a thing."

"It sure is." A hell of a thing that prickled and nagged at Indie. "Thanks."

She peeled off from him then, Broc at her side as she approached the deputy keeping the scene log. His badge read, *Pantano*.

Right. Augustus Pantano. Indie still struggled with remembering everyone's names from the sheriff's office. But she recalled he preferred to go by August.

"While we're awaiting confirmation that the scene's secure enough to have forensics process it, I'm going to go wash me and the K-9 up. Detective Indira Reign. Can I sign out?"

August handed her the log and a pen. "Good job on getting the kid out."

"If he makes it." She handed back the log and tapped her leg. "Broc, *los.*" *Let's go.*

They left the scene, glad to break into a run as soon as they turned off Delilah Street.

"Is the Guide happy?" Elliott's question echoed in Indie's head. *"I did everything they told me to."*

As Indie replayed that awful moment, her feet sped up, and her anger grew. These teens weren't grouping around the idea of ascending and taking dumb risks. Someone was worming their way into their heads and encouraging them to end their lives.

By the time they got back to the park where she'd left her Jeep, she was ready to tear the Guide apart.

She opened Broc's door. "Great job in there. It wasn't easy." She smoothed the fur around his snout and inspected him. "You feeling okay? Your breathing sounds all right."

He leaned his muzzle into her hand. *"I'm good."*

They were halfway home when Indie's thinking burst out of her. "I know you don't know, but I don't understand why Elliott would agree to build a bomb."

She looked at Broc in the rearview mirror for an answer. *"Ask him."*

"It would be helpful to know these kids before they became statistics. But while I wait to see if he makes it, I can look at his socials, talk to his friends and family. See if I can find this Guide that way. So you're not wrong."

"Am I right it's breakfast time?"

Indie had to smile at Broc's expression. What a gift he was, capable of lifting her spirits on even such a horrible morning. "You are. You're on a roll."

As she and Broc walked up the outside stairs to her front door, Satch's head popped out of the dog flap. His sunny look became almost hysterical in nature as he barked. *"What happened?"*

"I'm not injured." Indie patted her t-shirt, and a cloud of masonry dust bloomed from it. "I just look like I've been in an earthquake."

"An earthquake?"

"No, there's no earthquake. Just an explosion."

"An explosion?" Satch's eyebrows got higher and higher.

"It had already happened when we got there, but there was lots of dust. We're fine. If you let me in, I can get you all breakfast."

He backed up into the apartment so Indie could get in the door. By the time she did, Broc was already waiting by the kitchen cabinet that held all the dog treats.

With the boys busy eating, Indie scooped Salem up out of her tank.

"Do you know what I found? I thought we'd left it behind in the move." She looked at Broc, who had his nose in his bowl and was inhaling his food, all innocence. Indie placed Salem on her tiny skateboard.

"My skateboard!"

"Yes, it is. Now you're faster than a rabbit again."

Salem moved her front and back legs as though she were swimming and rolled across the kitchen floor toward the living area. Then she turned, amazing Indie with how well she could maneuver on wheels.

Indie could almost hear the *Jaws* theme playing as Salem shot across the floor right at Broc's paws. Satch's sixth sense warned him to sidestep away from the impending carnage, but Broc was oblivious to everything except his meaty gravy.

Salem gave him a little love tap.

He leaped into the air, legs splayed, then crashed down onto his bowl, which flipped, spraying the remnants of his breakfast everywhere.

Broc hurdled Salem. The reptile slid off her skateboard

and licked at the gravy trail, as though she'd planned this outcome all along.

Peeking down from the couch, Broc whined, eyeing the turtle. *"No fair."*

Indie covered her mouth to stifle a laugh, wishing she'd gotten the scene on video.

"Yes, it is." She righted his bowl, leaving Salem to the gravy. "Because it's life-enriching for her, like your treadmill is for you. Don't hurt yourself getting down from there."

He gave her a side-eye. *"It's not like getting out of a tree."*

"And don't step on Salem."

"You can count on that."

After Indie got all the grime off Broc, it took three washes to get the dust and soot out of her own hair. She watched the water get progressively clearer as it washed down the shower drain, the whirling currents mimicking the conversations she played out in her mind of how she could get Sheriff Sammy and Eli on board.

"Broc, time to go." Indie stopped in the living room. "Where is he?"

Satch looked at the dog flap.

As long as he was decompressing and not tearing up Aunt Edith's flowers.

Indie bent forward and drew an infinity symbol on the top of Satch's head. He put a paw on her leg. She laid her head on his, running her hands through the fur along his back. "I'm okay, Satch. And I'll be great when I figure this out. I don't understand what's going on, and someone else might die."

"You can only control what you can control."

"You're a wise boy. Maybe you should have the conversation with the sheriff for me."

❄

"So after Zach and Nila mentioned the Guide, and now with Elliott telling me that the Guide told him to ascend, that he had to do that to make them happy, it's clear someone is manipulating these teens."

The sheriff interrupted Indie's briefing to answer his landline. He only spoke one sentence before putting it back on the receiver. "Elliott Greene didn't make it."

"Damn." Eli shook his head, then put his hands behind it and leaned back in his chair to address Indie. "Do you have any direct evidence to back that up?"

"Nothing beyond them all knowing this Guide."

"You know if we arrested every person who suggested a teenager do something dumb, the jails would be overflowing more than they already are." Sheriff Sammy looked into his cup. "Seen it with my own. Micah would dare Rachel to do something stupid, and she'd get her revenge by upping the ante. He's the oldest, but he'd fall for it every time. They just don't know how to say no at that age."

"Their brains are still wiring."

Eli's cologne, deodorant, or whatever strong smell was emanating from him made Indie's nose wrinkle like Hen's always did around Broc.

"I give you Exhibit A. Kids eating detergent pods on a dare. Even as they were fishing them out of a box with warnings stamped all over it. That BS went viral."

Indie recognized it was impossible to lock up everyone who had a questionable influence on kids, but she felt so helpless, so powerless. Much like she imagined Nila Radler had felt, according to her poem.

"And this Guide could be an actual guide they're talking about, like a booklet." Sheriff Sammy reached for the edge of the stack of papers in front of him. "Unless the ATF finds something groundbreaking, I'm thinking you should wrap up this case once you get the ruling from the coroner."

Elliott wouldn't worry about making a booklet happy. But a point of grammar wasn't enough to counter the sheriff. Yet.

Wordlessly, Indie got up to head back to her desk.

"There is one thing you could do." He stopped Indie as she reached the door. "Swing by Elliott's high school with that dog of yours. Put his nose to good use doing a search of the premises in case there are any other materials there that belonged to this kid. Give our friends at the ATF a helping hand. It's always good to have positive interactions with other agencies."

"I'll get right on it." Indie hoped neither man noticed that she sounded as excited as Broc did around his beloved squid.

And no wonder. Permission to visit the high school might give her more answers about any one of the dead teens. More importantly, it might help her understand exactly what was going on and who was behind it.

16

Indie walked Broc through the main entrance of Sherwood County High School East's campus, where Principal Lori Martin was waiting for them. She gripped Indie's hand and shook vigorously.

Broc kept an eye on the shake.

"The students are in the auditorium as you requested. The teachers are monitoring them, but they're scarcely needed. We're this way."

She led Indie and Broc through a set of double doors.

"What do you mean about the teachers not being needed?"

The click of Lori's heels and Broc's claws ping-ponged around the hard surfaces of the silent corridors while she chose her words.

Indie gave her time to find them.

"Right now, even our most persistent rule-breakers aren't misbehaving. Everyone's just trying to make sense of what's happened, and I don't think I'm overreacting when I say some students are scared." Lori held her hand out to the right, a precise, no-nonsense action. "We're down here starting with the lockers." Her sigh was deep, long. "Teens think they have their whole lives ahead of them, so any death while they're with us is shocking. But this is so much harder."

"In what way?"

"Deaths caused by illness, crashes when they've just learned to drive…they're somehow easier to cope with. But suicides and guns and…this? A bombing?" Every word Lori spoke carried a weight of sadness and concern. "My counterpart at West is feeling the same. We'd hoped the start of this new school year meant we'd be back to normal."

Indie wished she could give Lori her promise that she could stop this. But she still didn't know what *this* was.

She looked at the long double-decker rows of gray lockers lining the hall ahead of them. "Can we start with Elliott's?"

"Of course." Lori led them to the second run and tapped on the door of one of the floor level ones. "This is his. Was his." She unwound her fingers from a large ring of keys and unlocked it.

Indie let Broc sniff the contents, but after what seemed a quick check, he stepped back. "Nothing?"

"What did I just say?"

Indie removed the can of body spray to rifle through the textbooks stacked behind it.

"Wasting time." From the look on Broc's face, she wouldn't have been surprised if he started tapping his front paw.

She pulled out a folder bursting with pages of handwritten notes and checked beneath the sweatshirt thrown on the floor of the thin metal cabinet, where she found a couple of pieces of foil-wrapped gum and a crumpled sales slip from a burger bar.

Nothing that could be used to make a bomb.

Indie put everything back and nodded to Broc. Point taken. *"Voran."* Search. "Anything that doesn't belong.

Anything from the house this morning. You remember the smells that didn't belong?"

Broc tossed his head. *"This whole place smells like that."*

"Search for bomb-making supplies."

"Got it."

"Doesn't he need something to smell, as a reference?" Lori eyed Broc with all the suspicion Indie could imagine she'd wield at one of her pupils trying to pass off a poorly forged note excusing an absence, signed, *Broc's mom*.

"He's an extraordinary tracker. He can manage without specific clues and smells in this case."

Lori's smile struggled to reach the corners of her mouth. "I'm just reeling. I can't believe his brilliance has been snuffed out like that. He had such a bright future."

"What was his passion?" Indie chose her question carefully, remembering what she'd found out about each of the teens who'd died before him.

Lori didn't hesitate. "Robotics. Elliott was mechanically minded. He spent most of his time working on tech projects, building gadgets, and solving complex puzzles. He'd always been a quiet boy, so when he joined the robotics team, I really thought it would help him come out of his shell."

The long line went taut, so Broc turned and sniffed at the lockers on the upper row on his way back to Indie.

"And did it?"

"They had a shared camaraderie, something to talk about together, but Elliott seemed to prefer the company of machines over people."

Broc stopped at a locker, tensed, staring at it.

Indie explained his indicating mode. "He's found something."

Lori used one of the keys on her ring to open the door. Among the textbooks and gym clothes that smelled like they needed to be soaked in bleach, Indie found an envelope.

Inside the medium-sized, ordinary-looking blue envelope—one that you'd expect to find a greeting card in—were three tiny baggies containing white pills.

She held them out to show the principal, who closed her eyes as though she couldn't bear to look at the contraband.

Lori tapped at her phone, checking the number, and gave Indie the student's name, which Indie wrote on the evidence bag she sealed the envelope in.

"Good find." She handed Broc a treat and motioned for him to continue.

"Was Elliott ever bullied?" Indie kept her voice level, though her own memories loaded the question with an undercurrent of emotion. Maybe being back in a school—among the familiar smell of floor polish, body odor, and cheap perfume—made them bite a little harder.

She'd been fast-tracked through high school and college. When she'd dropped out of her full-ride scholarship to Cornell, she'd already had an associate's degree and a bachelor's degree in biology, only a few credits shy of a second bachelor's degree in math. And that was all her choice. She might've eventually gotten used to the arrogance of academia—being told what to study and when—but she would never be able to endure the constant exposure to the suffering of animals in her veterinary science curriculum.

Being fast-tracked had been her saving grace.

But maybe it hadn't been like that for Elliott.

Broc stopped again, indicating on another locker. The find that time was weed, which Indie tagged and bagged. She gave him another treat. "Good boy. *Voran.*"

He trotted over to the opposite run of lockers and began working his way down them.

"No reports of anyone bullying Elliott ever came across my desk. But one incident seemed to change things for him." At Indie's side, Lori pursed her lips, offering the tidbit with no prodding. "He'd been excited for the school robotics competition, and he really believed his team had it in the bag. But when they lost…well, I'm sure you can imagine how he felt."

"Disappointed?"

Lori shook her head. "I wish that was all it was. I think he felt frustrated and angry. He believed the judging wasn't fair. The scholarship went to someone else. He was deeply unsettled by the outcome. Almost beaten down by the sense of injustice and failure. His intelligence has always been his security blanket, if you will."

"Where was he insecure in life?" Indie placed the evidence bags on the floor to coil up the long line as Broc worked his way back to them.

"He didn't make friends easily. Girls never gave him any attention. He dreamed of being a 'tech bro.' I worried about how he would channel such disillusionment." Lori's eyes widened. "You don't think that's what happened this morning…" She gripped Indie's forearm.

Indie twisted herself free. "We don't know anything for certain yet."

"Of course, of course." Lori pulled her hands back and wrung them together, clinking the master keys like chimes in a windstorm. "I tried to encourage him to look forward. That's an integral part of the care of our students here. But he just couldn't get past his team losing. Elliott was convinced had he entered the competition on his own, he'd have won."

Broc came back to Indie and waited for instructions.

"He hasn't found anything else." Indie fed him a treat and picked up the evidence bags. "Where next?"

Lori pointed. "The auditorium's down here."

Partway there, Broc sat in front of a closed door and gave a soft bark.

That wasn't his indicating pose. "What is it, boy?"

"That's a janitor's closet." Lori found the right key. "Would the cleaning chemicals confuse him?"

"Not usually."

Broc's tail thumped against the floor.

Lori unlocked the door and stepped back. Indie turned the handle, pulling the door open. Inside, she couldn't tell where one of the teenagers in front of her ended and the other began. A jeans-clad leg was intertwined with a yoga-pants-clad leg, the sleeves of a red hoodie wrapped around the back of a white sweater.

"Sheriff's office!" Indie had to shout for them to hear her above the moaning and heavy breathing.

The couple broke apart, shocked to have an audience, it seemed. Confusion and panic set in when they recognized the principal and registered a law enforcement officer with a huge dog showing all his teeth.

Unwinding limbs and adjusting crooked necklines, the two teens stood, but their gazes held steady on the floor.

"P-principal Martin." The girl swiped at her mussed-up hair. "We were just…"

"I can see what you were just. This isn't the time to be catching up on biology class."

Principal Lori Martin went up a notch in Indie's estimation. Her tone was exactly what was needed—a little strict, a little understanding, a little much-needed humor. And just the right amount of censure. "You should be in the stadium with the rest of the school. Both of you come see me before going to your classrooms after that."

The teens muttered apologies and sidled out of the closet.

Indie pulled out a non-squid treat for Broc. The disappointment in his eyes was hard to witness, but she wasn't about to make Principal Martin suffer through that smell. The woman was already stressed enough.

Lori locked the door and led Indie into the auditorium. They followed Broc, of course, while he searched the changing rooms, then the equipment closets.

"Do you think the effect of losing the robotics competition may've been profound enough for Elliott to think he couldn't carry on?"

Lori didn't answer Indie's question immediately. Instead, she gave her attention to a loop of bulky ropes that she pushed onto a pommel horse.

"I'd like to say no, but after Nila Radler, I realize I just don't know what any one of them are thinking. Perhaps losing the scholarship might've pushed Elliott too far, but I thought his love of science and technology was enough to keep him going." She shook her head. "Elliott never would've tried something if he wasn't confident it would work."

What does that mean?

Indie logged that comment for safekeeping. It sounded like she was saying that if Elliott created or invented something, he wouldn't release it to the world unless he was sure of its success. If Elliott was responsible for making the bomb that went off in his bedroom, the principal seemed convinced he knew it would detonate.

Which brought Indie back to that horrible word—suicide.

Indie and Lori lowered their voices while following Broc in his search of the eerily quiet empty classrooms.

Lori let out another huge sigh. "Losing these students has been terribly hard on me, but for their peers, their friends, it's shocking. And my worry is that in this world, where they're turning more and more online, there's a growing disconnect between my pupils and their support systems."

That worried Indie too. If the kids were going online for comfort and support, for camaraderie and even love, how could she stop the threat to them when she didn't know who or what she was looking for?

17

Indie held Broc on his short leash at one end of the auditorium, watching the students sit uncomfortably, some mumbling to each other, some staring blankly at walls, some even crying on the shoulders of the kids next to them.

She could feel exactly what Lori Martin had described. The buoyancy of their youth, with all its seemingly unending possibilities, was dialed way down. The unseen weight of what had happened, again, was everywhere Indie looked.

Slumped shoulders, muted conversations. No joking around, no shouted wisecracks. The men and women Principal Lori Martin would soon be introducing had a task ahead of them.

"The grief counselors will be in study rooms one through four for the rest of the week. And your homeroom teachers have their details if you'd like to continue talking with them after that." Lori didn't really need the mic she spoke into. The students watched her silently. "Thank you for your patience. We'll have you back to class shortly."

She fiddled with the mic's controls before approaching Indie. "What next?"

"I'd like to speak to the members of the robotics team, but I'll need the permission of their parents, since they're all minors."

"I'll get right on that." Lori stepped over to a lean man wearing bright-red glasses. "Mr. Barty Dowell, Elliott's science teacher. Probably the one who knew him best. This is Detective Indira Reign and her dog, Officer Broc."

Mr. Dowell blinked rapidly, the movement accentuated behind his lenses, making him seem worried or nervous. Broc didn't give Indie a steer, however, that she should watch more closely.

"You're wondering about Elliott?" Mr. Dowell stepped to Indie's side, away from Broc. "He was bright but quiet. No, bright isn't fair to him. He excelled in class, but he preferred to work alone."

"How did he work with the members of the robotics team?"

"If he could be said to have friends, they were it. But if he was grouped with other students, he'd take off to figure the assignment out by himself. Then he'd approach the rest of the group to tell them he'd discovered the solution. As they were invariably still trying to work on the problem, he'd appoint himself the leader, and they'd ultimately hand in his findings."

A loner. Another overlap with Nila Radler, Arun Chang, and Leila Perez.

"How did that go down with the other students?"

Mr. Dowell pushed his glasses up his nose and held them there with his index finger. "I must stress this is what you call hearsay, as I didn't witness it, but he apparently had a falling out with a couple of students."

Indie kept her question impassive. "Do you know their names?"

"I don't, and I'm struggling to think how you could find out, seeing as he didn't have a close friend as his confidant."

The next teacher on the list Lori Martin had given her told Indie an almost identical account, as did the one after that. And the overlap with Arun Chang was beginning to feel like more than coincidence. Isolated by their intellect, both boys had struggled to fit in.

After Indie had finished with Elliott's teachers, Lori marched up to her with a sheaf of papers in her hand. "I've got verbal parental approval for the students on the robotics team. The vice principal and I signed documents confirming the students' parents have given verbal agreement to you speaking to them. Is that sufficient?"

"That's good enough for me. Thank you. I can talk to them all together, with you, of course. Could we use a classroom?"

"Of course. I'll take you there, then round up the team."

By the time four boys and two girls shuffled into the room ahead of Lori, Indie had arranged the classroom chairs in a circle. She noticed one of the girls change her mind about where to sit when she saw Broc beside Indie's chair in front of the window, and she took the seat closest to the door.

"Whoa, he's huge."

Indie was sure Broc puffed his chest out at the boy's assessment of him.

Once they'd all sat down, she introduced herself and the Mali.

"He's like a detective too?" The boy with a mouthful of braces had chosen to sit closest to Broc.

"He is, though his official title is officer."

"The dog has a title? Cool."

Broc preened a little more. *"I am cool."*

"I'm very sorry to be meeting you in these circumstances,

and I'm sorry you've lost your friend." Indie's gaze shifted from student to student as she offered her condolences. She let it rest on what she thought to be the oldest student, if his stubble was anything to go by.

He shrugged. "Can't say we were friends, but he was okay. Crazy smart at the robotics stuff. Not into hanging out, though."

"He didn't want to socialize with *us*." One of the girls seemed to have taken offense to that. "He was all about his online friends."

Indie held her face still, keeping the significance of that hidden. "On what platforms?"

"Tech forums, obvs." The boy perhaps realized his sarcasm might be misplaced and sighed as a sort of apology.

Lori pulled him up gently.

"Camden, we can be polite."

He flushed.

"Do you know which ones?" Indie brought him back to her question.

"Nah. But it sounded like he was picking fights on all of them to me, not making friends."

"And you know this how?"

Camden pulled at a thread in his jeans. "I'm on a couple. He was easy to recognize. He used the same username on every tech forum. He thought he was smart calling himself Einstein175, but only a bonehead uses the same one all the time. Especially one that got other users mad. I saw him get into a fight about it on Starscrew."

Starscrew? That sounded made up. "Why would they be irritated by his username?"

The girl who appeared to be scared of Broc looked up from her lap to answer Indie's question. "Because Einstein's IQ was 160, though measuring intelligence in his day was less of a science."

"It was like he was bragging his was higher." The other girl patted her head checking that no hairs had escaped the band around her severely pulled back ponytail. None had.

"You were on the platform too?" Indie looked at her list to see if she could grab a name. She took a guess. "Britney?"

"That's me. Nope. Not really my thing."

Indie never really thought about how high she'd tested, but apparently that might've been important to this group. "And why did IQ matter so much?"

"To Elliott, it did."

Several of them murmured agreement.

One of the boys had looked at Indie several times, then away when she tried to catch his eye. She waited until he looked at her again. "Do you have anything to add…?"

"I'm Liam. I don't think he was picking fights." His gaze slid to Camden, who was currently intent on making a hole in his jeans. "I think he just got frustrated. He'd been going on about wanting to prove something big for ages."

"That was just Elliott," the girl by the door said.

"He thought everything he did was the next big thing." Britney recrossed her legs. She was beginning to look bored.

"Don't we all?" Liam looked at her.

He was defending Elliott, Indie noted. She thanked them and stood Broc back to let them leave.

"Go back to the auditorium," Lori instructed her students.

The girl by the door—Callie, by the power of elimination—waited until the other students had filed out before standing up. "You should talk to that pothead Logan Nagle," she said to her shoes before bolting into the hallway.

Indie checked the list Lori Martin had given her of other students she'd seen interacting with Elliott Greene. Logan Nagle's name was on it.

She mentally bumped him up to the top.

18

When it started hurting, Indie realized she'd been pulling on a dry, loose tag of skin on her bottom lip. She let it go and licked at it instead.

Both she and Broc watched the door to the classroom where they'd been waiting. When Lori Martin finally opened it, she directed the student behind her to go on in.

The kid was surprisingly tall compared to the image Indie had conjured in her head. And his attitude—cocky to the max—was dripping off him. Odd, considering he'd been called to talk to a detective.

"Logan, take a seat." Lori sat on the nearest chair in the circle. "This is K-9 Detective Indira Reign, and this is Broc." She looked at the dog. "Your parents have okayed you speaking with her under my supervision."

Logan folded himself onto a chair and hooked an arm over the back of it. He looked at Broc, then Indie, as though this were the most entertainment he'd had all year. "S'up?"

"I'm sure the detective would appreciate you using actual words."

"Whatevs."

Indie checked on Broc as she sat opposite Logan. His ears were up. She took in a big breath. The kid smelled faintly of marijuana.

Lori apparently hadn't noticed, even though she was sitting next to him.

Broc shifted a little to face Logan Nagle more directly, and Indie followed suit. "Tell me about the drugs."

His eyes widened, and his relaxed posture tightened. It took a second for him to regain his equilibrium. "If you found anything in my locker, it wasn't mine."

"Why do you think we found something in your locker?"

"You did a search, right? Don't have to be a detective to know where this is going."

Indie sniffed again.

"You got a cold?" Logan relaxed back into his chair, crossing a foot over the opposite knee. "Should we be masked up?"

Indie looked at his feet. His sneakers were like a work of art covered in symbols, strings of letters and numbers, and what looked like random doodles. "Tell me about those."

"Don't expect you to understand them."

"I don't. So what do the symbols mean?"

He grabbed the foot resting on his knee. "It's programming stuff. Even put one of my trademarks in there, but it's well hidden."

In the crisscrossing and overlapping of the gold-and-silver motifs covering the black sneakers, Indie doubted she'd find his logo, even with a magnifying glass and a map.

"Nicely done. Are you the artist?"

Logan guffawed. "At a keyboard, sure. With a paintbrush? Not so much."

"Custom-made art's expensive."

He held Indie's gaze before lifting a shoulder.

"Do you have an after-school job, maybe work with your mom or dad?"

Logan held his hands up and waggled his fingers at her. "And risk these babies? Nah. I can earn more at my keyboard in five minutes than Dad does under the hood all week."

"How's it feel to earn that kind of money at your age?"

"Didn't say I do. Said I could." He slid a look at his principal. "After graduation."

Broc tossed his head to get her attention. *"I'm telling you."*

She nodded to indicate she heard him and went back to her track. "You've been smoking weed today. Maybe this morning before school. It's faint but recognizable."

"I told you, it's not mine." He held her gaze steadily enough that he could've been telling the truth, and they hadn't found anything in his locker. "I don't do that shit anymore, but enough people do. I could've walked past someone puffing. Hard to miss it some days."

Lori looked as if she were about to intervene. The last thing Indie needed was for her to stop the interview, so she moved on to what she really wanted to know. "Tell me more about the 'programming stuff.'"

"I'm good at tech. Who's not? Unless you're old." His gaze flicked to the principal, then back to Indie. She waited while Logan sat forward in his chair, linking his hands together, his arms resting on his legs. "I only did white-hat stuff."

"White-hat stuff?"

"I didn't do anything to excite y'all." He cocked his head at Broc. "You think I'm like Hex Spectre?" He clapped his hands, looking delighted. "Look, I didn't break into the Pentagon or anything. I broke into a couple of companies, then contacted them to let them know they had security issues."

"That's very altruistic of you."

"Apparently. But that wasn't the plan. I'd have fixed their shit, if they'd paid me. They probably thought I was punking them when I asked. Joke's on them when a black hat finds the gaps. Black hat's not a friendly hacker. You don't want one of them in your systems." He sat back and nonchalantly added, "Anyway, I don't do that stuff anymore."

Indie lifted an eyebrow. "That stuff being...?"

"Hacking. White hat or black hat. Gave it up."

"Is that what you talked about with Elliott Greene on the tech forums?"

"Nah, he's not into that. Didn't see where the real power is. Can't help some people."

"How did you help Elliott?"

"Like I said, you *can't* help some people."

Broc gave Indie a side-eye. *"Think you'd get more answers from the chair."*

She thought the kid was lying or being evasive too. "How would you have helped him if he'd let you?"

Logan's gaze flicked to his principal, back to Indie. "Dunno. Hard to help someone who thinks they're better than you, even though they're not."

"What about others online? How did you help them?"

"Told you already." Logan slowed his words down so she could get it. "I told the companies I visited they needed my help. It's not my fault they didn't take it."

Indie was getting nowhere on that track. "What did you talk about on the forums with Elliott?"

"Can't remember." He sat back again. "Never thought he meant it, though," he said under his breath.

That comment clanged onto the floor between them. "Meant what?"

"Doing something big. He said it so much, I started calling him by another username."

"What?"

"GoHome, no space in between." Logan chortled. "Go big or go home, am I right?" He rolled his eyes at them both, presumably for not laughing too. "Yeah, he didn't think it was funny either. Got majorly pissed off. Tried to get me booted off the platform."

"What platform?"

"It's called Starscrew."

Indie was losing her patience, and she hadn't had time to check out that forum yet—to see if it even existed.

"For real. I'm telling you. Look it up. In the early days, computer hardware was put together with hex-head screws and the ones with the star-shaped heads. Thus, Starscrew. Maybe that's where the name Hex Spectre comes from." He grinned like he'd just won a prize.

"So you bullied Elliott on this platform?"

"He didn't know for sure it was me. Not until I sent him the malware ransom note."

Broc gave Indie a look that said his last comment still stood.

"What did he do then?"

"The ransom was only a joke. I gave him back his precious Einstein175 username. Told him to go bigger."

Indie dug deep into her patience. "Bigger how? Where? Doing what?"

"Life, everything. Dude made a serious statement today, am I right? Looks like he went…bigger." His animated look suggested he admired what Elliott had done.

Indie was beginning to understand why the sheriff and Eli kept talking about teens doing stupid things.

"Pussy move, you ask me. Didn't he only take out himself? If you're really gonna go big…"

Lori's gasp was loud in the heavy silence that punctuated Logan's careless admission. She looked at Indie as if she expected her to be bringing out cuffs, but all Indie could do was wonder why he had such blatant disregard for Elliott's life.

"Thing was, though, we had that in common, that we could go beyond what regular kids are capable of. Maybe that's the price of genius." Logan's grin might've faded, but Indie could see in his eyes that he believed what he was saying.

"Did Elliott say anything else about the big thing he was planning?"

"Not to me. But he wouldn't, would he? We were more rivals than friends."

Indie couldn't help feeling that Logan was pushing the interview around in circles. "How were you rivals?"

"We both wanted to prove who was better. Kind of like an old-fashioned duel but on keyboards. It's how we can ascend above and beyond the ordinary. You know that's how they got an American on the moon, by stoking our rivals. The technology to get there and back would've never gotten good enough if they hadn't."

In the middle of Logan's rant, one word stood out as if it had appeared above his head in a flashing neon sign.

Indie tried to make her voice as throwaway as his, as if the answer to her loaded question didn't matter. "Why do you say ascend?"

"Why not? English is a rich language. The shame is most people only use a fraction of the words. Whaddya say? You want to duel? Find out which one of us is best? I know it's me at programming, but how about with language?" He winked at her. "Have to say, I'm liking my chances."

"Did you and Elliott Greene converse privately, away from general forums?"

"Don't remember."

A self-proclaimed tech genius couldn't remember if he was on a private chat? That stank as badly as some of the gym clothes Broc had sniffed out. Indie looked down and saw that Broc agreed with her assessment. "Did Elliott ever mention anyone called the Guide?"

Logan opened his mouth, but snapped it closed. He leaned forward in his seat, then back. "If he did, I don't remember."

"Have you ever heard anyone else talk about them?"

Logan was good at deflecting, but his shrug seemed forced, like an actor learning how to display nonchalance.

She tried another sideways tack. "Is it easy to build a private platform?"

"You showed your hand. If you were half decent, you'd know how easy it is."

"I have other skill sets, Logan. Did you and Elliott ever chat on any private apps?"

"Don't remember."

Finding out where he and Elliott interacted outside Starscrew, or school, would have to wait. The verbal consent from Logan's parents wouldn't hold up if this chat transitioned from a voluntary interview to a custodial interrogation.

So far, their conversation was casual, even helpful—piecing together the gaps around Elliott Greene's death. But the more Logan talked, the more red flags Indie spotted.

If it came to asking direct, incriminating questions—the kind that could shift him from witness to suspect—she'd need his parents present and their written consent. Logan might look older than sixteen, but he was still a minor. And if he had any involvement in what was happening to these teens, she wasn't about to blow the case on a technicality.

"Thank you for speaking with me, Logan."

"What, that's it? You could employ me, you know, to find out what else he was up to. There's no place I can't go online."

"Logan, I think that's enough for today." Lori cut him off by standing up and thanking Indie.

She might not have been so amicable if she knew what Indie was actually thinking. With a thanks for Lori Martin's cooperation and a smiled goodbye, Indie picked up Broc's leash and walked out of the school.

As soon as she got back to the sheriff's office, she'd start the paperwork to obtain a search warrant for Logan Nagle's devices. Specifically, she wanted to look for any digital evidence connecting Logan and Elliott Greene or Logan and the ascension theme. And then there were the spaces where Logan and Elliott had interacted.

She just had to get Sheriff Sammy to agree.

19

"How'd your dog do at the high school?" Sheriff Sammy called to Indie as she walked into the bullpen, not giving her time to decide how she was going to approach this. "C'mon in. Give us the rundown."

Eli sat in the second chair in front of the sheriff's desk, both feet planted on the floor, knees at right angles.

Indie perched on the other seat, and Broc spread out near her feet.

"We found some contraband." She hefted the evidence bags she was carrying.

The sheriff looked pleased. "Less than you might've expected, I dare say."

She nodded. "No bomb-making equipment."

"Glad to hear it."

"But what I did find was someone I'd like to bring in for a formal interview." She took them through what Logan Nagle had said, watching both Sheriff Sammy and Eli for their reactions to him using the word "ascend." "He lied about knowing about the Guide. And he and Elliott were rivals."

Indie had googled the Starscrew platform before leaving the school campus.

"That's teenage boys."

Indie couldn't stop her eyebrows from arching. "Normal teenage boys don't hack each other and send ransom demands."

Eli and the sheriff exchanged looks suggesting the contrary.

"Anyway, I think we're justified in getting a search warrant for Logan's devices. But he's extremely tech savvy, so we need to act quickly before he wipes everything."

The sheriff didn't seem pleased anymore. He leaned back in his chair, steepled his fingers, and tapped them against his lips. "Well, now, I understand your concerns, and I understand why you might've leaped to this conclusion. But we have to remember that Logan Nagle's a teenage boy, and much of what he said to you could just be plain old bravado. We need more evidence before doing anything like you're suggesting."

"I understand that." Indie looked at Eli, hoping he'd back her up.

"I agree with the sheriff." Eli reached for his shoestring tie, but he wasn't wearing it today, so his hand flapped at his shirt collar. "I think you're overthinking this. Logan's a rebellious kid, and you're new, not to mention close to his age, so he's having his fun trying to get a rise out of you. He might've been crushing on you for all we know. And you know we all say stupid things then."

Indie's mouth dropped open.

"Before you get your feathers all ruffled up, I'm of a mind that we keep Logan on our radar, but low-key. So no search warrant for his personal tech and no looking into his financials." Sheriff Sammy listed Indie's requests that he was denying on his fingers. "And no formal interview. Not until we have something more concrete that an intern in a law firm couldn't blow out of the water before they sit down in the interview room."

Indie checked off what she had on her fingers. "Five dead teens used the word 'ascend' or 'ascension.' Leila Perez, Arun Chang, Zach Mitchell, Nila Radler, and Elliott Greene. Three of them mentioned the Guide. One asked if blowing himself up had made the Guide happy because he'd done everything they'd asked him to. Now I've identified someone using that same word and lying about knowing this Guide. The same someone has the technical knowledge to have built the online platform where these teens were communicating. And this someone is running around in very expensive, custom-painted sneakers. It's worth a look at his personal tech and his financials."

She might have been a trainee detective, but she had more reasons to talk to Logan formally than the sheriff had objections. Yes, her evidence was mostly circumstantial so far, but without further inquiries, she couldn't substantiate it.

Broc watched her foot tapping close to his nose. He waggled his eyebrows. *"You want me to...?"*

No, she did not.

He gave a huge yawn, only dwarfed by the accompanying noise of satisfaction as he smacked his lips. *"It's really no trouble."*

"Shh."

She had to follow their orders and, most importantly, the law. Then there was her status, only a couple of days into her probationary period. Indie was out of her chair and walking out when the sheriff's phone rang.

"Concerned citizen at the front desk," Sheriff Sammy said, stopping her. "Wants to talk to someone about the recent teen deaths."

Indie paused and turned. "I can take that."

The sheriff told the deputy on the line, "Reign's on her way."

The woman stood at attention in front of the glass partition protecting the deputy behind the welcome desk.

"Detective Indira Reign. Can I help you, Mrs...?"

"Oh, call me Marla. Marla Henderson. I'm thinking I can help you, but I'd rather go somewhere more private."

Indie showed her into the interview room, and Marla immediately checked the camera in the corner.

"Don't worry." Indie was quick to reassure her. "That's not on. But I'll take notes as we chat."

"Of course. I hemmed and hawed about coming in, but I'm a big believer in civic duty, and I'd never forgive myself if something happened to another of our young people and I'd said nothing."

She looked at Indie as expectantly as Broc did when he wanted some squid.

Indie's pen was poised. "And what did you want to say?"

"Just that at the Hogs and Hens Festival, I overheard an argument involving Jennifer Blake."

Indie wrote the name down. "And who's that?"

"Of course. You're new. You wouldn't know. Jennifer Blake." Marla tapped the table with flat palms in time with the syllables of her name. "She's like the town's chairwoman. Self-appointed, I might add. Into everything, on everything, trying to get us all to buy into her extreme agenda. I can't believe you haven't already heard her go on about the evils of social media."

"Extreme agenda?"

"Her son's only been at the high school five minutes, but all she's done is clash with the other parents. And as for the Hogs and Hens Festival, well, it was a wonder it even happened this year. She got everyone mad enough to spit nails with all her vetoing and arguing. She was puffed up like a bullfrog telling them it was her way or no way."

Marla stopped herself when she noticed Indie's almost-empty page. "What I wanted to tell you was that during the argument, I overheard her saying she was glad." Every pore of her face oozed outrage.

Indie wished Marla would get to the point. "Glad about what?"

"Glad some of the teens were dead, because it meant her son had a better chance at scholarships and opportunities."

Now Indie understood Marla's outrage. Could it have been Jennifer's son who won the scholarship Elliott had coveted?

Marla smoothed her hair, reining herself in. "I'm not one to gossip, but I'm concerned. Extremely concerned. I think that woman's unhinged, and I won't let her anywhere near my children. And my biggest fear is that she might know more about these deaths than she's letting on."

Indie jerked at Marla's suggestion. "What do you mean?"

"I don't know anything spe-ci-fic-ally." She drew the word out as though she spelled it with twice the number of letters. "But it stands to reason, doesn't it?"

The surge of adrenaline at the hope of a real clue that had rushed through Indie receded. "Do you have any evidence connecting Jennifer Blake to the recent fatalities?"

"That's your job. I'm doing my civic duty by bringing my concerns to you."

Indie made herself nod. Maybe going back to basics would get her something actionable. "Who was Jennifer Blake arguing with when you overheard her?"

Marla shifted in the chair, but that didn't tell Indie anything. The chairs were uncomfortable on purpose. "That's the thing. I couldn't see the other person. It was a man."

"Did you hear what he said in response to her comment about being glad?"

"I'm afraid not."

"Thank you for bringing this to us."

Marla brought her hands together. "It's the least I could do. I'm just sorry I don't have more details for you. But what I've told you will help, won't it?"

Indie looked at her scant notes, which translated only to hearsay from someone who clearly didn't like Jennifer Blake. But she took Marla's contact info and thanked her with real warmth, because a chat with Jennifer Blake might reveal something that could help.

The housekeeper who answered the Blakes' phone advised Indie that they were at a dinner out of town and wouldn't return until later that night. Indie thanked her but didn't leave a message. She'd try again tomorrow.

As she put the reminder into her phone, it buzzed with an incoming text from Dr. Kristin Parker. Elliott Greene's autopsy was scheduled for tomorrow afternoon, which gave Indie plenty of time to see Jennifer Blake beforehand.

20

At the end of the day, as Indie drove away from the Sherwood County Sheriff's Office, fragments of clues buzzed around her. The faces of the many people she'd met since early that morning shuffled through her mind, pausing on the one that mattered. Elliott Greene.

The urgency to stop anyone else from dying made her want to turn around and go back to her desk to carry on investigating, even though that would be counterproductive. She and Broc needed to recharge.

She turned onto the street that would take them home but, after only a few yards, pulled up on the side of the road, killed the engine, and looked at Broc in the rearview.

"This isn't home." His GPS was working as well as ever.

"It's not. You want a walk?"

He sprang up on all fours on his back seat.

Indie let him out, and they strolled into the welcome shade of the trees. A few feet in, the path divided into two.

Broc sniffed at the base of the first tree on the right.

"You getting good sniffs?" Indie turned a slow circle, looking up at the canopy above their heads before peering through the trunks ahead. She recognized the area. More than that, it exerted a pull over her, strong enough to make her want to investigate. Curious.

She pointed at the left path. "It's this way."

As they meandered down the path, Indie breathed in deeply, closing her eyes, letting the sounds and scents of the woods ground her. A touch on her leg got her attention.

"You okay?"

She rubbed the top of his head. "I'm good, bud. I'm just… it's been a long time since I've been here." But unlike seeing Baby Lake, this wasn't a memory that jarred or shocked her. This was a mosaic of happy times.

Broc was still looking at her, waiting for an answer.

"My Grammy Ada used to bring me here to teach me."

"Like tricks? I can do tricks if we find a stick." He wandered around the closest trees searching.

"Not tricks exactly. Though some might call Grammy Ada's deep connection to nature and her intuition that. Lots of people called it magic."

Broc ran back to her.

"How could I not remember all this?" She looked around at the trees, the ground plants, the underbrush, inhaling the pure air around them. "Why would I have closed myself off to what she taught me?"

He cocked his head to one side. *"You didn't forget."*

"Maybe I didn't." Indie sat on a small slope, her arms resting on her knees, and closed her eyes. As if unfurling the petals of a rosebud in her mind, she understood part of an answer. "It was when she disappeared. That's when I stopped trusting everything she'd taught me. When I severed the connection." She opened her eyes and looked around her, feeling a surprising wonder and relief. "But it's still here."

The swaying of the trees, the calling of insects, the peace of nature stilled Indie's mind and cleansed her of the day, the state of everything she'd touched being unresolved and uncertain.

"You lost your important person?"

"I did."

Broc leaned into her, ducking his head against her chest—his comfort mode. Indie lay her head on his.

"Grampy Everet too. He was my rock, enduring, unchanging, reliable. Just what I needed after my parents." She smoothed Broc's fur. "Don't get me wrong. They loved me and Aishani, my older sister, in their way, but their work was their firstborn, their legacy, their everything. Aishani didn't like that any more than I did, but she didn't love Grammy and Grampy the same as me. She didn't see their talents as worthy."

The realization was a surprise even as Indie said it.

"You know, I don't think my parents did either. That's brilliant scientists for you. Though Mom's, Dad's, and Aishani's deaths were shocking, only after losing Grampy Everet did everything really change. That's when the bottom of my world fell out."

She breathed in Broc's warm scent, letting the deep sense of peace he emitted ground her.

"Maybe him being a sheriff is why I was drawn to law enforcement." She dropped a kiss on his head. "Listen to me, treating you like a therapist. I think I see the perfect stick for fetch up there."

He ran on ahead, and another petal of Indie's memories unfurled as she followed him.

The last time she'd walked this path was just before they'd found Grammy Ada's belongings on the lake bank.

That memory made Indie stumble. The questions she'd asked a thousand times since were still as raw as the first time she'd searched for answers. What ritual had Grammy Ada been performing? Why would she vanish? And the one that cut the deepest...why would she leave Indie when she was all Indie had in the world?

Indie screwed her eyes up hard.

She was a different person than the last time she'd walked there. Six more years of life had changed her, taught her. What would she understand if she found Grammy Ada's things today? The pain of all the wondering clenched Indie's heart tightly.

What if Grammy Ada had left Indie other clues she hadn't understood then? Had she given up searching too soon? She'd been so torn, scared of never finding answers, but terrified of uncovering them too.

As they progressed along the path, the trees around them grew closer together. Broc's dark fur was a streak of movement in the cooler shadows as he raced ahead and back again.

A scent wafted her way, something herbal, almost cleansing. Pine? Sage? Indie sniffed at the air. No, the smell was more floral, reminding her of lilac. It took her back to seeing Grammy Ada's fingers deftly folding cloth over bundles of herbs, sewing around the edges, tying them off with ribbon.

Lilac flowers mirrored in the color of the ribbon, used for spirituality, wealth, and opening psychic abilities. Indie could hear her grammy's rhythmic voice as she worked, almost an incantation on its own. Grammy Ada, more than a grandmother, had been her guide in everything.

Elliott intruded, asking again if the Guide was happy about what he'd done. Indie shivered.

"Broc, this way." She turned around to walk back toward the Jeep. Her fingers found the top of his head as he trotted beside her, comforting, grounding. She wasn't ready to confront the memories of her grandmother yet, but the forest had awakened something inside her. She stopped and asked the trees, "Is it you, Grammy? Are you prompting me?"

But they kept their wisdom to themselves.

"How about," Indie pulled off her boots and socks, "a bit of grounding? Grammy Ada used to swear by it." She wriggled her toes past the brown pine needles into the soft earth and grinned at Broc. "Race you?"

With a delighted bark, he charged up the track.

She jogged behind his dust. She had a real journey ahead of her, not just to solve the deaths of the teens, but to find the truth about Grammy Ada's disappearance.

21

Hen patted her hip. Where was her holster? She checked again with her right hand this time. There it was, where it should be. Except it was empty.

Her gaze snapped down. No service weapon. Empty, empty, empty. Her hand flailed, reaching for her mom, even as she knew that wouldn't change things.

There was her gun, in front of her. Pointed at her.

Her focus shrank to the perfect roundness of the barrel filling her vision. The world sounded like she was underwater, as if life were going on without her already.

Had she been shot?

Was she dying?

She couldn't breathe. She reached for the comfort of her choker, but she wasn't wearing it. Her hand tightened on her mom's.

"Don't do it. Don't do it, please—"

Her dad barely looked at her as he pulled the trigger.

As the bullet ripped into her flesh, Hen jerked awake.

Her ragged breathing filled her bedroom. Just her breathing. Not the screams of her mom, not the panting of her dad as he lowered his arm. Not the clatter of the gun dropping onto the floor. Not the sickening smell of blood.

Hen gripped the bedsheet as though gravity had failed her, and that was the only thing tethering her to the world. Her ceiling looked as it should, just plain white. No blood splatter, no emergency lights strobing through the window.

She watched wide-eyed in case anything changed.

When she could pick her phone up without dropping it, she checked the time. Hours before she had to get up for work. But her memories were too jagged and sharp to let her sleep again. Why had her father fired at her this time? Hen couldn't even think about that.

Padding into the kitchen, she filled the kettle. While the water heated up, she wandered over to her carefully curated display on the mantel.

After six years, the presence of her mom was dwindling, even in the places they'd spent a lot of time together. And though her mom had never been in this home, here was where Hen felt closest to her. She ran her fingertips down her framed photo. Such love in her mother's smile. So much warmth.

"How could I have let you down?" She always asked the same question after the recurring nightmare. "Why couldn't I see the signs? What good are my gifts if they didn't help me see the worst thing before it happened?"

The kettle pulled her and her recriminations back into the kitchen. She splashed hot water into her cup, slammed the kettle down on the stovetop, and yanked the top drawer open. The clatter of the knives and forks and spoons brought her back to herself. She stared at the shiny flatware and let out an explosive cry.

Hen closed her eyes and put one hand on her stomach, one on her chest. She counted to four, pulling air in past her chest, ribs, belly. Out. Belly, ribs, chest. Hold the space. In again. One, two, three. Her hands rose and fell as she counted the air in, held it, released it. Over and over until her anger dissipated, until she was grounded again.

She picked up her tea and scooped up a heart-shaped rose quartz crystal. Tucking a throw around her legs, she turned the smooth crystal around and around between her fingers, focusing on its different shades of pink.

Rose quartz for self-compassion.

She hadn't yet found a crystal or a meditation or anything that could heal her fury at her father. At herself for never having considered he could be capable of something so horrendous.

And if she couldn't see it in him, the man she'd lived happily with for sixteen years? No wonder she didn't let many people into her life. If someone like him, who'd been warm and loving and caring, had a switch that flipped him into a monster, who could say it wasn't in 'most everyone?

Hen squeezed the crystal like she could turn it into a diamond. She reached for her tea, breathing in the warm aroma curling out of the top of the cup.

"You need to let it go for today," she told herself. "Right now, you're only hurting you."

She nodded at her wisdom.

Sitting up straighter, she recited Dr. Mikao Usui's five principles of reiki, one after the other. "Just for today, I will not be angry. Just for today, I will not worry. Just for today, I will be grateful. Just for today, I will do my work honestly. Just for today, I will be kind to every living thing. Even Broc, with his dander and fur and hives-setting-off presence."

Maybe the thought of the itching he'd bring out made her feel unsettled again. Hen picked her precious family heirloom out of the glass bowl where she kept it, sketching a symbol in the air over the battered red-and-gold pack of vintage playing cards to cleanse them, even though she was the only person who ever touched them.

While shuffling the cards, she stumbled over what question to ask. She fanned them out face down and pulled out nine, which she spread out on the table.

"What do you want to tell me, Universe?"

Hen turned over the cards she'd been guided to choose and nodded as they reassured her, confirming she was on the right path.

"What about my gifts?" She drew another card for this new question and laid it beside the spread. "Sharper than ever, huh?"

She tapped the deck. The real question bubbled just beyond her conscious thoughts. If she couldn't see the truth in her father, how could she trust her instincts now?

But Hen didn't dare ask that one.

22

Ava Johnson gazed out at the morning fog hanging over Robin Hood Lake. From up on the bluffs, she couldn't see the water beneath.

In the rehearsals she'd played in her mind, the sky was the most brilliant blue. No clouds, of course, and the water glittered and gleamed where the sunlight played on it, because this was a celebration.

This was when she'd get it all back…everything she'd lost.

The cool air stroked her skin, much less insistently than Jimmy Dixon had when he'd driven her up here for her first big date. She'd imagined a blanket under the stars, a late-night picnic, roses…

Real life wasn't like the movies.

Ava glanced at her phone. Her homeroom teacher had probably already marked her absent. She didn't care. School used to be her place to shine…before. At cheerleading practice, the whole squad deferred to her. Even in homeroom, she'd felt girls who wanted to be her, checking out her clothes, her hair. And the guys? Well, she didn't mind making them compete for her.

But now?

She'd never dreamed she'd want to be ostracized. But being ignored and isolated sounded way better than what was currently happening. Everyone was ridiculing her.

No, she didn't need to drag all that up here. This was for her, not them.

In ascending, she'd take back her power. How funny would it be when they were falling over themselves, pretending they hadn't said those cruel words? She'd be picky who she let back in after she ascended.

She opened the Ascension app, and the Guide's latest message made her tight chest loosen.

Today is the day, Ava. You've come so far, pushed yourself beyond your fears. I'm so proud of you. This is the ultimate test of trust. You're going to fly. Believe in yourself. Take the leap, and you'll be free.

Putting her phone on the ground, Ava picked up her backpack. She made sure the zipper was open and peeked inside to check the fabric tied in there was still exactly as the Guide had described it should be.

She'd taken so much care with it, because everything in her ascension had to be right. Satisfied, she shrugged the backpack on, adjusting the straps and clicking the clasps across her chest.

The sun was beginning to melt away the early morning fog, and the scene was turning into what she'd envisioned. The lake looked a long way beneath her. Plenty of distance for her parachute to open.

This is the ultimate test of trust. The Guide's words came back to her. Trust in herself. Well, that was easy, as she had no one else now. Trust in the process. RisingStar77 had told her that their ascension was unlike anything else they'd ever done, the rewards so much greater than they'd believed they could be.

That, more than anything, Ava trusted. While she'd always loved having everyone look at her, now their stares were through eyes crinkled with laughter. She didn't like that.

Worse were the snide comments and catcalls as she walked down the halls at school. As for the awful memes of her having sex? How long 'til they trended and everyone on the whole planet saw them?

She gripped the clasps of her backpack, brushing her breasts. She'd worn her favorite bra. The one that made them look bigger, held them higher, so her waist looked smaller, her hips more hourglass. She'd been so proud of them, even though she didn't think they were her best asset. But guys couldn't get enough of them—that's what she'd said while she flicked her long blond hair and crossed her legs in the locker rooms after gym.

Another before.

Now she could barely look at herself in the shower.

Clitasaurus.

It haunted her everywhere. She'd like to push whoever came up with that nickname off the bluff without a parachute. No one she'd slept with had ever complained about her clitoris, never been surprised it was apparently so huge. The embarrassment made her curl up inside.

She picked her phone up off the ground and saw a stream of new messages.

RisingStar77 was right at the top. *I'm so excited for you to ascend and join me.*

NeverLookBack said the thing she'd waited to hear. *No one will ever call you terrible names again. They'll be so jealous of you. They'll realize they want to be you. But how could they be so perfect?*

She'd show them. Jimmy Dixon and all of them. She stepped up to the edge of the bluff.

One last check of her phone.

Leap, Ava, the Guide told her. *Leap into our love, and join us.*

Yes, yes, yes.

The wind blew against her face. Ava breathed in deeply.

Yes.

23

Ava Johnson's face came through on my laptop screen as clearly as if I were standing in front of her on the edge of the bluff over Robin Hood Lake. Her mind must've been so occupied with what she was about to do that she probably hadn't noticed I'd activated her phone camera.

Her backpack straps were pulled tight against her chest, which rose and fell as she shuffled to the edge. She stopped, her face pale, lips parted. She must've reached the end of solid ground.

Ava's jagged breathing, faster and louder now, came through my laptop speakers. Conversely, I was breathing slowly, deeply, evenly.

She frowned, then moved backward, in the wrong direction. Away from the edge.

"What are you doing, Ava? What's spooked you?" My heart started to race.

I moved my mouse so the cursor hovered over the command to reactivate the bots. RisingStar77, everyone's favorite, would have something to say about this.

The view behind Ava rushed past her faster, the plateau narrowing as she reached the shrubbery. She looked less fragile now as she bent over her phone and typed. *I'm so sorry. Not today.*

"Ava, Ava, Ava." She'd broken my trust. Failure to ascend meant only one thing for her.

But something in her face made my finger pause before hitting the command to delete the app from her phone. She knew she was fooling herself. I could see it in the way she gulped air, in her trembling lips. And that was before I'd pushed her as hard as I could.

Reaching this pivotal moment—when the ascensions were speeding up—changed things. We'd reached the tipping point where it was becoming more about the collective number than about each individual. Deleting Ava now would mean pushing someone else along faster. Which was more likely to backfire.

My finger hovered over the return key, which would initiate the removal command. The little arrow looked so innocuous.

"You're lucky, Ava." I deleted the command and instead activated the program to send her comforting and supportive messages.

The bots responded instantly, and derivatives of the same message flooded Ava's phone screen.

It's okay, CatwalkQueen.
You're so brave.
We're so excited for you to join us. Make it soon.

The words were exactly what she needed to hear. A watery smile didn't quite light up her face, but she responded with heartfelt thanks, grateful that someone understood.

That was all right for now. Later, I'd program them to shift their tone, but slowly, carefully. I didn't want to spook her. She needed to take her place with the other Pathfinders in her time.

But just to be sure, I clicked into the back end of the app, to where Hex Spectre had loaded the most useful function—even given the AI a human-sounding interface.

How can I help today? The cursor blinked, waiting politely for my input.

Monitor texts, phone calls, and conversations of Ava Johnson, username CatwalkQueen, for any reference to Ascension, the bluffs over Robin Hood Lake, ascend, ascending, parachute, a failed challenge. For any reference found or heard, activate app deletion command.

As easy as that.

No one had ever reported me to their parents or the authorities, and I was certain Ava wouldn't be the first. After all, she was already battling embarrassment and humiliation. Her so-called friends in the app would be there to channel the disappointment.

My gaze flicked to the clock display on my screen. Almost time to begin my day.

I reached out to trace the contours of the photo frame beside me. Its hard edges, its pointed corners, contained the smile of the boy who was everything, the boy who should've been more. The boy I had lost because of them—all of them—the faceless monsters behind the screens who pushed him to the brink and mocked his pain. Left him with nowhere to turn. He'd been so trusting, so vulnerable.

And me? How could I have not seen the signs before he was gone?

"I'm doing something about it." My voice was steady, my tone fiercely reassuring. "I couldn't save you from the pain that should never have been yours. But I'm turning it into a force to make sure it wasn't in vain."

The irony wasn't lost on me that my Pathfinders were

achieving the kind of immortal infamy influencers on the different platforms craved. And Ava would join them next.

"Thank you, Ava," I said to her photo on the screen, because I suddenly understood why she hadn't ascended. My fingers dived for the keys, tapping out the message to her that she'd be waiting for. After all, the Guide was there to guide.

I salute your courage in choosing to bear the cruelty on your own. We're here for you to support you when you need us. When they come for you again, we'll be here, and once you've joined those who have ascended, you'll understand how little those bullies matter, how great your future can be.

Her thanks came straight back.

My gaze skipped over the photos lined up in my Pantheon. A feeling of heaviness settled over me that I recognized as regret. When my Pathfinders had fulfilled their purpose and I no longer needed to add to their number, how would I occupy my talents?

There was one way. My breath caught, the thought surprising, unbalancing. I had never had such lofty political aspirations before, at least not that I'd admitted to myself. Running for Congress had always been in my master plan, but…

"The White House?" I whispered the words. I closed the app and looked at the photo. Once I had secured his legacy, why not the top job for me?

"Your name will be the one on the laws to ensure no child can be bullied that way again. Your legacy will outlive all of us."

A surprisingly hot lance of fury cut through me. I didn't want his name to be immortalized in that way. I wanted him here with me, for us to be anonymous in our normal lives, happily reaching the milestones other people celebrated.

College, graduation, his first job, meeting the love of his life, having children.

A knock at the door stilled me. I closed my eyes, breathed out my anger. Shutting my laptop down, I closed the lid and tapped it to be sure. Only then could I steady my voice to call out, "Come in."

24

Indie and Broc walked up to the front of the Blake McMansion. The flower garden looked like a page out of a glossy magazine. Not one leaf dared to mar the perfection of the lawn, mown in stripes of deep emerald and bright lime.

She held Broc's leash lightly as the notes of the doorbell chimes echoed around the inside of the house.

"You're not thinking of using her lawn, are you?"

He looked away from his study of the inviting grass with big, innocent eyes and a toothy grin.

"Let's not annoy the woman before we've met her."

What kind of woman says she's glad that teenagers have died?

Especially as she had a teenage son of her own. That was all shades of wrong. But there, standing in front of the kind of house surrounded by the kind of yard that should appear in the dictionary next to the word *aspirational*, it didn't fit.

Something nudged and poked at Indie, as if she were looking at a perfect facade where the colors were just a shade too bright, hinting that they hid something darker. Like you'd look at the made-up face of a clown, amused until you realized the red smile was painted in blood.

Where did that come from?

Being surrounded by perfection should not give her the heebie-jeebies.

The door opened, and Indie recognized Jennifer Blake. Or at least the type. *Straight from the hairdresser* styled blond hair, pristine, sweat-free workout clothes, plump pink lips, eyebrows plucked to perfection, and those lashes...Indie never looked that put together on her best day.

Indie introduced herself and Broc. "Are you Jennifer Blake?"

She stiffened. "Yes, I'm Jennifer."

"I'm investigating the teen deaths in the area, and I'd like to ask you some questions."

Jennifer's gaze flicked to Broc and back to Indie. "Just you can come in."

"That's fine." Indie handed him a treat as she walked him to where Jennifer indicated he could wait. "Stay there. Maybe don't spray the railings. There could be squid in it for you."

His front paws danced, but he settled into a sit so she could tie his leash around the wooden balustrade. *"Not thinking about it."*

She followed Jennifer into the living room, checking that her boots weren't leaking dirt on the hardwood floor.

Jennifer strode across the room in her bright-white sneakers. "Please sit." She waved a hand wearing such a huge ring that it looked like a splint on her finger.

Indie chose the smallest couch, which had perfectly aligned decorative pillows along the back. Each had the top corners pulled to attention around a straight karate-chop mark in the exact middle. It seemed the housekeeper used a ruler as often as a duster.

The bottoms of the long white drapes pooled on the floor in perfect circles at the edges of the French doors leading to the back. Though sunlight streamed in through the spotless glass, the room felt cold and sterile. Indie imagined it wasn't easy for a teen to relax there.

Jennifer sat opposite her, legs angled to one side, hands clasped in her lap, as though she were posing for a photo shoot. "What about these teen deaths?"

Indie took out her notebook and opened it at the page where she'd noted Marla Henderson's remarks. "In light of what's been happening, the Sherwood County Sheriff's Office is looking for community support to help us understand the town's teens, their needs, their struggles. I've been told you're very active in the community and wondered if you could help us."

"Would your visit have anything to do with Marla Henderson?" Jennifer answered her own question with an icy smile and a tight nod. "Of course it does. When did I last see her? That'll be at the Hogs and Hens Festival. Oh, she was on her high horse that day."

Interesting that Marla hadn't told Indie she'd been out of sorts too.

"You should know that woman always has 'some concerns' about everything and everyone, and lucky me. I'm often at the top of her list." Jennifer rolled her eyes and sat even straighter. "Honestly, if she must eavesdrop, I wish she would do it properly instead of walking into a conversation halfway through and giving her unwanted opinion. If she'd bothered to listen to my entire conversation with Johnny O'Donnell, she would've heard what I actually meant."

"Which is what?"

"What I've been saying all along. That these deaths are yet another example of the dangers of social media. In that respect, it's good that they're highlighting the unprecedented pressure teens now face that we should all be paying attention to."

"I understand you're very vocal against social media."

"As we should all be." Jennifer brushed an imaginary speck from her workout pants. Her ring flashed cold fire. "Anyone can set up a platform, you know, with no oversight and no protocols to protect young people." Her eyes hardened. "They barely need the dark web these days. The vilest things are on the one we all use without even thinking about how we're in their territory."

"Their?" Indie realized she was tapping her pen and stilled it.

"Bullies, trolls, criminals who should be locked away."

Jennifer changed the angle of her legs. Her knuckles were white where she clasped her hands. As though conscious of Indie's scrutiny, she parted them, placing her palms flat on her thighs.

"As you can tell, it's a subject I'm passionate about. I'm trying my hardest to advocate for our young people, but it's like standing at the top of the bluffs above Robin Hood Lake and hoping a whisper might reach the other side. It's utterly ridiculous to suggest I had a hand in what happened to those teens. You should be checking their social media presences, following the trolling going on there."

"We've done that." Indie kept her response vague, not wanting to make it public that the teens had deleted their accounts on every platform.

"It's easy to hide apps. It's easy to hide behavior you don't want tracked."

Jennifer wasn't wrong, but for all the deceased teenagers to have withdrawn from online interactions felt against the odds, considering what their families were saying.

"It's becoming understood that these activities in the ether are more of a danger than anything children have had to face before. Dylan's therapist agrees with me. All the therapists do. Even if they hold their appointments online."

"Dylan, your son? Do you mind sharing the name of his therapist?"

"Of course not. He sees Dr. Josephine Strickland. I insisted on it before he started high school. He was homeschooled for many years, so I needed to ensure he was ready to face the huge adjustment. Young people can be so cruel. Dr. Josie has been really helpful."

Indie added the therapist's name to her notes. "How is he coping with the deaths of his classmates?"

"Far better than I expected, though it's likely he didn't know them well. He's a good boy, and he understands our rules keep him safe."

"Rules?"

"I'd have thought that was obvious. No phone, no video games. It's a win-win. Having fewer distractions helps him concentrate on his studies while avoiding cyberbullies and trolls. It's a mother's job, after all, to keep her child safe from every danger. Negative influences, criminals. It's all the same. I'll do everything in my power to make sure he stays safe."

Indie couldn't help feeling she was hearing an often-delivered speech.

Jennifer brushed at her perfect hair. "If I could be charged with anything, it would be acting as a caring, protective mother, but I don't believe that breaks any laws."

Caring and *protective* didn't tally with this home environment. It all felt too controlled, too rigid. As though it hid something just below the surface that the tiniest crack would break wide open.

Jennifer stood. "Is that it? My personal trainer doesn't like to be kept waiting."

"If you think of anything that might help, please call."

Jennifer took the business card Indie held out to her, dropping it straight onto a side table as if she thought it might infect her.

She led Indie to the door, opened it, and closed it after Indie had only just stepped through without another word. She was a strange one. What was Jennifer Blake hiding?

Broc waited exactly where Indie had left him. He cocked his head at her, and she welcomed his straightforwardness like a balm. She untied his leash. "You definitely have squid in your future."

"But not now?"

"Yes, now."

He trotted happily beside her to their Explorer. But nagging unease was snapping at her heels. Indie didn't like an unsolved mystery. She'd figure out what that was all about.

She gave a delighted Broc his treat and put him in the SUV. As she slathered her hands in sanitizer, she looked back at the house.

"You'll be seeing me again much sooner than you'd like," she promised Jennifer, even though the woman couldn't hear her. "And I'll find out what you don't want me to know."

25

Broc lay stretched out on his seat behind Indie, his head on his crossed front paws, eyes closed, probably dreaming of the ecstasy of two helpings of squid before half the morning had passed.

At the next intersection, Indie looked right where she'd turn to the station, then left toward the subdivision where Zach Mitchell had lived. Should she detour to pay his family a visit? Whether she would or not wasn't really a conscious decision, especially considering she didn't need Eli to tell her a good detective checked everything.

Indie called up a number on her phone before turning left.

"Dr. Strickland's with a patient. Can I take a message?"

"It's about Dylan Blake." Not just about him, though, and that was where it got too complicated to explain in a message. "Don't worry, I'll call back."

She turned onto the Mitchells' street and noticed two vehicles in their driveway. Speaking to both of his parents might give her something to tie the loose ends together.

Indie could see who Zach might've become in the face

and physique of the tall, broad man who answered her knock.

"Nolan Mitchell?" Indie tapped her badge and gestured at Broc beside her. "K-9 Detective Indira Reign. I'm sorry to disturb you. I'm looking at your son's case and had a few questions. Is now a good time?"

He mumbled something Indie took to be a *yes* and stood back to let them in.

As she walked Broc in with her, he leaned against her thigh. He hadn't done that since the night she'd met him, when she'd seen how rough his first handler, Riker, had been. The sight of Broc's tail between his legs cut through her.

She squatted in front of him. "What's wrong?"

"I don't like this."

Indie placed her hand on the floor, but Broc didn't react. The place wasn't the problem. She moved it to the side, closer to where Nolan Mitchell was watching them. Broc leaned his head into her. Interesting.

Indie smoothed his fur until he looked at her. "I've got you." Standing as though this was all regular behavior, she looked from the open doorway beside them to Nolan. "In there?"

He nodded.

A glass-fronted display cabinet took up the length of the living room, filled with trophies, medals, framed certificates, and footballs on stands. It was like she'd stepped into a sports museum.

The rest of the room was decorated in cast-off clothes, with an odd number of sneakers under the coffee table that had half a dozen used cups on it. Glasses congregated next to an armchair. Beside them, a handful of stacked plates leaned as if they might cascade onto the floor at any moment. The place smelled like the day after a rager.

Indie focused on what was most important in the room. "Was Zach the athlete?"

"The first shelves, those're mine, before this." Nolan swept a hand at his knee. "They say those who can't, teach. I could, until an illegal tackle." He hissed out a sigh, clearly still not over it. "Most of the rest are Zach's. He was a total badass, better than me." He lifted one shoulder at Indie. "I can admit that, but I could still teach him a thing or two."

"What about those?" Indie pointed to the far right of the display, where the accolades were spaced farther apart.

"They belong to his brothers. It's up to them now to make the Mitchell name synonymous with greatness."

Was that tension the reason for Broc's distrust of Nolan?

"Were you happy about Zach doing parkour? Isn't that a magnet for injury?" As Indie spoke the words, she realized how insensitive she sounded. She hoped Nolan didn't pick it up.

"Of course I wasn't happy." He cracked his knuckles. "He wouldn't listen when I tried to talk to him about it. Said it was building his strength, honing his reaction times. He swore he'd never go higher than he could handle. So I was as okay as I could be. And I believed him."

"Why?"

"He was scared of heights."

As Indie had suspected. Though she watched Nolan, she could feel the pressure of the shiny wall of accolades nudging at her. "Why did he do it, then?"

"You tell me. He said it was a release from the pressure of football, but there's no future in parkour." Nolan spat the word as though it were packed with nails. "Nothing on the scale of what he could've achieved through his gridiron game. Scholarships," he hit the side of his hand against the palm of the other with each syllable, "sponsorship deals, stardom. He'd have been set for life. We all would've been, after just a few years of discipline and self-motivation. We could've hit heights heady enough to make his head spin."

At the conclusion of what appeared to be a well-practiced speech, Nolan snapped his mouth shut, as if he realized how inappropriate the words were now.

Poor kid. That was a lot to live up to.

"It was right there for him." He placed his fingertips on the glass unit beside him. "He just had to reach out and take it." Nolan's words rattled from the flat, wrung-out numbness of grief straight to anger.

"I'm so sorry for your loss." No matter how off-putting this man was, Indie meant the words with everything inside her.

He deflated, seeming to shrink several inches. "I wish he'd put as much pressure on himself for football as he did for his parkour. Taking risks there was plain stupid. I'd have said he'd never put himself in harm's way intentionally, but…" His words fell onto his tennis shoes. "Who knows why teens do anything?"

It sounded as if he'd been talking with Sheriff Sammy and Eli.

"Was it Zach's idea to go to the construction site?"

Nolan dropped heavily into the armchair. "When he started parkour, I set some rules."

Just as Jennifer Blake had for her son. "Rules?"

"He wasn't to do any stunts on his own."

There'd been no evidence of anyone else with him on the video Indie had seen. "Why did he?"

"You think I know?" He launched himself out of the chair to pace beside the trophy cabinet. His thumping footsteps rattled something in the end unit, making Broc grumble a low warning.

Nolan checked his watch, anger sparking his words. "Is that it? I have to get to school for a coaching session."

"Could I speak to Sarah?"

Any fire he'd conjured up burned right out again at the mention of his wife. He stood still and awkward. A flush crept over his cheeks, tinging the tops of his ears. "She's asleep. I thought it best to let her be. She's depressed, drinking more than usual." He waved his hand at the cluttered table. "At least asleep she can try to heal."

They exited together after that, parting ways silently as they found their vehicles.

"You okay?" Indie asked Broc once he climbed into the Explorer. "Was it the man's feelings that upset you?"

Broc walked in a circle. *"He smelled like Riker."*

No wonder Broc was feeling upset and antsy. Within a few seconds of seeing how Broc's former handler treated him, she'd wanted to punch Riker out. Indie parked herself on the edge of his flat area and held out a hand. "You want scritches?"

He turned the other way.

"Is that what angry smells like?" She watched him turn back in the first direction. When she'd met Broc and his first handler, angry had seemed his default. But Broc had seen furious people with her since and not reacted this way. "What is it you didn't like?"

"The man smelled of it too." Broc dug at the floor with his front paws, rocking the big SUV with his energetic pummeling.

Indie understood. "Alcohol."

"Anger."

"There were a lot of emotions in there." Indie encouraged him to shake off the emotions, the impact they'd had on him.

He did, his tag clinking against the clasp on his collar.

She held her hand out again. "Scritches now?"

He looked at her with such trust, it made her heart break

that he could've experienced anyone being mean to him. Exactly why she'd bought him from Riker.

Broc put his chin in her hand, and she petted him until his tension leaked away.

"I hear your duck calling you from under my desk. Are you ready for fun with it?"

"Duck? What are we waiting for?"

But when they got back to the station, Indie's welcome didn't feel like any fun.

"Did you forget you work here?" Eli Walker paused at her desk, a cup of coffee in one hand, the other hooked over his big belt buckle.

She made sure Broc had his duck before she addressed the accusation. Though he seemed completely engrossed in chewing the bright-green plastic, Broc was keeping a careful eye on the level of emotion being aimed at her. And on what she was giving back.

So she spaced her words out, keeping them light. "I've been out interviewing."

"On what?"

"Following up on the tip from our concerned citizen the sheriff told me to run with yesterday."

He went to look at his watch and thankfully realized he was holding a coffee. The dark liquid slopped over her desk, but just barely. "And that took 'til now? Did you go all the way back to their childhood?"

"It takes as long as it takes."

"Sheriff wants to see you."

Indie looked at the open door of the sheriff's office before glancing back at the exit behind her. She was closest to the exit.

"You can update us both on this follow-up." Eli led the way.

"Bleib." Stay. She looked at Broc, who was gnawing on the

duck's head so hard, she resigned herself to buying another on the way home. "Mind you don't choke on it."

Once Indie got into his office, Sheriff Sammy started asking questions before she even sat down. "What's new?"

She recapped what she'd learned that morning, starting with Zach Mitchell and ending on the bombshell of Jennifer Blake's beliefs. But instead of being intrigued or asking Indie to take it further, the sheriff gave her a look she was sure he used on his kids. One of practiced disappointment.

"Well, now, I'm sure I don't need to tell you about procedure and protocol. We have rules for everyone's well-being. You know you need approval before conducting investigations independently."

"I wasn't. You told me I could continue on the case as long as it didn't interfere with my other duties. And it isn't, because I don't have any."

"Be that as it may, we can't have you rushing around willy-nilly. We must have a coordinated approach, and our left hand needs to know what our right hand's doing."

The sheriff had slipped into politician speak. It might've been useful for him to muddy things in the media, but it just made things confusing to Indie.

"You mean you telling me I can do something doesn't necessarily mean it's okay?" Her tone added an extra question mark. Why couldn't people just say what they meant?

"I'm telling you that you must prioritize your caseload."

"And run past me, as your training officer, what you think your next step is," Eli added, adjusting his huge belt buckle.

"That'll do it. Congratulations. You've caught a new case." The sheriff flicked her a toothy smile and tossed a file across his desk, which she grabbed just before it slid onto the floor. "Another missing person. Just the kind of thing your dog excels at. Mary Jackson at Sherwood Pines Care Home was very pleased at how quickly you found Burt Draper. Let's hope you repeat that with this little lady."

Indie opened the file and read the name Ava Johnson. But the girl's age made her run out of the sheriff's office to her desk.

Could sixteen-year-old Ava be another "ascension" victim?

Indie read the meager details noted in the file before calling Sophia Johnson. Last seen this morning, Ava hadn't arrived at school. That was all the file told her.

"Sophia Johnson. How may I help you find the home of your dreams?"

That's strange. Her daughter's missing, and she's all business.

"Mrs. Johnson, I'm K-9 Detective Indira Reign with the sheriff's office, calling about your daughter. Does she have a Find My Phone app?"

"She does. That's how I know she was up at the bluffs above Robin Hood Lake. I went up there to find her, but before I arrived, she'd switched her phone off, so all I could do was shout for her where it last pinged. I didn't see her anywhere, and she didn't answer me."

"Was she upset about anything?"

"Not that I know of, and we didn't have a fight recently or anything like that, if that's what you're asking." Sophia's voice dropped, and she spoke slower, almost like she was spilling a secret. "That's why I'm worried. She's become more withdrawn. I'm sure it's just the whole being-independent thing, but it's not like her to miss school. She likes it, or at least she did, which is why I called y'all."

Indie's antennae went up. "Why doesn't she like school now?"

Sophia sighed, and when she answered, she sounded close to tears. "She's been having a hard time lately with bullying."

A prickle ran down Indie's spine. "Tell me about that."

"I don't know specifics. You know how teenagers can be so secretive. It's just a couple of things she said, and she seems to have deleted her social accounts, so I can't see what she won't tell me. Lately, she's seemed upset and distracted, but she doesn't want to talk about it. Trust me, I've tried."

Indie's mind spun from one question to another, but the one that burst out of her made her hold her breath. "Does Ava have any fears?"

Sophia answered right away, as though not needing to think about it. "I mean, she's going through the whole teenage-drama thing, but she's not afraid of anything."

Relief that Ava might not be about to try and conquer a phobia—like Zach and Leila had done—flooded Indie. But frustration tempered it. Knowing that could have given her a solid starting point to look for the girl. "Can I come and get something of hers so my dog can follow her scent?"

"Well, I'm not at home right now. And I have a showing here at this new listing that I really can't leave." Sophia blew out a loud breath. "It's a hard thing, being a single parent."

"What about Ava's father? Can he help?"

Sophia laughed like Indie was a stand-up comedian. "Unless it has something to do with his church, good luck with that. Since he remarried, they don't have Ava for overnights, so he won't have any of her clothing. And I won't give him a key to my home. Oh, I probably have something of hers in the car."

"Don't touch it. I'll stop by where you are on my way to the bluff. Send me your address and a screenshot of Ava's last known location."

"I'll do that now."

Indie hung up and studied the screenshot that pinged in. She tilted her phone so she was looking at the north side of the lake, figuring out the closest place to park.

Grabbing her bag, she squatted and held her hand out for Broc to give her his duck. "Let's go do what you do best."

※

Indie looked up, but the top of the bluffs wasn't visible from where she'd parked. She hoped she'd made the right decision. The hollow look on Sophia's face when the car search came up empty had been enough. Indie had volunteered Broc without hesitation—willing to chase the faintest chance of finding Ava, even without a scent to guide them.

"I can do this." His reminder came as she clipped him on his long line. He licked his lips, watching her tuck his treat-containing toy into her tactical vest.

"I hope so. *Fuss.*" Heel.

Indie led him along at a brisk pace, following the trail up to the top of the bluffs. She reached the spot where Ava's phone had last pinged just a few feet from the edge. But there was no one there now on the plateau.

"Ava!" Indie called, but the breeze whipped her words out over the water. "*Sitz.*" Sit. She held her hand up until Broc sat before walking carefully to the edge of the bluff and peering over.

It was a long way down. Indie forced herself to scan the water, dreading what she might spot. Nothing. No flash of color. No floating body.

But she knew better than to feel relief. Not all bodies rose to the surface—at least, not right away. If Ava had jumped or fallen, she could've been caught in the rocks, pulled under by the current, or dragged down too deep under some kind of weight to locate right away.

Still, Indie exhaled slowly and stepped back from the edge, holding on to the thinnest thread of hope.

She'd guess that possibly no one had come up there since

Ava, given how early it was on a weekday. "Can you pick up Ava's scent from here? It's probably the strongest human scent around here besides me."

Broc put his nose to the ground, sniffing backward and forward, around and around before he latched on. *"Got it."*

"Good job. *Such.*" *Track.*

Broc moved backward, thankfully away from the edge, into the brush that bordered the woods. Indie followed, pulse ticking faster. Had Ava walked away from the danger? Maybe. But it was just as likely he was following her scent from when she'd first approached.

Either way, Ava had been here. Indie just hoped she still was, and that she was okay.

Broc tracked Ava's scent down a narrow trail. The path angled downward, and he pushed his way through the thickening foliage it bisected for some way, until they heard faint snuffling and jagged breaths.

"Ava," Indie called so as not to alarm the girl. The noise they were making could easily be mistaken for a wild hog. "I'm a K-9 detective with the sheriff's office."

Broc dived around a dense bush, and Indie lost sight of him. She pushed her way through, snapping twigs, showering the ground with leaves.

And then, thanks to Broc, Indie spotted the teenager.

Ava was curled up at the base of a tree like a wounded animal that had crawled away to hide.

Broc sniffed at her.

She lifted her head, but seeing them both made her cry harder.

Indie did a quick visual check. Other than red, puffy eyes, she couldn't see any obvious injuries. "This is Broc. He found you."

He would've been preening, but he appeared to be as worried about the distraught teen as she was.

Indie called Eli. "Broc's found Ava Johnson. She's alive and uninjured. Shall I call her mom?"

"Hold on." Eli spoke away from the phone, relaying her news to the sheriff, she presumed. "She's got the kid."

"That was mighty speedy," the sheriff's more distant voice responded. "I'll tell the mother the good news."

Eli came back on the line. "No need. Sheriff's got that. Good job."

"Broc found her." Indie wished others would give Broc his credit.

When she disconnected the call and returned her attention to Ava, Broc was lying on his tummy, and Ava's sobbing had reduced to sniffling. Indie sat down on her other side and waited until he caught her eye to ask what he thought. She tapped her temple, their signal for "what are you thinking?"

"She's hurt, but I can't find where."

Indie touched her heart, wishing she could speak to him, help him understand that the inside could hurt real bad.

He sniffed at Ava's chest and stood to sniff her head again. He looked at Indie. *"It's everywhere. Hurt is making her small."*

Was he echoing what Hen had said about auras? It made sense, given that dogs were so attuned to human energy that they could pick up on the subtlest changes in emotions.

Ava looked at him. "What's he doing?"

"He's checking to see if you're hurt."

"Aren't you supposed to ask if I'm okay?" Her words sounded as if she had a bad cold.

"Why? I can see you're not." Indie touched the girl's hand. "Not inside, at least."

Broc lay back down beside Ava, looking back and forth between her and Indie.

"He wants to know if you mind him lying on you. He wants to help you feel better."

Ava let out a harsh sound but patted her lap. Broc wriggled forward until he rested his head on her leg.

Indie smiled at him. "Good boy. Everyone needs some Broc love." She turned back to the bushes in front of them, tracing the pattern of leaves with her gaze. A bird sang close by, repetitive notes, over and over. Indie ran her fingertips over the ground beside her, laying her palms flat on the cool earth, letting it ground her.

Nature and the warmth and closeness of Broc worked their magic. It took only a few minutes for Ava's voice to sound stronger. "You're not like a regular deputy."

"I hope not."

Ava's face was more animated too. Her eyebrows shot up. "Don't you want to be? I mean, don't you want to fit in?"

That made zero sense. "Why would I want that?"

She seemed startled by the honest answer. "Well, because…because it makes things easier. If we fit in, we belong."

"See that shrub there?" Indie pointed at one on her far left that was taller than the others, spindlier, but with the brightest green leaves.

Ava nodded.

"Do you think it's worried that it's not the same genus as the bush next to it?"

Ava shook her head slowly.

"It's just growing alongside the others because maybe they all benefit. It could require different nutrients, or maybe its flowers attract different insects. Variety makes everything stronger."

"I never thought of it like that."

Indie glanced at Broc for an update. Ava was drawing tiny circles in his fur.

"She's feeling better."

Time to ask what Indie wanted to know. "What brought you up here?"

She was quiet for the longest time. "It'll sound silly."

"Anything you feel strongly about isn't silly."

"I came here to ascend, but I don't know what that is. Not really."

The word didn't belong here. It carved a jagged gash right through the peaceful space, through Indie.

Ava rushed on, her words making her breathless. "Move on to something better, I guess."

"How were you going to ascend?" Indie struggled to keep her tone light.

"Like a leap of faith." Ava rummaged in her pocket and pulled out her phone, powering it up. "I've been chatting with friends in this app. They've been really helping me. Giving me challenges to face my fears so I can be stronger. I mean, I go to therapy and all, but it's my friends on the app who've helped the most. I can show you."

Yes! Finally, some answers. "Please do."

She passed her phone to Indie. "Ascension. It's behind the journal icon so only those invited know it's there."

Just as Jennifer Blake had said—something easily hidden on the regular old internet.

Ava pointed at the outline of a book floating on a green square. Indie pressed the icon, and it changed to a bright-blue one on which a distinctive white *A* was centered between angel wings. Indie tapped it, and the screen flooded with notifications.

You hanging out after school?

I want to top up my tan. We should go for a swim in the lake.

Did you see what Serenity's wearing today? The guys' tongues were on the floor!

She didn't slay it. She still had the price tag on it.

Indie read the top of the screen. "SnapBack?" She showed Ava.

"Oh, that's not it. It's called Ascension." Ava took her phone back and thumbed out of SnapBack, back to the screen filled with icons. Her frown deepened as she scrolled through the screens. "I don't understand. It was right there. You saw it, right?"

Indie nodded. "An *A* with angel wings?"

Ava's fingers trembled as she stabbed at the screen. "It's gone."

"Can you download it again?"

"Maybe." Ava navigated to the app store, but as she flicked through the options, she pulled on the ends of her hair. "It's not there. I mean, I had an invite the first time, but why can't I find it now?"

Broc lifted his head to get Indie's attention. *"She's getting upset."*

Indie acknowledged his concern with a nod. Time to take her somewhere safe.

"Don't worry about it. Can we take you home? Do you feel you need to be checked out at the hospital?"

Ava shook her head so hard, Indie worried she might need treatment for whiplash. "I just want to see my therapist. Can you take me there? I see Dr. Strickland at the Evergreen Counseling and Wellness Center."

"I'll need to run it past your parents."

Ava's face told Indie exactly what she thought of that. "They'll say yes, because then they don't have to deal with me. But don't call my dad. He'll go nuts. You only need permission from one of them, right?"

Indie placed the call to Sophia Johnson. She picked up right away. Indie explained the situation. "I'm happy to take Ava to her therapist, if you agree."

"Of course." Sophia sounded relieved. "Dr. Josie's been

wonderful. She's the best person to deal with this. Can I just speak to Ava?"

Ava gave monosyllabic answers to her mom's many questions before handing Indie's phone back to her.

"One more call. Then we can go. Wait here." Indie stomped down to the trail, not wanting Ava to hear her.

When Eli answered, Indie asked if she could drop Ava at the Evergreen Center, as per her mom's request.

"Makes sense." Eli surprised her first by agreeing, then again by adding what she hadn't even thought of. "And ask this doc her professional opinion of what's happening to the kids at the high schools. She might know about something similar going on elsewhere."

If asking for permission made it easier for Indie to progress things so quickly, she'd keep him on an open call all day. She'd been itching to talk to Dr. Strickland.

When she crouched again by the teen and Broc, she placed her hand on Ava's shoulder. "I can take you. We just need to drop Broc off at home on the way. He's earned his reward."

Broc waggled his eyebrows expectantly, eyeing the bulge in Indie's vest that held his chew toy filled with treats.

"Yes, you can have it at home, but I'm thinking I need to add a couple of extra treats, since you've been such a good boy. What do you say?"

He said *yes* in all the ways a dog could—a noisy yawn, a shake, and a grin, his tongue lolling out of the side of his mouth.

"Thank you." Ava looked at Indie, but her arms went around Broc. "Both of you. You really helped."

Indie ruffled the Malinois's fur. "He really does."

26

Walking into the Evergreen Counseling and Wellness Center reminded Indie of the peace and tranquility she'd experienced sitting in the woods with Ava. Perhaps because the photographic mural on the wall behind the reception desk was a perfect scene of sunlight streaming through rows upon rows of bright-green trees. It was mesmerizing, inviting Indie to stand and stare at it until she felt lost in its peace and warmth.

The woman behind the desk broke the mural's spell. "Can I help...Ava, are you all right? You don't have an appointment today."

"Ava would benefit from seeing her therapist, Dr. Josephine Strickland, if possible."

Worry wrinkled the woman's brow. "Of course. Please take a seat."

Indie had barely done so before the double doors opened, and a slender woman in her late forties breezed into the area. In her white palazzo pants and pale-blue silk blouse with matching scarf tied around her neck and her dark-brown hair styled in a neat shoulder-length bob, Dr. Strickland could've been on her way to Fashion Week in New York City.

But her eyes, light brown with flecks of green and gold—Indie noticed they were almost exactly like her own—were warm and concerned as she walked straight to Ava.

"Ava, are you all right? What's happened?"

"Dr. Josie, I just needed...you won't believe..." Ava broke into sobs.

"Come now. Let's get you settled. There's nothing we can't deal with, remember?" The doctor's gaze, along with her warm smile, swung to Indie. "Would you like to come in?"

Indie followed them into a spacious room that was as inviting as the main reception area. Ava moved a pile of cushions from one end of the comfy couch to curl up in their place. She pulled one of the cushions onto her lap and held it close. Light through the blinds bathed her in a soft glow.

Dr. Strickland nudged a box of tissues across the table and handed Ava a fluffy white blanket. "There you go. You get comfy, and I'll get a cup of tea for you." She looked at Indie. "Would you like to come with me?"

Indie followed her back toward the reception area, where the doctor asked the receptionist to take tea to Ava. She turned to Indie. "Would you like coffee or tea?"

"Coffee would be good."

Dr. Strickland returned her focus to the receptionist as she added to the order. "And coffee for myself and the deputy. Thank you, Florence. We'll be in the conference room."

"It's Detective Indira Reign." Indie followed Dr. Strickland into a room along the hall.

"I beg your pardon, Detective Reign. Please sit." Dr. Strickland pulled out the closest chair and sat with her fingers interlaced in front of her on the polished conference room table. "Is there a reason you brought Ava in? Why is she not at school?"

Indie sat opposite the doctor. "I found her up at the bluffs over Robin Hood Lake. She was very upset. She mentioned that she went up there to ascend. It's a word I've heard used in connection with a handful of recent teen deaths in the area."

"It's certainly concerning that we seem to be suffering from a cluster of teenage deaths." She tipped her head to one side and leaned toward Indie. "Have you determined if there's a specific cause, or whether it's simply the averages ironing themselves out?"

"This is only my first week here, but I can't find anything to point either way." Indie's frustration leaked into her words.

"Situations such as these are very difficult to navigate. On the one hand, we hope something is causing these deaths so we can stop them. On the other, we hope they're random, because anything else is too awful to contemplate." Dr. Strickland reached for the scarf around her neck.

Indie understood the need to touch things for comfort. "What's your role here?"

"I'm a child psychologist and behavioral scientist. Lots of fancy words to say I try to understand what makes children tick."

"In your professional opinion, what do you think is happening?"

Dr. Strickland turned around at clinking noises in the doorway. Florence came into the room and deposited a tray on the table. "Lovely. Thank you. Does Ava have her tea?"

"She does."

"Could you let her know I'll be with her shortly?"

Florence nodded and closed the door.

"Cream and sugar?" Dr. Strickland picked up the coffee pot and poured.

"Just cream." The smell of the coffee wafting over to Indie made her realize how thirsty she was.

"In my professional opinion, such as it is," the doctor added cream to both coffees and pushed one across the table, "it's almost impossible to understand what drives children's impulses, particularly teenagers. The prefrontal cortex, responsible for impulse control, decision-making, and risk assessment, isn't fully mature until the early to mid-twenties."

"Hence teenage behavior, where they do things they know are stupid." Indie found herself parroting the sheriff and Eli.

"Precisely. During this developmental stage, teens are especially vulnerable to the effects of social media and excessive gaming. There's mounting evidence of a causal link between increased social media use and reduced well-being, particularly depression and anxiety. And I've seen both can lead to addiction-like behaviors, which impact them in every area of their lives."

"Would you include the use of apps in that?"

"Certainly. There are all kinds of gaming apps, and of course messaging. Teens find it almost impossible to not check for messages, even if their phones haven't notified them of anything new."

Indie sipped the coffee. "This is delicious."

Dr. Strickland smiled before sipping her own. "I'll let Florence know you said so. She chooses the beans. Unfortunately, in both social media and gaming, we're fighting against the feel-good factor of the dopamine hits such interactions give their users. They're particularly alluring to the developing brain, as their reward systems are highly active, yet their impulse control is still lacking."

"And there's no chance we can put either genie back in the bottle."

Dr. Strickland shook her head. "I fear you're right. In the absence of that, what we need to ensure for our children is balance and awareness, as in all things. Demonizing the online world isn't productive. After all, social media can provide good learning opportunities and valuable social connections, especially for marginalized youth."

"Do video games have similar benefits?" Indie cast a longing glance at the coffee pot.

"Only with moderate usage. If we can guide our teens toward healthy usage patterns and encourage diverse activities, along with open communication about their online experiences, they'll be able to benefit from using the online world without letting it take over their own."

Dr. Strickland had an engaging manner. She let the sense of her words talk for her, a huge contrast to Jennifer Blake's rise to anger and outrage after a couple of exchanged sentences. Indie found herself nodding along with Dr. Strickland's words, even though she was hearing her ideas for the first time.

"That's how I try to help them," she finished simply.

"Have you ever heard of an app called Ascension? Ava mentioned using it. And she said that she'd gone to the bluffs to 'ascend.'"

"Ascend?" Dr. Strickland frowned, as though she'd never heard the word before. "Did she explain what she meant?"

"She doesn't know."

"There we have it. The perfect example of the teenage brain at work. She wanted to do something, yet she has no idea what that something is. She understands it's for the potential of a reward, but she doesn't know that, either, yes?"

Indie nodded. That was exactly it. "She mentioned something about making things better for herself if she did."

Dr. Strickland finished her coffee, her expression clouding. "I wish they'd listen to me when I say, 'Think about what you're doing, then think again. Talk to someone, then think again.' But I fear I'm shouting into the wind. I've never heard of such an app, but I'll see if I can find anything out for you." She turned her cup around on the table. "There is…one other thing."

Indie leaned forward in her chair. "What's that?"

Dr. Strickland rubbed her temple like it genuinely pained her to continue. "I have to be very careful what I share about my patients, obviously, but if there's any chance you'll be called to help Ava again, I feel a responsibility to make sure you're fully informed." She reached her hand across the table to Indie. "This mustn't leave this room, but I trust you to be discreet. And I know such information is vital for you to do your job properly."

"If what you're telling me doesn't break HIPAA or my duty as an officer of the law, I can be discreet."

"Thank you. Lately, I've seen troubling shifts in Ava. Sudden mood changes, evasiveness, that thousand-yard stare I wish I didn't recognize. She's been spending time with a… let's say, less than ideal peer group."

"You suspect drug use?"

"I can't confirm anything. But after years of working with teens, you learn to read between the lines. The things they don't say are often louder than what they do."

Indie didn't answer right away. She didn't like going down rabbit holes without evidence, but she also couldn't afford to ignore a potential warning.

"She's lucky to have you."

"Unfortunately, I far too often see parents so self-absorbed in their own lives that they neglect their children. We do what we can here, of course, but it's an ever-growing problem." Dr. Strickland stood so gracefully, Indie couldn't help wondering if she used to be a dancer. She smoothed her pants. "Now, I must go and talk to Ava to see how I can help her."

"You've been very insightful."

"Don't hesitate to contact me again if you need to know anything else."

As Indie walked out of the center, the traffic and people going about their day were noisy and busy, but the sunshine was warm on her face. Eli and Sheriff Sammy would benefit from speaking to Dr. Strickland. She had a much more compassionate view of teens than they seemed to hold.

Indie checked her watch, and the time made her run to her SUV. She needed to hurry to get to Columbia Medical Center in time to attend Elliott Greene's autopsy.

27

The risk of being late meant Indie didn't have time to psych herself up for the smells and sounds and sights of the pathologist doing her job. She knocked and went into the morgue.

Dr. Kristin Parker looked up from where she was peering at the body on the table and, with a finger held in front of her lips, nodded her hello. "Minimal external injuries on the chest." She tapped on a pedal on the floor in front of her and addressed Indie. "I thought you weren't coming. From what I've seen so far, I'm not expecting to find anything to dispute cause of death."

Indie crossed to the bench along the back of the room to pick out a mask and apron. "I felt I needed to be here." Washed clean of the soot and dust from the explosion, Elliott looked hopelessly young.

"I understand."

"I saw his back at the scene." Indie stayed a few feet away as she knew Kristin liked attendees to do. "It's surprising his front is so free of injuries."

"Primary blast injuries are more than likely what killed him, and they're predominantly internal." Kristin pointed at Elliott's chest. "What we call total body disruption is the most severe and invariably fatal injury after an explosion, affecting the ears, followed by the lungs and the hollow organs of the gastrointestinal tract."

"Is that from breathing the heated air?"

"Partly. It's the overpressure from the blast that causes most injuries close to the seat of the explosion, rather than flying debris that becomes shrapnel farther away. The most traumatic injuries from the overpressure are to the lungs and brain."

"Neither of which are very survivable."

"They're not."

Indie glanced at Elliott's body, unable to stop herself from wondering how much damage had occurred to his vital organs. "I've just come from the Evergreen Counseling and Wellness Center, where I had an interesting conversation with Dr. Josie Strickland about the developing teenage brain and how they don't fully mature until their mid-twenties."

Kristin nodded. "And when you understand that, it becomes easier to be patient with them. Let me show you."

After pulling on a fresh set of gloves, she chose a scalpel from her instrument tray and cut through Elliott's scalp with practiced strokes. When she started tugging on the skin flaps, Indie's gaze darted to the floor.

"This is a bit noisy." Kristin powered up a bone saw that sounded similar to a dentist's drill, and Indie couldn't help flinching. Which became an actual shudder when the sawing was replaced by a kind of sucking sound and a rubbing, like two halves of a coconut shell. "There we are."

Indie struggled to pull her gaze up from the shiny floor to see what Kristin was talking about. She'd removed the top of

Elliott's skull, leaving his brain protruding from the remainder. The pinky redness of it always surprised Indie. Before seeing her first autopsy, she'd assumed the brain would be a washed-out gray.

"The brain is remarkably soft and can be damaged just by touch, which is why it floats in cerebrospinal fluid to keep it from bumping into the skull. This here," Kristin waved the end of a scalpel over the front portion of Elliott's brain, "is the prefrontal cortex. When I tell you that controls complex cognitive behaviors such as decision-making, reasoning, and personality expression, and that it's still developing in the teenage brain, you can understand why teenagers find those years so perplexing to navigate."

Indie stepped closer, the clinical detail oddly grounding. "That's a lot of work for such a small part."

"It also helps us maintain social appropriateness and controls our goal-directed behavior. Beneath the frontal lobe here," Kristin pointed with the scalpel, "we have the nucleus accumbens. It's part of the brain's reward system and is highly sensitive in teenagers. When they engage in behaviors that offer validation or rewards, it stimulates the release of dopamine, reinforcing those behaviors."

"Even if they know those behaviors are dangerous?"

"Even then." Kristin waved her scalpel over the middle of Elliott's brain. "There are two other areas both very active in teens. The striatum and the amygdala."

"The amygdala." That was a term Indie had heard before. "That's the lizard brain, isn't it?"

"That's right. While it processes emotions, it also detects threats. This is why teens react so emotionally. And the striatum makes them highly sensitive to peer approval."

"Why they take things more to heart?"

"Exactly." Kristin stood back and put the scalpel on her

instrument tray. "Once I've finished the autopsy, I'll send my findings to Clifton, but I think he'll rule Elliott's death an accident rather than suicide. Even before opening him up, I'd say the pattern of injuries is consistent with him turning away or attempting to flee at the moment of detonation."

"Which suggests hesitation or an unintended outcome." Given what Indie had learned about Elliott, perhaps he'd just tried to build something to see if he could, and it had gotten away from him. That would explain why the seat of the blast had seemed to be the back of the house. He could've thrown it away from him when he realized he couldn't stop it and then tried to outrun it.

"Most suicide cases involving explosives show direct frontal injuries, where the victim faces the device. It can't be ruled out here definitively, since we don't know what he was thinking, but the evidence leans more toward an accidental death." Kristin picked up a different scalpel. "You want to stay for the rest?"

"One other question first, please. Did any of the teens that you know of have drugs in their system at their time of death?"

"That's an easy answer. No, none did. I remember, because I'd been expecting something, even if only weed or alcohol. They were all clean." Kristin glanced down at Elliott's body. "Want me to call if his tests turn anything up?"

Indie nodded. "Yes, please."

She looked away while Kristin made the Y-incision, a long cut from one of Elliott's shoulders, then from the other, then down to his pubic bone. Even though Kristin performed her grisly tasks with professionalism and compassion, neither she nor Indie wanted to see another kid on her table.

Whatever the verdict, Elliott's death was a tragedy. From everything Indie had learned from Dr. Josie Strickland and

Dr. Kristin Parker, teens had a lot to cope with beyond navigating the world and trying to find their place in it.

If someone was trying to take advantage of that by driving them to extreme ends, they couldn't hide from Indie. She wouldn't stop until she'd found out what was happening to the teenagers in Sherwood County.

28

"What'll you have?" The voice over the restaurant drive-through intercom was asking the silliest question Hen had heard that day, and it had been a grade A day for stupid.

"Everything."

"I'm sorry, ma'am. Can you repeat that?"

Okay, ordering everything on the menu might have been a little over the top, even though she was starving. Hen went with her usual, adding an extra order of fries.

She set the bag of food on the passenger seat and parked.

Hot enough to burn her fingers and salty, the fries were perfect. She'd been dreaming about them for the last three hours.

Movement in her peripheral vision made her pause with a handful of fries partway to her mouth. Near the restaurant entrance, a man and woman were having a more-than-amicable discussion. The woman leaned toward him and held his arm with a lingering touch. His attention was snagged on her low-cut dress.

Recognition hit. "Jayleen Levin, what're you doing?"

When the couple began to walk toward the closest row of

parked cars, Hen almost tripped over herself getting out of her cruiser and charging over.

"Sheriff's Deputy. Jayleen, what're you doing?"

The middle-aged man held his hands up as if Hen had drawn her service weapon on him. "What's the problem, Deputy? We're all consenting adults here—"

"Considering Jayleen's fifteen, I don't think so."

He paled as he understood the implications of what she was saying. "Fifteen? No, she's eighteen."

"Tell him, Jayleen, how old you are."

Jayleen told the whole parking lot what was on her mind. "It's none of your business. You've got no right. Go chase some traffic or whatever you do."

Hen pointed at her cruiser. "In you get, unless you want me to make this official. I don't want to do that to your grandmother. Do you?"

If there was any doubt about her age, Jayleen stomping toward the cruiser, muttering and gesticulating, made her look like a child throwing a tantrum.

"License and registration." Hen held her hand out to the man.

"I was only giving her a ride to the mall in the next county." His Adam's apple bobbed as though he were gulping down water. "That's all. I swear."

"Do I need to repeat myself?"

"No, no." He scuttled to his car and brought the documents right back to Hen, holding them out with a shaking hand.

"You wait here. If you're not on that exact spot when I come back, I'll put out an APB on you."

He looked as if he might collapse right there on the pavement.

Jayleen stumbled in her heels as she reached Hen's vehicle, but she was still shouting. "Just because you know me, you've got no right. It's harassment. I'm gonna report you."

"Go right ahead. Mind your head now." Hen shut the door after Jayleen had taken a seat. She ran a background check on the man, which returned no red flags.

She turned in her seat to face her young neighbor. "You're going to give yourself a sore throat with all that shouting. I just want to know what's happening here, to make sure you're safe."

"There is no 'here.' I walked from school and changed in the bathroom. I told him I was eighteen so he'd give me a ride to the mall. I wasn't going to screw him. What do you think I am?"

Hen held Jayleen's gaze while her belligerence faded away. She was more concerned when she thought she saw a flicker of fear behind the girl's bravado. "You know you can talk to me. About anything. As a friend."

"I'm good. Now can I go?"

"In a minute."

Hen got out and handed the man's documentation back to him. "Don't let me catch you picking up young girls in Sherwood County again. If she'd have gotten in your vehicle, this wouldn't be something that would just go away. Do you understand?"

He nodded so hard, beads of sweat flicked off his hair. Muttering his thanks, he rushed back to his car.

Hen placed a call while she strolled back to her cruiser with tiny steps.

"Hi, Mildred. I'm sorry to have to call you with this, but I just stopped your granddaughter going off with a stranger. She's safe, but I didn't want to just drop her off at home without a heads-up."

Mildred let out a familiar sigh, one that Hen had heard many times, riddled with equal doses of exasperation, frustration, and heartfelt despair. "Thank you for looking out for her...again." She sounded tired to her core.

"Of course. Are you all right?"

"I wonder if you could take her to the Evergreen Counseling and Wellness Center instead of bringing her home? She's supposed to be there for a group session at four. It's part of a court order after the last time she was in trouble. The Lord alone knows what'll happen if she breaks it again."

Hen also had a pretty good idea, and it wasn't great for Jayleen. "Of course I will. You take care now."

"Can I go?" Jayleen asked when Hen got back into her cruiser.

"We can. I'm taking you to your group session, but you need to change first and wash your face." She drove over to the restaurant's entrance and parked right in front of it. "I'll wait here. Unless you want me to escort you in and help?"

The girl's eyes narrowed. "You wouldn't dare."

"I absolutely would. Go to the bathroom to get changed, with or without me."

Jayleen rolled her eyes so hard, Hen thought she might strain the muscles. "You the CEO of being stupid? How old are you anyway?"

Doesn't matter if she's rude. Don't get into a shouting match. Hen repeated the mantra as she got out and opened the rear door.

Jayleen apparently didn't understand the assignment. "You can't tell me what to do." Once outside, she stomped her foot and nearly fell over when her ankle rolled.

Leaning back, Hen held the girl's gaze. "But the court can. If you don't attend your group session, it's juvie. I can take you straight there."

"Fuck's sake." Jayleen gathered her bag and stormed into the restaurant.

When she came out in normal clothes with most of her

makeup washed off, Hen fought to keep her mouth from dropping open. More surprising, Jayleen sat inside the cruiser with no more protests.

Hen gave her a few minutes into the drive to let her anger evaporate. "How's school?"

The teen didn't react—just played on her phone.

She tried again, louder. "Jayleen, I'm asking how school is." She watched Jayleen in the rearview mirror, but the girl kept looking at her phone. "Everything okay there?"

Jayleen tapped.

"What's your favorite subject?"

Jayleen scrolled.

"Are you playing a game?"

Jayleen snorted. "That's for losers. I'm part of an online community filled with people who get me. We're all leaping into a better future together. But I can't talk to them if you're asking me dumb questions all the time."

When they'd parked at the Evergreen Counseling and Wellness Center, Jayleen slipped her phone into her bag and didn't even grouse at Hen for insisting on walking her inside.

A blond woman just ahead of them turned around, and her expression of mild interest changed the second she saw Jayleen. Hen recognized Jennifer Blake, wrinkling her nose, curling her lip. She couldn't have looked more disgusted if the girl had been covered in cockroaches. Gripping the boy beside her by the elbow, Jennifer bustled him down the hall toward the stairs.

A group of teenagers milled around a brown-haired man in jeans and a t-shirt whose behavior suggested he should be wearing a clown costume.

He grinned at the teens, calling them out by name, pointing a finger at a girl with long auburn hair, holding his nose and wiggling through the famous *Pulp Fiction* dance move. She didn't copy, but a coy smile broke through what had been an icy glare. The would-be clown twirled and did a fist-bump explosion with a chunky boy who flushed bright red.

Jayleen rolled her eyes but tagged onto the end of the group.

Hen moved toward the stairs when she saw Dr. Strickland coming up.

"I need a quick word in private."

"Of course." Dr. Strickland turned to an alcove away from the melee. "Will this do, or would you like to go downstairs to my office?"

Hen glanced over her shoulder. No one was paying them any attention. "This is fine."

She summarized what had happened with Jayleen. The doctor listened with complete focus, not even one glance at the noisy scramble behind them.

Hen licked her lips, realizing she was clearing her throat for the second time.

She felt as if the doctor were treating her like one of her patients. But that was unfair. She was only giving Hen her full attention, and as a psychologist, the woman was trained to analyze human behavior. She was probably wondering right then why Hen stood so stiffly, as though she had secrets to hide.

A chill trickled over her scalp. Not now. She'd definitely remembered to put her spiritual protection around her before going on duty—it was as much a part of her routine as clipping on her badge and tying up her hair. She usually relished the feeling of the cool embrace of either a cleansing or a download of new information from the universe. But there were too many people around for her to open herself up to it now. Far too many conflicting energies.

As soon as Dr. Strickland confirmed she'd speak to Jayleen about her behavior, Hen made her excuses and rushed down the stairs. But she hadn't made it to the door when an urgent, "Deputy, Deputy," made her turn back.

"What's being done about the Greene boy's death?" Never known for being subtle, Jennifer Blake had outdone herself in just eight words.

"The sheriff's office is investigating the case."

"Not that. You know very well what I mean." Jennifer moved her oversize purse from one arm to the other. "What are you doing about yet another death because of social media?"

"Have you seen something online that proves that's so?"

"No, but are you looking?"

"We're pursuing all lines of inquiry. What makes you think social media caused Elliott Greene's death?"

"Isn't it obvious? It's probably the parents' fault. Yet another example of bad parenting, letting that child be unsupervised on his phone and computer. I'd never be so lax with Dylan, but I'm in the minority." She jabbed the air between them with her free hand. "I'm doing my best to tell the parents the responsibility is theirs, but I'm one voice. Social media platforms have to be accountable for what's posted."

Jennifer launched into a rant against social media that Hen had heard her deliver variations of before.

"Ma'am, if you have any information relating to an ongoing investigation, you should report it to the Sherwood County Sheriff's Office. Excuse me. I have an urgent call."

Hen rushed out of the center, hoping Jennifer Blake wouldn't follow her. Her "urgent call" awaited her in her cruiser, but her lunch was now stone-cold.

29

Two black noses poked through the fence as soon as Indie arrived home.

Broc jumped up, resting his paws on the top of the gate. His goofy welcome grin made her smile.

"Hello, my boys." Indie signaled for him to get out of the way so she could get in. "Did you have a good afternoon?"

"Did you?" Satch cocked his head, reading her.

She did a Broc-type wriggly shake.

"Not bad." Broc did one that put hers to shame.

"Show-off."

"You didn't answer my question." Satch still looked concerned.

And she was still deflecting. "He didn't tell you of his great deed today?"

Broc nudged Satch with his snout, and Satch put his paw over his eyes, making Indie laugh out loud.

"Finding Ava meant it was a great day." She stroked both dogs—the shorter fur on Broc that her touch barely ruffled and Satch's long fur she could entwine her fingers in. "You've gotten a bit matted there, bud." She held the base of the knot behind his ear so she could ease out the tangle without hurting him. "Think someone needs a brush."

Broc looked hopeful. *"Can we play first?"*

"That's the best idea I've heard all day."

She opened the garage door, and Broc ran inside and jumped on his treadmill before she'd even opened the chest. He hit the big red power button and trotted happily on the belt, watching while she picked out a selection of toys. "Seems you're as antsy as I am."

No matter how many dots she connected, she was only linking things at the margins. This had been frustrating her all day.

Indie laid out various toys in a huge circle in the yard, then called to Satch. "You want to play too?"

He grinned and came right over.

Broc turned his treadmill off and raced to join them.

With one on each side of her, she walked around the outside of the circle. "Satch, get lion."

Broc tossed his head while Satch went through the circle and seized the lion, which had long ago had its stuffing pulled out. It flopped in his mouth with every step back to her.

"Good job." She gave him scritches and took the toy. "Broc, get the *big* rope."

She and Satch walked around while Broc went to the green rope tug toy, which he snatched up before trotting back to Indie. *"Easy."*

Indie laughed as she petted him. "You want me to make it harder? Get the *small* rope." She turned to Satch. "Satch, get the dragon."

As Indie reached the top of the circle, Aunt Edith beckoned her over to her porch. "I'm guessing you haven't eaten yet."

Indie shook her head.

Aunt Edith was in the house and back out in a flash. "Here you are, fresh from the stove."

Indie met her on the porch, and Aunt Edith thrust a bowl of something red and hot that smelled wonderful at her.

"Tomatoes and basil from the garden with those lentils you were telling me about. Come. Sit."

Indie sat in one of the comfy chairs beside the back door. Like everything that came out of Aunt Edith's kitchen, the soup was delicious.

Aunt Edith patted her apron straight. "How're you settling back here?"

"I'm liking it." Indie stirred her soup. "I found a place Grammy Ada used to take me. I know that's not surprising, because she used to take me all over, but that one felt special."

Aunt Edith smiled at the dogs, who seemed to be making up their own game with the toys. "It must be comforting to find memories again. It's always good to know where we come from. You know your parents would be so proud of you."

Indie looked away from Aunt Edith's all-knowing gaze. She wished she shared her certainty. She'd always thought they would've directed her to a scientific career, so how would they have felt about her becoming a detective? That was the heavy burden of having them snatched out of her life when she was just nine—the wondering about everything that now could never be.

A deep barking made Indie clink her spoon against the bowl. What had upset Satch? And the snarling didn't sound like either of her boys, who were suddenly nowhere to be seen. She thrust her half-finished bowl at Aunt Edith and ran toward the sounds at the far side of her apartment.

Broc had something cornered near the trash cans. A raccoon.

Small, gray-and-white, with black-ringed eyes locked on

Broc like it was daring him to try something, the animal snarled, chest puffed, tail bristling like a bottlebrush. Broc growled back, low and deadly.

Indie raced in their direction. "Broc, no!"

He wasn't listening.

Before she could call another command, a second raccoon burst from the shadows, snarling bloody murder as it lunged at Broc's flank. Satch barked a warning from behind her. Broc whirled, narrowly missing a bad bite from what Indie could only assume was the smaller coon's mom.

Knowing she shouldn't step into the fray to separate them, Indie continued forward, but a spitting blur of orange and white sprang out of nowhere and beat her to it.

A cat! And it hit the raccoons like a heat-seeking missile.

Shrieks, yelps, barking, and hissing exploded in a fury of fur and claws. The chaos lasted only seconds before both raccoons bolted toward the fence, tails tucked.

The cat landed on top of a garbage can like it had been aiming for it all along. Fluffy, furious, and clearly in charge.

"I had it." Broc's proclamation came as the aggressively fluffy cat licked a paw.

Satch barked a final time. *"I don't think he did."*

"Clearly, I had it." The cat put its nose in the air. *"And you're welcome."*

Indie stared at the cat. His voice in her head sounded as though he were visiting from New Jersey.

Still perched high like a warlord, he pawed at his ear. A nasty gash split it.

Indie winced. "Your poor ear. Great. Now we're going to the V-E-T."

The cat didn't even flinch at the word. Broc nearly fainted.

"You okay?" Indie squatted in front of the Malinois, but

she didn't need to get close to see his nose was bleeding. "Hope you learned a lesson."

"I'm fine. No V-E-T needed here."

Great. Now he knew how to spell.

"Everyone all right?" Aunt Edith appeared. "That was some ruckus."

Indie noticed a streak of blood running down the cat's face. "Do you happen to have a cardboard box? For the cat?"

"Just a minute." Edith turned on her heel and bustled back into her house.

When they'd gotten the cat into a box, Indie nodded at the garden. "You might want to shore up the fence around the sweet corn. It's apparently popular with the local wildlife."

Edith snorted. "That explains a lot."

Indie called Broc to follow her to the Jeep. "Come on, then. Let's get this hit to my bank account over with." She looked at Satch. "Rain check on that brush?"

Satch flopped onto the porch and sighed. *"Sure. After all that excitement, I need a nap."*

Indie grimaced. *Hard same.*

30

Indie let out a sigh of relief when she pulled into the parking lot of The Green Paw Clinic, surprised the cardboard box holding the scrappy cat was still in one piece. Maybe Broc's savior had gone to sleep.

"You wait there," she told Broc. "I'll be right back."

After wrestling the box out of the Jeep, she buzzed the intercom on the front door.

"Yes?"

At the question, Indie explained who the patients were.

The door clicked open, and Indie held the box tightly against the cat shifting position inside, making it lopsided.

"Who do we have here, Indie?" The man who greeted her smiled shyly, his dark gaze on her, not the box.

"Ari?" Indie matched his smile, a flush heating up her neck and face, even the tops of her ears. "Of course it's you." The *Dr. Amarasiri Sakaran* on the plaque outside the building had sounded familiar but so formal, and she'd only ever known him as Ari.

"It's been a while." He ducked his head at her. "Nine years. But who's counting?"

"Nine years since we thought we could right the world?" She looked up at him. "You got tall."

He tipped his head from side to side. "And you…you got…" Her flush seemed to be contagious, deepening his light-brown skin.

"You got a beard too." She pointed out the obvious.

He stroked his close-cut and well-shaped beard, and she caught sight of the red bracelet he always wore.

"I heard you came home," he looked at her uniform, "and are a cop."

"K-9 detective. Oh, here. This one's a stray." She thrust the box at him. "I left the other in the car." She strode outside and came back in with Broc marching at her side. "This is Broc, my K-9."

Ari smiled at the pup's ridiculous grin, all teeth and flat ears. "You are a handsome boy."

Broc preened.

"Come on." Ari led them through the quiet building into a consulting room. He put the box on a table, leaving the lid closed while he addressed Broc. "Shall we check you out? Can you sit for me?"

Broc gave Indie a side-eye. *Can I sit?*

Indie rolled her eyes back at him.

Ari checked Broc's snout with careful, well-practiced hands. "Just a scrape. Nothing to worry about, but I'll need to wash it out. His shots are up-to-date?"

Indie nodded.

"Can I see your teeth, young man?"

Broc tilted his head so Ari could lift his jowls up.

"Lovely. Someone's doing a good job with the cleaning."

Indie lifted an eyebrow at Broc's preening and poked herself in the chest. *Me.*

"But I let you."

Indie couldn't exactly point out that he only did because he liked the meaty toothpaste. He was her good boy, after all.

After cleaning Broc's scrape, Ari opened a bright-orange, dog-face-shaped box on the desk. "Can he have a treat for being such a good boy?"

"Yes, he can."

"Here you go. Paw?" Broc didn't hesitate to slap his paw in the vet's hand. Ari tossed the treat, and he snapped it out of the air. "Good boy. Other one?" Broc did the same on the other side for another. For good measure, he raised both paws, holding his balance on his back legs for a moment, which made Ari laugh.

"Now he's showing off." But Indie couldn't help the note of pride in her voice.

Ari handed Broc another treat, then threw one up in the air. "Can you catch?"

"Can I catch?" Broc snatched the treat out of the air.

Indie gave him a *behave yourself* wag of her finger.

Plopping back on his butt, Broc looked at Ari eagerly, at the orange box, at Ari's hands.

"You have a new best friend now."

Ari grinned. "Excellent." He coughed and turned to the cardboard box, scooping out the cat. "You're a furry one." The cat's ears flattened, but he didn't take a swipe at the vet. "You don't know him, but you brought him anyway?"

"Right. I have no idea if he or she," though his voice in her head sounded male, she couldn't tell Ari that, "has a home or not, but I'd hope someone would do the same for my animals if they happened across one of them hurt. If you could check his chip, I'll take him home until we can find out."

The cat's eyes narrowed. *"Home? What's that?"*

Well, Indie guessed that answered the question. Of course, from the looks and smell of him, he'd been homeless for a long time.

Ari peered at the injury. "Racoon did this too?"

"It was all a bit of a blur."

"The good news is that it looks a clean cut. The bad news, my friend, is that you're missing a chunk of your ear."

The cat gave Ari a *What're you going to do about it?* stare.

"If I was a betting man, I doubt this guy's had any vaccinations."

"I agree."

"Then I'll get him cleaned up and vaccinated. Better safe than sorry, especially after a raccoon fight. I'll check for a microchip too."

The cat bellowed a meow when Ari washed his ear.

"It's just saline," he soothed. "It'll do it good. Then you get a treat too."

"It's okay," Indie told the cat. "It'll make you feel better."

He scowled harder. *"Just a treat? Yo, I deserve salmon."*

When Ari ran the scanner over the back of the cat's neck, the furry feline remained silent. He tried farther down, on his sides, all over him. "No chip. He's probably a stray."

"Can I take him?" Indie couldn't help smiling.

"There's a five-day stray hold, so you couldn't…you know what? Since I know you, I'll bend it a little. You can take him home for now. If no one comes in with a substantiated claim of his ownership in five days, he'll officially be yours. How does that sound?"

"That sounds great." She stroked the cat's back and lifted its tail to take a peek. A boy, confirmed. "What shall we call you, then? Do you already have a name?"

The cat licked his paw, ignoring her.

"Well, if you won't choose, I'm going to call you Moriarty. Though you look a bit mobster-like." She stroked the top of his head. "I think you're more likely to be the brains behind an operation. Am I right?" He moved his head into her scritches. "I think so."

Ari sat at the desk to type on the computer. "Moriarty Reign, all registered with us. A couple of shots and a dewormer, and I'll get some samples to send to the lab to make sure we're not missing anything." Ari looked at Indie. "Then you can take him home for now."

Indie spent the whole time he treated Moriarty trying to think of something witty to say, but he'd finished before she'd managed to. Instead, she blurted the first thing she thought of as if she were sixteen again, like when they'd last seen each other.

"Did you ever catch the poacher you were trying to track? Do you remember?" Indie glanced at Ari after he'd treated Moriarty.

"Of course." They'd joined forces to save the bald eagle from certain extinction, because Ari was trying to prove himself while home on summer break. "It was so hot, and we didn't wear sunscreen, so the only thing I found was a sunburned nose."

"And we didn't take enough water, and I insisted we had to ration it." She smoothed her uniform. Teenage her sounded so bossy.

"We were much better prepared for our next mission." His voice softened, though he didn't add that they'd spent days searching for Indie's Grammy Ada. "Was there ever any news about your grammy?"

Indie shook her head. "Never anything to say what happened to her. Where she went."

"I often wondered…I'm so sorry. I can't imagine." Ari's eyes were filled with such warmth and sadness that Indie had to turn her head away. "Seems we're still trying to save the world in our own ways." He looked at both their uniforms.

A phone ringing elsewhere in the building startled them both.

"Sorry. I'm taking up too much of your time."

"Not at all. We have a centralized answering service. If it's an actual emergency, they'll message me."

"Thank you for seeing us. I'll be sure to bring them to you when we need a vet. I have a German shepherd and a turtle, too, so you'll probably be seeing us a lot."

"That would be my pleasure." Ari glanced at Moriarty, sitting on the table, licking his paw.

The cat glared at him for having dared to give him not one but two shots.

"Perhaps the next time I see Moriarty, he'll have forgiven me." He pulled a card out from the desk drawer and scribbled on it. "That's my personal number." He held it out to Indie.

In her haste to take it, she grabbed his fingers. "Sorry." She let go, yanking her hand back like the touch had burned her.

He let go at the same time, and his card fluttered to the floor. She bent to retrieve it as he did, the heat of his closeness warning her to swerve away just in time to avoid banging heads.

"So sorry." He held the card out again. "There you are."

Indie was certain her face was as red as Ari's nose had been after their mission to save the bald eagle. "Thanks."

All the way home, thoughts of Ari and his link to her past warmed her. What would life have been like for her if her parents and sister hadn't been killed? Would she have stayed here? What would their friendship have become without the interruption of her going to New York to study and work? And then to Florida?

She'd discovered there that being a K-9 officer was much more her. Without that, she never would've met Satch. Or Broc.

Still, the questions were playing through her mind when she crawled into bed. Both dogs were snoring at her feet. The evening's events had worn them out. She turned her head to look at the cat, curled up on the cushion she'd given him until she could get him a permanent bed.

"Welcome to our family, Moriarty. I hope you'll be happy here."

He watched her, his gaze flicking to the dogs, then back to her. *"They always this noisy?"*

"Sometimes. It's nice. There's plenty of room for you over here, when you're ready," she reassured him.

He turned on the cushion, arching his back before settling in a ball, wrapping his shaggy tail around himself. The cat desperately needed a bath and a good brushing. But not tonight.

"You okay?"

"It's not too shabby. I might stay for a bit."

Indie smiled at him and closed her eyes.

31

I double-checked the door was locked before I booted up my laptop. It wasn't likely I'd be disturbed so early, but it didn't hurt to be sure. Especially in view of what I was about to do.

The back end of the Ascension app loaded fast, giving me little time to deliberate. But did I really need to? I'd already decided.

"I gave you every chance, Ava," I told the girl, even though she couldn't hear me or even read my words now. "You could've spared yourself this, but you let me down."

Flexing my fingers, I clicked the command to activate the bots. The photos they released uploaded one after the other, whisking through the ether to appear on devices all over the county. From there, the wider circle of the device owners' followers would spread them through the country and even on to other continents. The speed with which information now flowed around the globe was as impressive as it was terrifying.

I couldn't help feeling how shameful it was that the guys with whom Ava appeared would come out of this with their reputations intact, perhaps even enhanced. For her, the dice wouldn't fall favorably.

With another ascension lined up and ready to go, what Ava did next wasn't important. The shame and social backlash might push her to leap after all. Perhaps I'd treated her with too gentle a touch. Maybe the brute force of stigma had been required all along.

It was unlike me to have misread things so badly. But we lived and learned.

There was an element of anticipation in this one. The ascensions were almost becoming rote as they succeeded one after the other, but as Ava no longer had the app on her phone, she wouldn't know about the bots' work until she saw it on other socials. Or someone confronted her about it in person.

Today would be a hard day for her. And for me. I had no way to guide or even know what was happening.

I checked the time on my laptop screen. This waiting game was a new challenge for me, but life had hammered me to be supremely patient, and I would draw on that today. Bringing up my calendar, I was surprised how many entries would swallow the day. The only time I had for my personal appointment was now.

Such a busy schedule meant I wouldn't be able to check what was happening on the app until this evening.

I had no doubt, though, that Jayleen would be delighted when my first automation fired at lunchtime, inviting her to leap tonight. She was so eager to follow my instructions. I knew it wouldn't take much to push her. I typed in her challenge to be triggered once she said yes to ascending.

Congratulations, Jayleen. I'm so happy to welcome you to the real Ascension. To truly ascend and join with all your friends at the next level, you must take control of your fate by overcoming fear.

I read and reread the words. They had to hit just the right

tone, and yes, they did. More than that, they were perfect. Especially when I added extra praise that she wouldn't be able to resist.

This is your final challenge. You alone have earned this honor, and no one else can take credit for it. This challenge is a test of your strength, an opportunity to prove to yourself that you aren't afraid to step into the unknown. Your friends know you can do it. Now you need to prove it to yourself. Your challenge is simple. Borrow your grandmother's heart medication, and take enough to prove your commitment to the leap.

This next step of the message was the most important. They needed to believe they could survive what was coming next. That they would live, and through that living, would ascend to a place beyond future hurt.

Your friends believe in you. We believe in you. And when you come through this—when you feel the fear break and the pain slip away—we want to hear from you. We'll be waiting to celebrate with you. When you're ready to proceed, reply with, "I'm ascending."

I set the automation to send them to her later that afternoon. She would follow through, because her desperation for control would drive her to the edge.

With the potential of two ascensions happening in the next twelve hours, today could prove to be remarkable.

I touched my fingers to the images of their pretty faces. "Thank you both for your sacrifices."

32

Indie's desk phone rang sharply through the quiet background murmur of conversation and typing in the sheriff's office. A Mr. Tom Mitcham was at the front desk and wanted to converse about the uptick of local teenagers dying. This had Indie rushing into Sheriff Sammy's office, followed by Eli's, for permission to talk to the man.

Neither was around to rubber-stamp it.

Their visitor looked like everyone's good neighbor, the one you'd trust with your key while you were on vacation. He was clean-cut, in his mid-thirties, with short brown hair. Nice-looking in a nonthreatening way.

"Mr. Tom Mitcham, K-9 Detective Indira Reign. I understand you have some information for us."

"That's me." His face twitched up into a smile. "I wanted to come last night, but I have responsibilities at the Evergreen Counseling and Wellness Center, and I didn't want to let the kids down."

Indie led him to her desk.

"Whoa. He's a big guy." He approached Broc with his hand out.

"Broc's a working dog. I'd appreciate you not petting him while he's on duty." She pulled a chair over and put it beside the end of her desk in Broc's eyeline.

Tom sat, placing a laptop bag he had slung over one shoulder between his feet. "Completely understand."

Flipping open her notebook, Indie wrote his name at the top of a new page. "You work at the Wellness Center?"

"I'm in IT, but I volunteer there. I have a real rapport with the kids. We do great work together."

"What brought you here today?"

"I overheard a conversation yesterday between one of your deputies and Dr. Josephine Strickland."

Indie nodded. "I've met her."

"You'll know, then."

"Know what?"

"She talks a good game, but she's a bit lacking. You know, I have real empathy for the kids. Life for them is tough, what with all the online pressures. Way worse than high school ever was for us." He laughed, apparently not noticing Indie was a decade younger than he was. "The other therapists there…it's all just a paycheck for them. The kids don't get their focused attention." He laid his hand on his chest. "But I really care."

"What about this conversation concerned you?" Indie steered him back to why he'd come in.

"The deputy was telling Dr. Strickland about the wayward behavior of one of our teens, but Dr. Strickland didn't do anything about it. Jayleen Levin, the girl involved, needs personal attention. She's had a tough start. Both parents are in jail, so she lives with her grandmother. She talks a big talk, but underneath, she's just a frightened girl."

Indie glanced at Broc. He was watching Tom Mitcham as though the man might snatch his toy from the end of Indie's desk and run out of the building with it.

"Jayleen needs a gentle guiding hand."

A guiding hand? Did that mean what she thought it might? "How do you guide them?"

"However they need. They're all different."

Indie kept her voice even. "Say a teenager is a loner because they're very smart. How would you guide them?"

Tom shifted beneath Broc's scrutiny. "Does he always stare like that?"

"It's a dog thing." Indie held her pen poised. "So this hypothetical teenager?"

"It depends. Like, do they want to be alone, or would they like strategies to make friends?" He leaned forward. "How are you progressing on the cases of the teens who died? I could help. While I didn't personally know all of them, I know teens."

A tiny red flag began waving in Indie's mind. People who offered to help with open investigations were often well-meaning. But sometimes…they weren't. Sometimes, they inserted themselves into cases to control the narrative, to stay close to the investigation, or just to feel important.

"Do you have children of your own, Mr. Mitcham?"

He sat back, adjusted the hem of his t-shirt, and ran a hand down his jeans. "This isn't about me."

Indie glanced at Broc, and he seemed to agree. The man was hiding something. "Are your children teenagers?"

"Child."

"For you to be so good with the kids, I'd guess he or she is around their age?"

"It's irrelevant. I lost him." He pressed his hand to his mouth. Was he annoyed at her for pushing or at himself for answering?

"I'm sorry to hear that. It must be the hardest thing, as a parent." Indie leaned toward him.

"Being a parent is hard, period." Tom pulled at his t-shirt, then crossed his arms and legs. "Look, I came in because I can help you. Tell me. Were the teens who died showing signs of stress, anxiety, worrying more than usual?"

"What do you mean by that?"

"Well," Tom looked from Indie to Broc, "suicidal intent is usually evident in cases like these before the actual event. If you wanted to chat through the specifics, I can give you my expert opinion. But I was wondering what the parents had to say about it."

Any LEO would rather have an expert opinion from an actual expert. Unless they were talking to the perpetrator. Indie studied Tom's clean-cut image. Had he cultivated the perfect disguise to get teens to open up to him?

"I know these kids, what makes them tick, where they're at risk. I can help guide you as to where you should be concerned. You need a good guy on your side."

"He's not a good boy like me."

Broc was right.

"What do you do in IT?"

Tom's gaze shot to the bag at his feet. "Programming, mostly."

"Can you explain it to me like I'm five? Me and tech don't get along." Indie hoped her smile looked less fake than it felt.

"I write instructions in the language computers understand to get them to perform functions."

"Is that for apps?"

"Apps, software, databases, anything that's required." His hands slipped into his lap, and he uncrossed his legs as he warmed to his subject. "Don't want to sound bigheaded, but I'm damn good."

Indie used the same questions she'd asked Logan Nagle. "What about tech forums?"

"What about them?"

"Are you on them?"

"Sure, on them, and I've set them up for clients. You know, community spaces and private chat areas."

He might not have looked so pleased with himself if he knew his admissions were ticking boxes on Indie's suspect list. But that was as far as she could take it without making it a formal interview.

She stood. "Thanks for coming in, Mr. Mitcham. If you know of anything specific or you think a teen's at risk, please, let us know."

He checked his watch. "Yep, got to get back." He picked up his laptop bag, slung it over a shoulder, and walked out past the front desk.

Indie waited until he'd left the building before she sat down and looked at Broc.

His thoughts were all over his face. *"He's not what he says."*

"Shifty is the word you're looking for." She handed his toy back to him. "Good job. I think we'll be calling him in before long, but I need to check into his background first."

33

Jayleen Levin propped herself up on her elbow and rested her chin in her hand. Was the lunch bell ever going to ring?

Mr. Dowell was going on about something as if he thought he were solving world peace. His gaze landed on her. She glared back. *Move on. I'm busy.*

Could her plans yesterday have exploded any more spectacularly?

If that loser from the restaurant had just said yes right away, they'd have been long gone before Hen got there. Jayleen would make sure Hen knew how it had bitten her in the ass. Then she'd feel bad.

Jayleen still couldn't believe Dr. Strickland had brought it up, in embarrassing detail, in group therapy. They were supposed to share their own things, and she never shared fully. Everyone had turned to look at her, like she was in one of those bad dreams where she'd turned up at school naked.

And that Tom Mitcham. Where did he get off with his muttering about making better choices? He wasn't even a shrink. He was only a volunteer poking his nose in.

She wouldn't say one word the next few times she went. That'd show them. Now if she could just stop the events from yesterday from living in her head rent free and focus on the only good thing about group therapy, she'd be fine.

Logan Nagle.

He was so fine. Just thinking about him made her sweat. Funny how yesterday was the first time he'd spoken to her. If only Hen hadn't made her change out of her sexy dress and heels, he'd have been drooling over her too.

Imagining she was still wearing them had made her brave enough to give him her number. She replayed his smile when he stuffed the scrap of paper into his jeans pocket. It was enough to make her melt. Bummer he hadn't texted yet.

The lunch bell made her jump. Finally. Jayleen scooped her stuff from her desk into her backpack and bolted to the cafeteria. She grabbed a tray of food and rushed to her usual empty corner.

Once there, she checked her phone, but still nothing from an unknown number. Logan would get to it.

She clicked on the journal icon that led to the Ascension app. While it loaded, she pulled out a book and stood it up in front of her. She couldn't help smiling at her brilliance. The lunchroom assistants left her alone, thinking she was reading. The other kids sat somewhere else, not wanting to be seen with "the nerd who studies during lunch." If only they knew. She'd take that win.

There they were, as she'd known they would be. All her friends with their messages of support after her confession about her mortifying day. Her heart jumped at one from the Guide.

Jayleen, you're so much stronger than that situation. You're so capable. You can rise above all the people who don't get you.

Jayleen smiled, hope flooding her, making her eyes

prickle with relief. Yes, she could. She typed her reply. *I will. They don't know anything.*

The Guide's reply came straight back. *Are you ready for your final leap?*

Jayleen caught her breath. Her heart felt like it had gotten too big for her chest. *I'm ready.*

So ready to be done with this shit. Her mother and father were in separate jails for different crimes—wastes of space, both of them. Probably never thought about her at all. She was only too happy to return the favor.

Her grandmother was okay, but too old and too tired to understand anything about her. None of them mattered now. What mattered was that the Guide could see her potential.

Jayleen leaned her forehead on top of the book to hide her grin. The Guide was giving her the ultimate honor. RisingStar77 had told her when she first joined that it was a huge thing to be invited onto the app and that ascension would take time. And now to be invited to ascend so quickly? That was really something. Jayleen felt so special. She wanted to jump up on the table and announce it.

The bell rang for afternoon class. She rushed to type the last message. *I'll ascend tonight.*

Congratulations, Jayleen. I'm so excited to show you everything you can be.

The Guide knew who she really was. After yesterday being so awful, Jayleen never could have guessed that today could be the best day of her life. She slipped her phone back into her pocket and put the unread book in her backpack. She grabbed her untouched tray of food and shoved it in the rack before heading to class.

How different would tomorrow be for her? A rush of excitement made her want to skip down the hall. She'd gotten herself to this point, and she didn't need anyone else.

And after she ascended, Logan would break his fingers in his rush to text her.

She folded around her secret, hugging it to her, so excited her grin felt almost crazy.

34

Broc sniffed the air breezing in through the open windows as Indie drove them home after another busy day that somehow still felt unproductive. *"Will it be there?"*

She turned onto their street. "Salem?"

"Not the she-devil. The new one."

"Moriarty? Cats don't always stay at home. They roam wherever they want to."

"I can do that."

Indie pressed her lips together to stop her smile. "Cats can't guard the property. That's a dog job, so dogs stay on the inside of the fence, but cats can go outside or climb the trees."

"Dogs go up trees."

"You do, but not all dogs can."

Broc tilted his head into the breeze, maybe thinking through that conundrum. Her smart boy had helped slow the restless whirl in her mind, if only for a while.

When Indie parked and let him out, he sniffed the air. *"Dinner."*

Indie ruffled the fur on his head. "Your nose is better.

We're having dinner with Hen and Aunt Edith. You can probably smell that she's got your food ready. We just need to grab some stuff from home."

When Indie had finished packing a bag, she let herself and Broc into Aunt Edith's. He dashed into the big kitchen ahead of her.

"There you are, Indie dear." Aunt Edith was carrying a large dish to the table. "Come on in. Sit. Did you have another busy day? Hen's already here."

Indie took in the warm and welcoming space. Satch looked up at her, back at his dinner, at her. "It's okay, boy. You finish eating. I can see where your priorities lie." Indie handed Aunt Edith the bag she'd brought.

Aunt Edith looked confused at the groceries inside. "I don't invite you to dinner to bring your own."

"No, it's just that I…" Indie felt Hen watching her from her place at the table. "I have a meal plan and I've eaten here so much, it's all messed up. I can't use these things up now before I go shopping again. I thought you could."

"You don't want to change your shopping date?"

That hadn't occurred to Indie, but then she'd be in a new normal, and everything around her was already new enough. "Then everything gets confusing."

Aunt Edith patted her on the arm. "This is kind. Thank you. I'll definitely be able to use them."

Indie's shoulders dropped as tension she hadn't realized she'd been holding dissolved. "Good."

"Now sit yourself down, and we can eat."

Broc whined at Indie as she passed him on her way to the table.

"You're okay. Eat your dinner. It's the food I always make. Hey, Hen. You good?"

Hen looked a lot better than the last time Indie had seen

her, when they were both reeling from having lost Elliott Greene and covered in dust and soot.

Hen put her glass of lemonade down and waved her hand in a so-so motion. "I'll be better after this." She picked up the jug. "Homemade lemonade?"

Indie nodded and sat opposite her as a bundle of white and orange leaped up on the back of her chair. "Well, you're looking much better. You want scritches?"

Moriarty looked at her outstretched hand like it was another racoon.

"Maybe not."

Hen frowned at the animal. "That a new one?"

"As of yesterday. Is he going to be a problem too?"

Hen touched the base of her reddening neck. "I took my allergy meds, so I'll be fine."

Broc whined a baby howl.

"Is Salem in here?" Indie looked around but couldn't spot her turtle. "I did put her outside this morning so she could explore."

"Haven't seen her." Aunt Edith came to the table. "Ah, one's returned. Maybe Salem's hiding from Moriarty."

Broc barked.

"What's the matter?" Indie went over to him. Satch was eyeing Broc's bowl of untouched food. "What's wrong? Salem's not in here."

Broc whined again, looking at her with pitiful puppy dog eyes. *"Get it out."* He nudged the bowl with his nose.

"What is it?" Indie poked at his food, and a sprout of green jumped up.

Broc pounced in front of the bowl, keeping his head very still to give the offending vegetable a serious warning. That awful trainer had created a serious trauma for the poor dog around 'most anything green.

"Why don't you try it?"

"Get it out."

Indie fished it out and held it up to him. Broc backed away.

She held it out to Satch, who swallowed it without chewing. *"More?"* She fished the others out and tossed them into his bowl.

"Aunt Edith, how much broccoli did you add to the boys' food?"

"Only a couple of pieces each. I checked your list. It's good for them."

"It is, but I forgot to mention that Broc has an aversion to it." She pushed the bowl to Broc. "Broccoli free."

"Still happy to eat it, just to be safe." Satch licked his chops as he offered.

"Stop it, you." Indie went to put her hands on her hips but remembered her gravy-covered fingers. "Your dinner's perfectly safe now, Broc, but if you don't eat it, Satch will."

When Indie got back to the table after washing her hands, Hen handed her a slice of fresh bread. "That sounded like a full-on conversation."

Indie flushed. Because she talked to her boys so much as if they were people, it was hard to remember not to do it in front of others. "If you pay attention to their body language, they're very clear what they want."

Hen passed Indie the salad bowl. Indie had a feeling she understood more than she was letting on.

She very much wanted to take the focus off herself. "How're you?"

Hen shrugged. "I caught my neighbor's fifteen-year-old granddaughter's wrath for stopping her going off with a guy."

Indie buttered her bread. "She didn't understand you were just looking out for her?"

"'Course not." Hen cut a slice of cucumber into tiny

slivers. "They say no good deed goes unpunished, so when I took her to group therapy, Jennifer Blake went on and on about us doing nothing to protect the teens. She'd been dropping off her son, Dylan."

"That woman has a lot of prepared speeches."

Hen speared a floret of broccoli. "I've spent all day wondering if she isn't right. I mean, Jayleen was going on about an online community where her friends really 'get her.' But I think Jennifer's right, that their connections in the real world are what the kids should prioritize."

An online community? Was that what Indie hadn't been able to find? "Did she say anything about ascending?" She braced for Hen's reply.

"No." Hen shook her head slowly, then faster, with more certainty. "Nothing about that."

Indie told Hen what she'd seen on Ava Johnson's phone.

"So it *is* an app?"

Indie nodded. "And what I learned from Dr. Josie Strickland, and Dr. Kristin Parker at Columbia Medical Center, about the teenage brain tells me exactly why it works so well on them." She summarized what she'd learned and took another gulp of her drink, her mouth suddenly dry. "But I don't have the evidence we need."

Aunt Edith clasped Indie's hand. Her touch was healing and gentle. "Sweetie, you need to give yourself grace. You've been on the job one week, and look at all you've found out. I already see you running yourself into the ground with the long days, and I'm sure you're overthinking things during the night."

When she frowned, Indie found herself nodding. "Some."

Aunt Edith's face wrinkled into concern. "I take no pleasure in being right about that. You need to give it some time."

Time. Indie turned the word over in her mind. *We go*

around thinking it's elastic, stretching to years, decades, the best part of a century for some of us, forgetting it can snap back to just days, hours, minutes, seconds. The weight of however many young lives were counting down—even in that moment—pressed on her.

"I don't know if the kids in Sherwood County have time," she whispered over the beautifully prepared food in the chipped, clashing dishes in the middle of the table. The bright colors of the wholesome ruby-red tomatoes, emerald-green salad leaves, and vivid-orange peppers seemed to fade with the knowledge that something dark lurked beneath the surface of their small community.

35

Another sneeze, and Hen was doubled over again, right outside her apartment door. She wiped her nose, shook off the allergies, and inserted her key into the lock.

Indie's growing menagerie was going to kill her. Or maybe it'd be like desensitization therapy and accidentally cure her.

Hen sneezed again before she got the door closed. She waved an arm at the ceiling, but the motion sensor lighting must've been out. Again. Though she liked where she lived, today it was sad and lonely, probably because she'd just left the life and vitality, the fun and warmth, that was part of Nana Edith's home.

In the quasi-darkness of the hall, she could see light shining under Mildred Levin's door. But Mildred didn't like callers after early evening, so Hen would wait until tomorrow to see how she and Jayleen were doing.

But on the heels of that thought came a nudge, telling her to change her mind. Hen had learned to never ignore that ping from the universe.

She rapped lightly with her knuckles. "Mildred, it's Hen. Just checking on you." She knocked again. "Mildred, everything all right?"

Could she be sleeping? She did get tired easily. And after yesterday, Jayleen wouldn't be answering the door to Hen for a long time.

Hen banged harder. *Come on, Mildred. Shout back, and I'll leave you in peace.* "Mildred, it's Hen."

She exhaled when the security chain on the other side slid along its bolt keeper. When the other locks disengaged, Mildred peered out. Her face relaxed into softer lines, but a smile loaded with gratitude crinkled it all up again. "I can't thank you enough for taking such good care of Jayleen."

"It's my pleasure. How is she?"

Mildred looked behind her at a closed door. *Stay Out* was scrawled in red on a piece of paper stuck to it, and the boom of a strong base thumped out from the other side. "She's been quiet since coming home today, apart from that racket. Would you like to speak to her?"

Hen could only imagine how much eye rolling would be thrown at her if she broke Jayleen's order to steer clear of her.

Go check.

The nudge was stronger. Not actual words in her ears, but coming from deep in her soul.

"Sure. I'll make it quick."

She stepped into the Levins' apartment and approached Jayleen's bedroom. The air thickened, as though she were wading through water.

Hen's pulse hammered in her ears, louder and much faster than the beat of the music. She swallowed hard, putting her protection around her. There was something very wrong here.

She did a full-on deputy knock, hammering with the side of her fist. "Jayleen, it's Hen."

Nothing.

Her nerves tightened. "I'm coming in." She turned the door knob, but it was locked. She laid her palm on the wooden surface. An energy crackled against it that made her skin itch and tingle.

Trying not to alarm Mildred, Hen made her tone bright as she asked for the key.

"I don't have one." Mildred's voice broke in worry.

"I need to check on Jayleen. You all right if I…?" Hen mimed kicking the door in, and Mildred nodded.

The door burst open on Hen's second kick. A heady booming throbbed into her eardrums.

Jayleen lay on her bed, eyes closed, white pills cascading from the bottle by her head, scattered like confetti all over the red comforter.

"Jayleen, *what did you do?*" Hen rushed over, pressing her fingertips to Jayleen's neck. She had a faint and thready pulse, but a pulse nonetheless.

"She's alive. Mildred, call 911." But Mildred had already left the room.

Hen turned Jayleen onto her side into the recovery position.

A movement caught her eye, and for a second, Hen wasn't sure if it was ethereal or physical. But the sudden brightness was Jayleen's phone waking up as though unseen hands worked it. An icon, a blue square with a distinctive *A* flanked by angel wings, flashed across the screen. It winked away, and a stream of notifications replaced it.

Congratulations. You did it.
We're so proud of you.
I'm so excited to welcome you.

Hen's mouth dropped open as she read them. She

fumbled for her phone to snap a photo, but the messages had already blinked away. *Leaping into the future.* Jayleen had meant ascending. *Oh, Jayleen, what a waste of your life.*

Hen checked her pulse again. The fragile beating of her heart had stopped. Mildred wailed as if she knew, but Hen kept her expression rigidly neutral, her tone reassuring. "Mildred, could you go and wait for the paramedics by the main entrance? We don't want them going to the wrong apartment. Please. It'll really help Jayleen."

As Mildred hurried out of the room, Hen was already moving Jayleen off the bed. She grunted with effort, her muscles sore from carrying Elliott down his stairs just a couple days ago.

She eased the unresponsive girl onto the floor, needing a hard surface for the compressions to work effectively. She began rescue breaths and alternating chest compressions, but every time she checked, Jayleen's chest remained motionless.

Hen couldn't help believing that the architect of the app was somehow watching, mocking every move she made to save the girl.

The energetic darkness in the room roiled against her. *You'd better believe I'm going to save her.*

Mildred crying out in the hall, the worry that the paramedics would be too late...Hen pushed it all away. There was only the rhythm—one breath, two breaths, thirty compressions.

Over and over.

Come back to us, Jayleen.

Hen pulled on every ounce of strength, every moment of her training, to keep going. Sweat ran down her back, trickled from her temples, dampened her armpits. Her arms ached and her back hurt, but she focused on the compressions, on breathing for Jayleen, pushing blood through her body.

You haven't won yet! She screamed her thoughts at the orchestrator behind this. *You don't get to have her.*

Gentle hands rested on her back, giving her the strength to keep going.

She had her own help in the here and now, but she desperately hoped EMS would get there soon.

36

As Indie charged into the ER at Columbia Medical Center, she spotted Hen standing next to an older woman. Indie held her badge up as she blasted past the receptionist. "Detective Reign with the sheriff's office."

The woman beside Hen sobbed openly. A tall man in a white coat reached them just as Indie did.

"You came in with Jayleen Levin?" He looked at Hen. "Good job on the CPR."

"This is Jayleen's grandmother, Mildred. How is she?"

"Alive but critical. She's extremely lucky. Most of the pills she swallowed came back up only partially dissolved." He nodded at Hen. "If you hadn't checked on her when you did, the dose would've been fatal. She'll be transferred to the ICU shortly." His gaze shifted to Mildred. You should go home and sleep. There's nothing you can do for her this evening. She took your medication?"

"Yes." Mildred paled, but the doctor's look held no censure.

"You'll need your rest as much as she does to be strong for her recovery."

"Thank you." Mildred dissolved into fresh sobs.

Hen sat her down in the waiting area before leading Indie a few steps away. She pulled out a sandwich bag from the crossbody purse she wore.

"This is Jayleen's phone. As I was working on her, a whole load of messages came through congratulating her on taking the leap."

Indie took the bag. "Ascending?"

"Sounds like it to me. Talking about welcoming her, being so proud she did it."

"What monster is doing this?" Indie tapped the phone screen through the plastic, but it remained stubbornly dark. "Is the battery dead?"

"It had plenty when the messages were coming in."

Indie went back to Mildred. "Do you know the passcode for Jayleen's phone?"

Mildred sobbed in a breath. "It seems I don't know much about my granddaughter anymore."

Hen sat beside her and took her hand. "As her legal guardian, could you give us your permission to access her phone?"

"We'll obtain a warrant, too," Indie added, "but if you give us permission, it could speed up the process, and we could find some answers."

"Of course." Mildred looked at the bagged phone. "Please go ahead. Do whatever you need."

Indie wrote out a quick permission slip that Mildred signed.

"Would you like us to take you home now?" Hen held out her hand to help her up, but just the set of Mildred's jaw and the thin line of her lips made it clear. This woman wasn't going anywhere.

"I know the doctor means well, but while my Jayleen is in

there fighting to stay with me, I'll be right here waiting for her. I made a promise to her parents."

Hen squatted in front of her. "But you need to rest, and we have to get you some more meds for your heart."

Mildred gave a sad smile. "Well, if it's going to let me down tonight, I'm in the right place."

"Can I ask the nurses to set you up a cot?"

"I don't want to be a bother. I'd rather they spent their time looking after Jayleen. I'm perfectly fine here."

Hen squeezed her hand and stood. "Call me if you need anything, and when there's news."

Mildred nodded. "I will. Thank you, Hen, for everything."

"It's what we do for each other." Hen looked at Indie. "Let's go."

37

Indie waited while Hen asked an orderly if they could arrange somewhere more comfortable for Mildred to wait. Once that was done, she pressed the exit button to let them out of the ER. "She's fond of you."

"And I am of her. Tech team won't be working now, right?"

"Probably not, but we need to preserve the chain of custody. Locking it away at the station is best practice." Indie stopped so abruptly, Hen stepped on the back of her heel.

"What the—"

Indie raised a hand and nodded toward the man rushing toward them. "Tom Mitcham."

"Detective." His face screamed that he wished he'd bumped into anyone but her.

Too bad. "What are you doing here so late?"

Beside her, Hen looked confused. She was probably wondering why Indie's question sounded like an accusation.

"No law against it." He aimed for a grin, but his face wasn't cooperating.

Indie's eyebrows arched hard, and Broc and Satch

would've been squirming beneath her silently sarcastic annoyance. "Can you answer the question?"

"Just being a good friend. My buddy broke his leg, so I'm giving him a ride home."

Indie handed the sandwich bag containing Jayleen's phone back to Hen and pulled out her notebook and pen from her jacket pocket. "I'm going to need his details."

Tom's hands shot up as though Indie had drawn her service weapon. "That necessary?"

"I'm asking, so yes. Name, contact details, room number."

Hen looked behind them. "Now that I think about it, I didn't make a note of Jayleen's. I should prob…" Her voice trailed off when Tom's gaze rocketed to the doors behind them.

"Jayleen Levin? Jayleen's in the ER? What happened?"

Indie gave Hen a sharp shake of her head, but Hen was already pressing her lips together as if she'd realized her mistake.

"Is Jayleen okay?" Tom's voice rose. "Why won't you tell me?"

"Because we don't know." Indie watched him carefully.

His face worked. "That's terrible. She seemed okay yesterday, apart from making herself look like a fool."

"Your buddy's name." Indie wrote down the name Tom gave her as he circled around them and marched toward the ER double doors.

"What was that about?" Hen hustled to catch up with Indie.

"You need a ride?" Indie threw the question over her shoulder, striding through the parking lot as though her sneakers were having an argument with the pavement.

"I drove. I can follow you. You're taking it slow, though, right?"

"You want to come with me, and I'll drop you back here to get your car?"

"Sure." Hen raced after her.

Indie threw herself into the driver's seat and tapped the steering wheel, waiting for Hen to get in and click her seat belt. Putting her foot to the floor was much more in keeping with the way she was feeling, but she drove below the speed limit off the hospital grounds.

"You always carry your notebook off duty?"

Indie had to give Hen points for being diplomatic. "Had a feeling I might need it."

Hen nodded. "Turned out you did."

Indie rubbed the back of her neck. "You met him before? Tom Mitcham?"

"I saw him at the Evergreen Health and Wellness Center goofing around with the kids."

"He came into the station today, trying to insert himself into the investigation." Indie let out a groan. "Who'm I kidding? We don't have an investigation. That's why I'm mad. We should be looking at this officially, but the sheriff and Eli shut me down every time I say so."

"They like straightforward and easy."

Indie jerked a thumb behind her. "That guy, Tom Mitcham, he's not straightforward. Threw the therapists under the bus, telling me he does better with the kids than they do. Then there's Jennifer Blake and her ideas on social media." She stopped at an intersection, flicking a glance at Hen, grateful to be able to chat about what she knew so far. "Have you ever come across Logan Nagle?"

Hen considered that for a minute. "Don't think so. Is he connected?"

Indie nodded, shrugged, and wriggled in her seat, her body language showing exactly how conflicted she felt about it all. "I don't know for sure, but I wouldn't be surprised. He's a self-proclaimed tech genius, though he's only sixteen. When I talked to him, he raised a lot of red flags, but the sheriff and Eli—"

"Dismissed them as good old boy stuff?"

"How'd you know?"

The smoothness of the steering wheel against Indie's palms and Hen's understanding of her dilemma soothed her. She pushed herself against her seat back and turned into the station parking lot.

She was so over it. In the morning, she'd go through everything she suspected and convince them to let her investigate fully. What she'd learned so far screamed that someone was playing deadly games with the kids in Sherwood County. And with Sheriff Sammy's agreement—or not—Indie would track down whoever that was wherever they were hiding.

38

Ava Johnson leaned against her headboard, pressing an already-damp tissue against her wet eyes, but it was too sodden to mop up any more tears. She threw it at her trash can. It landed on the corner of her open laptop, leading her gaze right to the incoming flood of messages and notifications.

"Just stop," she pleaded with the device.

She might've styled out one or two photos, but whoever was doing this had apparently gotten ahold of every single photo ever taken of her—and altered them dramatically.

Her eyes were swollen and gritty, and it hurt just looking from one side to the other after crying the whole night.

Zero stars. Would not recommend.

Her head pounded, and her tongue stuck to the roof of her dry mouth. She pushed off the comforter to head to the bathroom, but the loud grinding of the coffee machine in the kitchen made her freeze.

Since when did her mom get up so early on a Saturday? Was she working? *Please be leaving for work soon.*

Ava tensed against a yell, stomping footsteps, slamming

doors. But the only sound winding up the stairs was her mom's warbling to some awful boy band she used to love when she was Ava's age. So she hadn't seen the mess online. Yet.

Ava lay down again, her hand curling up under her pillow, recoiling at what she'd hidden there last night. She tucked her hands between her knees.

Gradually, her sobs faded into exhaustion. The comforter warmed her, and she relaxed her tight muscles, one by one. Sleep danced in front of her eyes, and they grew heavy. And then, the ring, ring, ring of the doorbell over heavy pounding snatched it all away.

Groggy, confused, she sat up, each sore blink of her eyes reminding her of the living nightmare. She wouldn't be surprised if it was the police come to arrest her.

But it was worse. Much worse, because she recognized the voices.

She closed her eyes and crossed her arms over her stomach, which was churning worse than when she'd had norovirus. She was too exhausted even to stick her fingers in her ears to block out her father and his wife's screeching.

"Where were you when our daughter turned herself into a whore?"

Way to go, Dad. Make it Mom's fault.

That her mom defended her should've made Ava feel warm, but dread solidified in her until she was almost choking on it.

How could she have been so stupid?

If she'd ascended yesterday, she'd be beyond this trauma, this humiliation. If she'd been braver, she would've drifted down from the bluffs as light as a dandelion seed. After being welcomed into the lake's embrace, she would've been washed clean of her past—and her future would've been so bright.

Footsteps and yelling up the stairs sounded like a full-on

SWAT raid. Her door slammed open, and her father and his wife burst in, trailed by Ava's mom.

"How dare you disgrace us like this?" her father roared, his face an unhealthy red, his breathing erratic. "Whoring yourself out at sixteen? You disgust me."

"You're going straight to hell for the shame you've brought us!" Melody screamed at her with so much hate in her fiery eyes, she looked like the devil incarnate.

Ava gathered her knees to her chest and wrapped her arms around them.

"We raised you better than this." Her dad played the disappointment card next, his usual ace. It always hit her so hard. While the hammer blows of her dad's fury and Melody's judgment struck, she sought out her mom, still trying to defend her, trying to soothe what couldn't be calmed.

"Can everyone take a moment? You're overreacting."

"Overreacting?" Melody's anger had her scrambling for her phone. "How would you deal with this abhorrent behavior?" She jabbed at the screen and held it up.

Ava had never seen her mom's face change so fast, a kaleidoscope of anger and disbelief that settled on outright horror. Her eyes met Ava's, and while they were the same baby blue, Ava didn't like what she saw reflected in them.

Mom, I'm sorry.

Ava might've missed her chance to ascend, but there was a way she didn't have to deal with this fresh new nightmare. She reached under her pillow and seized her salvation.

Having drawn on herself at least a dozen times during the last night, she wasn't surprised by the gun's weight now.

"Where did you get that?" Ava's mom seemed shocked at the sight.

"Where do you think?" Her dad turned on her mom. "It's yours. From your nightstand, right?"

It was. But it was cruel of him to use that against her, especially when he had guns too. Several. 'Most everyone in South Carolina did.

Ava didn't want her mom to think this was her fault.

"I'm sorry, Mom. This isn't on you." She lifted the gun and rested the muzzle against her temple. A gentle touch that silenced the clamor in the room.

Her finger curved around the trigger, fitting as perfectly as if it had been custom-made just for her. In the darkness, the barrel had felt like just another enemy in her ever-growing list. But now, in the face of judgment, it promised the only way out.

It made perfect sense. Her parachute had been light to get the job done. This new option was weighty. The heaviness of the metal in her hand offered her the only way to overcome the unbearable reality of trying to endure this scandal.

Her life was tainted. Wherever she went, whatever she achieved, her path ahead would always snap back to those moments when she'd been having fun. Moments that had now been cast as filthy and degrading and wrong, wrong, wrong.

"Ava, sweetie, put it down." Her mom held her hands out, showing her what to do. "Please, honey, don't listen to them. We can get through this." Her voice cracked. Desperation coated the words she didn't mean, couldn't mean. "This isn't the way. I love you. We can get through this together, me and you."

"Put it down, Ava." Her father's face had flushed a deeper red. He threw one hand out toward her, fingers splayed. "You mustn't."

"He's right, Ava." Melody's voice had dropped a few octaves. "You'll burn in hell if you pull the trigger."

"Stop with your fucking fire and brimstone," her mom snapped. "Ava doesn't need that. She needs our support, our understanding." She turned back to Ava, and her voice softened, edged with tears. "And you have it, Ava. Anything you need. Sweetie, look at me. Listen to the sound of my voice. This isn't the answer."

Ava's gaze swung to her. "I'm sorry, Mom. I wanted to ascend, but I wasn't brave enough." She turned to look at her father. "I've fallen, and now I have nothing."

He met her eyes with his own heavy expression, still as full of judgment as when he'd walked in. But a quiver of his lips told Ava that he understood. He knew why she was doing this.

"We can fix this, Ava. Don't risk eternal torment. Pray with us. Please." He grabbed Melody's hand, and the two of them bowed their heads.

"You really think now's the time to bust out your hopes and prayers?" Ava's mom's voice was strangled by fear. "Your condemnation, your saintly ideals...that's what's driving this. Ava needs you to be her dad for once, not this pathetic pastor, only worried about what people might think."

"I'm doing what I can for her soul." He sounded as if he believed it.

"Her heart needs you now."

The heartbreak in her mom's words cut through Ava, but her dad shook his head, closed his eyes, and began muttering well-practiced phrases.

Her mom pushed in front of him. "Ava, honey, please. Whatever you think's impossible right now, you have to believe me. It's going to be okay. Nothing's forever. Please, just put the gun down. We can get through this together, me and you. Don't worry about them, about anyone outside this room. You and me, we can do it together."

Clarity rushed through Ava, and all fear faded away.

I can't hurt if I'm not here to feel it.

She gave her mom a tiny smile, closed her eyes, and pulled the trigger.

39

"Eli, you're in. Great."

The lead investigator looked confused by Indie's welcome.

"I mean, it's Saturday, but I was hoping to update you and the sheriff."

"Go for it." Eli shook his head at the few drips he'd coaxed out of the coffee pot, then followed her to the sheriff's office, boots clomping on the floor, spelling out his disappointment. "Reign has an update. You good to hear it?"

"Sure." The sheriff waved them in.

Once Eli had settled himself, Indie perched on the other seat. "We almost had another teen death last night."

Sheriff Sammy sat up.

When she'd recounted what happened to Jayleen Levin, the sheriff leaned back in his chair again. "Hen did that?"

"She saved Jayleen's life." Indie looked from him to Eli, but neither man seemed to have anything further to say, so she plowed on. "I understand what we had before was circumstantial, but with Jayleen being on the Ascension app, the same one that disappeared from Ava Johnson's phone when she tried to show me, I think we can agree it's more than that."

Sheriff Sammy gave her no sign that he agreed, but he spread his hands in an open invitation. "Remind us."

"You'll recall Logan Nagle raised some red flags when I spoke to him, and Jennifer Blake has also made some problematic comments. She's a very outspoken critic of social media, and she's even gone so far as to call out the parents of the teens who've died. Then there's Tom Mitcham, a volunteer at the Evergreen Health and Wellness Center. He comes into a lot of contact with those teens, including Jayleen Levin, Ava Johnson, and Logan Nagle."

"Okay, so he worked with those kids as part of his volunteering. Plenty of people volunteer. Doesn't make 'em killers."

"He's been trying to worm his way into the investigation, offering his expertise. He was at the ER last night, where Jayleen is. Allegedly picking up a buddy, but I haven't been able to confirm that yet."

"Does he know anything helpful? Can't say as I've heard his name before." Eli turned to the sheriff. "You?"

Sheriff Sammy shrugged before waving at Indie to continue.

"He told me he knows teenagers, but his job is in IT, and he confirmed he has the skills to build such an app." She took a second to let that sink in before getting to her next important point. "Jayleen mentioned leaping, and Ava Johnson, the teen who briefly went missing, talked about ascending."

The memory of Elliott's hopeful face as he died derailed Indie's logical thoughts for a breath, and the emotion of it strangled her words.

"Elliott Greene asked if he'd ascended right before he died. With the permission of Jayleen's legal guardian, we signed Jayleen's phone into evidence last night for the tech team to look at."

While Indie laid out everything she and Hen had discovered, the looks between the sheriff and Eli intensified.

"Can I have your approval to make this an official case? These deaths are becoming more frequent. And there's an ascension link to them all. We don't know how many other teens are at immediate risk."

The sheriff made a clicking noise with his tongue. "Laid out like that, I'll agree this is unsettling. But you're talking about deaths that have been tied up, all with verdicts that don't warrant further investigation. And no evidence to suggest we should escalate things."

He looked at Eli, whose expression was unreadable.

The sheriff turned back to Indie. "We have to live in this community, and you know we police by consent. Upsetting that system opens the door for things to get ugly. And what about the families? Don't you think they're suffering enough? Stirring things up'll poke the media, and things'll get crazier than a rat in a coffee can. We don't want a firestorm of unnecessary controversy in our lovely town."

Was he actually saying he was more worried about his public image, more concerned about the tourist numbers, than about the teens who lived here? Indie fought to keep her mouth shut. Jumping up and yelling at him to open his eyes would get her thrown off her probation faster than Broc could eat a squid.

"You know…seems to me there might well be more going on here than we've considered." Eli gave Indie the smallest of glances before he laced his hands around his empty mug, elbows on his knees. "I don't believe in coincidences, and everything Reign's uncovered might be circumstantial right now, but what if what's happening *is* being orchestrated? We owe it to our kids to check. It's good training for her, too, learning what to discount as well as what to take further."

Indie gaped at him in surprise. She didn't dare say a word or even make a sound.

He leaned back in his chair and added what was apparently the money shot. "If she uncovers something that finds a culpable individual we then bring to justice, the town will remember who backed this for a lot of years."

The sheriff stroked his chin, as if he were missing a beard he'd recently shaved off. "Put like that, I can see the benefit in digging a little further. But we don't want to upset folks unnecessarily."

He looked at Indie, and she witnessed the moment he made up his mind.

"I'll give you a little leeway on this, long as you understand that if any other cases come in that require K-9 support, you're to drop everything and attend to them. It's important to focus on real business."

"Of course. Will you now support me in getting warrants for device searches and allow me to officially question Logan Nagle?"

The sheriff opened his mouth, but his phone rang before he could give Indie the *no* she was sure was coming. Instead, he offered a bright, "This is Sheriff Sammy," to the caller.

Whatever they said made his eyes widen and his face go pale. He dropped the phone on the cradle with a loud clatter. "We have another dead teenager."

His words hit Indie square, making her shoulders curl. "Who is it?"

"Ava Johnson."

Indie's stomach dropped. She closed her eyes briefly

before forcing herself to sit up straight in the chair. "Can I have the techs examine Jayleen's phone now? Would you put in a request for search warrants for the other teens' electronics?"

The sheriff sank back in his chair, but finally, he nodded.

40

Indie signed the log at the Ava Johnson scene and pulled on shoe covers and gloves.

"Has forensics finished?"

Deputy Pantano checked her entry in the log. "Not yet."

"I'd better leave him with you, then." She handed the leash to him, telling Broc, "*Sitz. Warte.*"

She and the Mali exchanged knowing looks. Wishing she could take him in with her, Indie patted him on the head and entered the Johnson home.

The quiet murmurs of professionals at work on the second floor led her up the stairs. The sound of a camera and the gentle babble of someone making notes were demure, respectful. And at odds with the shocking aftermath of violence that greeted her.

While she couldn't see Ava, hidden as she was behind Clifton Harina's bulk, the rest of the room showed her it must've been a lovely space, calm and tasteful, at one time.

But Indie knew that no matter how many times Ava's mom redecorated, she'd never be able to forget seeing the spray of her daughter's blood and brain matter arcing across the headboard. Or get over the devastation of Ava pulling the trigger.

Indie ran her index finger back and forth over the stitching of her pants pocket. She didn't think anything would ever dislodge the guilt in her gut that she'd let Ava down.

Minding where she stepped, she approached the tech working beside the window and pointed at the laptop on the carpet. "Could you bag and tag that? I'll be signing it out to take with me for the techs."

He nodded. "Sure thing."

The coroner straightened at her voice, stepping away from Ava.

Indie could now see her. She was on her side, knees drawn up, similar to how she'd looked by the tree.

"Indie. Can't say as it's good to see you, considering the circumstances." Even Clifton's booming voice was muted. "The events seem clear-cut here."

"I met Ava yesterday when she was really upset, but Broc calmed her down. And when we left her with her therapist, she seemed much better."

"We can never know what another person is thinking, and teenagers...they can be so secretive, you know?" Clifton reached for his bow tie, a green-and purple-checkered pattern today. "I'll let you know when I've determined my ruling."

"Did she leave a note?"

Clifton shook his head. "Not that we've found so far."

"Appreciate that." Indie headed back out.

At the door, August handed Indie Broc's leash. "He was good, just like you said."

Broc twitched an ear. *"That deserves squid."*

"Nice try." Indie led Broc into the living room.

Sophia Johnson sat in the chair with her arms wrapped

around her stomach, wearing pale-pink lounge pants and a matching sweatshirt. Though early on a Saturday, she must've had time before the tragedy to add chunky earrings and a necklace. Her makeup no doubt had been meticulously applied, but now it slid down her cheeks in black and gold streaks.

She looked through Indie with Ava's baby-blue eyes, raw with pain.

"I'm very sorry for your loss, Mrs. Johnson."

Her lips trembled, and she struggled to pull in a deep enough breath.

"Mrs. Johnson? Sophia…" Indie could've been talking to the wall.

Broc sat close enough for the grieving woman to feel his warmth on her leg. In just a few seconds, she became aware of his presence and looked up at Indie as though surprised to see her there.

"Can you tell me what happened?"

"My baby's gone." Her tone was flat, hopeless. "She took my gun and shot herself. But she's in therapy. That's supposed to stop something like this. I pleaded with her, but she looked me in the eye and did it." Her next words were small. "She looked so sad."

It took everything inside Indie not to pull the woman into her arms. Instead, she let Broc do that comforting.

"Do you know why she did it?"

Sophia blew her nose. "There are photos of her online. Melody, the bitch, showed me one of Ava with a boy. And then Mark…" She finally met Indie's gaze for the first time. "That's my ex-husband. He said they had to pray for her soul. They had to pray for her, not help me stop her." She shivered. "I wanted to grab the gun out of her hand, but I was so scared it would go off." Her voice dropped to a whisper. "And then it did."

Losing a child was the worst thing that could happen to a parent, but to watch it happen…be unable to stop it…it wasn't something Indie could imagine.

"When I saw Ava yesterday, she showed me her phone to check something out. Is it on your account?"

Sophia nodded.

"Would you give permission for me to access the device?"

She reached for another tissue. "Whatever you need."

"I'll just get a form so it's all legal."

It took time for Sophia to read the sparse wording on the form and sign it. The woman was completely shell-shocked.

Thanking her, Indie took back the form and her pen. "Again, I'm very sorry for your loss. I'll likely be back with more questions once I've had the chance to review Ava's phone, so I thank you in advance for your patience and cooperation."

Indie tapped her leg, and she and Broc went into the kitchen to interview Ava's dad.

He was as stuck in the terrible event as Sophia seemed to be, but where Sophia had seen Ava's sadness and despair, Mr. Johnson kept asking Indie why Ava wouldn't just pray with him.

After going in circles, hearing the same replies to different questions, Indie went into the den where Ava's stepmother waited.

Melody Johnson's dark hair flowed around her shoulders in large waves, making her look almost like a model. But her makeup-free eyes were narrowed, and her mouth made such a tight, thin line, her lips had all but disappeared. She recounted the events as though she were telling Indie about the bullet points from the news.

"We found out about the photos of Ava circulating online this morning and rushed right over to confront her. Mark has his position in the church to think about."

Indie and Broc shared a look in agreement that they didn't care for the new Mrs. Johnson. "Can you tell me what happened when you went into Ava's room?"

"We confronted her and her mother. She didn't even know what her daughter had done."

"What had she done?"

"She was being indecent with lots of different boys. The whole world could see her naked and having sex." She spat the words out as though they'd burned her mouth. "She didn't deny it. She didn't even have the grace to apologize. But then she pulled the gun out from beneath her pillow. I mean, that woman, her mother? Who has an unsecured weapon in a house with a child? Then we all pleaded with Ava to stop."

"How did Ava seem then?"

"She was upset."

"Upset?" To Indie, upset at high school meant failing a test or being made to look stupid in gym class.

Ava's stepmom's gaze dropped to her tidily folded hands. "Despairing, then. She was crying. She said something crazy about wanting to ascend but not being brave enough. And something else about having fallen and having nothing. I was praying and didn't hear it all."

Indie shivered. It would be a long time before she could hear that word without reacting. It was all connected. She was certain.

"Thank you for your help. I may have more questions once I've reviewed Ava's phone."

She didn't expect a reply, so she was surprised when Ava's stepmom thanked her for her service to the community. Not sure how to respond, Indie simply dropped her business card on the table and led Broc back to her SUV.

Even his trot was more subdued than usual. *"Sad in there."*

"It is." She opened the door for him. "I have a feeling time isn't on our side."

He tipped his head at her.

She stroked under his chin. "I know you don't understand time. But today, it feels like I'm running behind. And I'm worried we might miss something critical that could help us save the next victim." She let out a long sigh, but her body was too tense to relax. "Back to the station to get that warrant moving."

Indie filled up Broc's water bowl. Luckily, he was thirsty and drank it all down in about ten seconds, because she drove fast, took corners way too tight, and stopped hard, which would've tested the manufacturer's non-spill guarantee.

She rushed into the tech department with Broc at her heels. She was so relieved someone was there on a Saturday that she greeted him like a long-lost friend. "Oh, thank goodness. I'm so glad to see you here."

He tipped his head like Broc did when he was trying to understand, but a grin quickly followed. "I'm Matt. You must be Indie. Your greeting beats 'good morning,' or 'who drank all the coffee?' and 'why are there no clean cups?' You know, the usual."

"I was worried no one would be here since it's the weekend. But what I have is so urgent, it can't wait."

Matt clutched at his heart. "And here I was thinking you were pleased to see me, not here for my mighty technical prowess." He looked from Indie to Broc and back. Neither could bring themselves to even acknowledge his attempt at humor. "And we're straight to business. What do you have that's so urgent?"

"This is the phone and laptop of the teen who died this morning, Ava Johnson." Indie handed over both, along with the signed form from Sophia Johnson. "I have written permission from her mother to access it, and her password's on the form. She had an app called Ascension, which she accessed through the journal icon. But when Ava went to show it to me yesterday, the app disappeared."

"A hidden disappearing app? Now you've got my interest." Matt picked up the evidence bag on his desk that held another phone. "This belongs to the other teen, Jayleen Levin. You might want to see this." He held the bag close over the screen so Indie could read the notifications.

Text from Logan Nagle, the top one read—and the second and the third. Not app notifications but text messages. Logan. Once again at the heart of this.

"Have you read them?"

"Not yet, but these two phones are at the top of my list."

A hidden disappearing app, something Indie assumed would be "easy" for a hacker to create. The perfect way to keep the community exclusive, for invited participants only. That sounded right up a secretive teenager's alley.

41

I glanced at the closed door, even though I knew no one would interrupt me. I was alone.

Unlike after Elliott's ascension, when his death story took time to drip into cyberspace, Ava's had already hit the digital headlines. The media clearly considered a cheerleader killing herself in such a dramatic and violent way to be worthy of attention-grabbing news.

Even in death, things weren't fair.

But was all this attention on Ava while Jayleen was in the hospital a good thing? I bit my lip, tugging on the tiny hairs at the nape of my neck before I forced myself to place my fingertips in the comforting ready position on the keys of my laptop.

Nothing could be traced back to me. I'd been so very careful in the way I'd orchestrated Ascension, and Hex Spectre's helpful suggestions had made it impenetrable to outsiders. So long as I remained behind the curtain, no one would ever know the identity of the app's mastermind. And I was content to remain anonymous in that capacity, because none of this was about me.

I leaned back in my chair, scrolling through the news articles and comments about Ava.

The invisible poison of social media shaped and distorted our children's thoughts, filling them with insecurities, addictions, and fears. Why was the world so blind to how it made them vulnerable to manipulation? Children—toddlers, practically—were allowed to navigate these digital minefields, exposing their developing minds to toxins disguised as entertainment.

I pushed my shoulders down and swiveled my head from side to side. Tight muscles protested, but there'd be time enough to care for myself properly afterward.

One of Ava's articles had the perfect photo of her for my Pantheon of Pathfinders. Ready for cheerleading practice with her hair tied back and wearing little makeup, she looked younger and a lot more wholesome than in the photos my bots had doctored and released.

"A casualty of war." I copied and pasted the image into my gallery. "Another sacrifice to make people see. And that's why you deserve your place there, Ava. I won't hold it against you that you let me down initially. Thank you for your sacrifice."

Closing it down, I opened my encrypted spreadsheet and added her name to the tab for Sherwood County. The tally here was creeping nearer to my most prolific location, but I waited to check exactly how close the numbers were. In a world that wanted instant gratification, I understood the value of anticipation.

Starting at the beginning, I opened the tab for Nashville, Tennessee. Only two names occupied that page, but they felt more...was "important" the right word? Maybe "momentous" was more apt to describe my first two ascensions.

Next, I clicked Cary, North Carolina, and read the four names listed. Seven on the next page in Macon, Georgia. And then, when things had all fallen together perfectly, twelve in other South Carolina counties. And now six in Sherwood.

My shoulders dropped of their own accord, relief flooding my body over all I'd accomplished so far. I closed my eyes to replay my well-worn daydream of the utopia where children were protected from the insidious grip of social media, where parents no longer had to worry about their offspring's minds being shaped by influencers and algorithms. That was worth fighting for.

So on I had to continue, though I knew the path would be slick with more blood. The next ascensions were vital to the larger war we fought—and I needed to rush them through before Jayleen's failure had any impact.

Being a soldier on the front lines was exhausting. But I owed it to future generations to keep pushing until the world woke up to the truth.

42

Hen closed the door to Jayleen's hospital room, quieting the conversations outside.

She didn't need to be a medical professional to see that Jayleen was in desperate need of what Nana Edith would call a "good old Appalachian healing."

Once she'd muted the TV to focus on cleansing herself and the room, Hen could begin to help her heal.

She drew the reiki symbol for emotional and trauma healing over her heart chakra. Scooping away the energetic pain Jayleen had been feeling and refilling it with white light, Hen held her left hand over the girl's heart. Clean, clear energy spun against her palm. She smiled.

Much better.

Mildred would wonder what she was doing if Hen hadn't sent her home to rest. It might look odd, but Hen's ministrations went way beyond her promise to keep watch on Mildred's granddaughter.

She worked her way through all Jayleen's chakras, clearing what shouldn't be there, injecting positive healing energy. Jayleen's eyes fluttered as Hen attended to the crown chakra at the top of her head. The lightness Hen began feeling told her Jayleen would be okay.

Hen sat beside her then, pouring more reiki energy into Jayleen's bruised and battered body. The girl pulled the energy through Hen's palms as though she were starving.

If Hen had anything to do with it, Jayleen would come back to them feeling as if she'd been bathed in peace, love, and a sense of security. Immeasurably better than the negativity Hen had already cleared.

A knock at the door made her drop her hands, closing off the reiki energy. No sense in alienating the medical staff with all her woo-woo.

But Indie stepped into the room instead. "How's she doing?"

"Better."

Jayleen's eyes flickered open, and she glanced around the room, seeming confused.

"You're okay, Jayleen. It's Hen. This is Indie. You're in the hospital." Hen pushed more reassurance into her voice. "It's okay. You're safe."

Jayleen licked her lips. "Did I ascend?"

That was her first worry? Hen opened her mouth to ask what that meant, but Indie beat her to it.

"You did. You did a wonderful job. Everyone's so proud of you. Especially Logan Nagle."

"He is?" Jayleen's face brightened with the smallest trace of color. "I hoped he would be. I knew he'd see me once I ascended. My friends on Ascension told me everything would change."

"Ascension?" Indie made her question sound so unimportant, but Hen was itching for Jayleen to expand on her comment.

"An online community that challenges me to be better."

She looked at Hen. "The other day, with the old guy in the parking lot, that wasn't a challenge, by the way."

"What challenges have you completed, Jayleen?" Indie nodded at Hen as she asked the question.

Hen expected the usually sullen teen to shut down, but to her surprise, the girl lit up, like she'd been holding this part of her life in for too long. Like a secret she'd sworn to keep and had finally been given permission to let go.

"Disconnect was first. I had to avoid speaking to anyone for a full day. That was easy. No one bothers me much at school, and there's only my grandmother at home. She's usually too tired to chat."

"How did that help you?"

Her eyes widened. "Made me see only Ascension could give me true connection."

Indie nodded as if that made perfect sense. "And what about the others?"

"Embrace the Pain."

"How did you win that…challenge?"

"Held my hand in ice-cold water until I couldn't take it anymore. The Guide told me that pain is a teacher, and it's true. It taught me my friends on the app are the people I should have in my life. They get me."

Hen had to focus to push her outrage down so it didn't pollute her next question. "What about your last challenge?"

But Jayleen closed her eyes, a smile curling her lips. The few minutes of conversation seemed to have drained her. They watched the teen sink back into sleep before they moved to the closed door to chat.

"What was that about Logan Nagle?" Hen asked under her breath.

Indie pressed around her bun, making sure all the pins were in place, triggering Hen to check the state of her own.

"He's been messaging Jayleen since her ascending challenge. I wanted to know why before officially questioning him."

"Did what she say help?"

"I don't know. Did you hear about Ava Johnson?"

"Another shocking waste."

Indie rearranged her polo.

Hen noticed she did that a lot. She'd have to get her something to put in the laundry to soften it. New uniforms could feel like you were wearing the clothes hangers they came on. Hers must've been really stiff.

Indie rubbed her pants pocket back and forth, which Hen didn't think was a laundry issue. "I thought she'd be okay when I left her the day before. She'd calmed right down, and her mom didn't seem concerned."

Something in her reply made Hen open herself up to look at Indie with her third eye. A muddy green streak had appeared in her aura. That hadn't been there before.

When Indie first joined Nana Edith and her for dinner, Hen had needed to check Indie out on all levels, seeing as she was staying on her nana's property and given that Indie had been kind of off when they'd reconnected. Indie's energy had been clear, with good emotions radiating freely from her then. But Hen didn't need to be a reiki master to understand Indie felt much more comfortable and was much more used to communicating with animals than people.

Now, though, the streak was expanding. The weight of guilt was a difficult thing to withstand, and if the muddy patch was growing as fast as it seemed to be, Hen had reason to worry.

43

"Are you sure I can't bring you something back?"

Indie was beginning to understand that Hen liked to ask the same question over and over until she got the answer she wanted to hear. She was a nurturing carer, just like her nana.

"I'm all good. You go eat. Take a minute for yourself."

"They make a pretty good pizza." Hen stopped by the door. "I can bring you back a slice."

Indie knew she was beaten. "That'd be nice."

Left alone, Indie watched Jayleen sleeping peacefully. She could've sworn more color was coming back to the girl's cheeks second by second.

Pulling out her notebook and pen, Indie thought about the best strategy to adopt when she spoke to Logan Nagle. She wrote his name on the page, interrupted before penning the final letter by a knock at the door.

The woman who entered seemed entirely different from the first time they'd met. Her outward appearance was as polished as it had been then, but Dr. Josie Strickland's gaze rocketed from Jayleen to Indie and back again. And her tiptoed steps to Jayleen's bedside were small and tight, muting the click of her heels.

"Detective Reign, I just heard. This is so awful. How is she?" The doctor's hand fluttered to her chest, where she grasped a large pendant she wore on a long chain over a black silk t-shirt.

"We're waiting for an update, but there are good signs she's going to be okay." Indie stood and pushed the chair toward her. "Here. Sit."

Dr. Strickland grasped Indie's hand and collapsed into it. "That's so good to hear. I just can't believe what's happening to our community. I mean, in group therapy, Jayleen doesn't say much, but she participates just enough that I saw no hints of something like this on her horizon. In sessions, her body language screams that she's lost, even scared, though her demeanor suggests she's defiant, a rebel. But…this?"

Indie crossed her hands in front of her, holding her notebook. "That's a troubling mix."

"It is." Dr. Strickland reached up to tap the page where Indie had written Logan's name. "He's another I'm very concerned about."

Indie had almost forgotten what she'd written. "Why?"

"I can't share anything specific, but I can't help but wonder if he has anything to do with these deaths."

Indie clamped her lips together. She held her shoulders and back rigid, kept her facial expression set. Not one movement, barely a breath in, out, nothing to stop Dr. Strickland from sharing what could be dynamite, something that might blow the case open.

Dr. Strickland finally shifted on the chair. "I hesitate to get involved with rumors, but I think you need to know that Logan had grudges against several of the teens who died. Specifically, Zach Mitchell, Elliott Greene, and Ava Johnson."

Indie wrote down their names, though she didn't think

she'd ever forget them. "I appreciate you sharing that. What were the grudges about?"

"I don't know definitively. All I've heard are rumors." Dr. Strickland seemed much more centered now. Her gaze held Indie's without flitting around the room. "And I'm sharing this with you with the knowledge that much of what teenagers say in a group of their peers can be discounted as bravado. Logan's probation only specifies group therapy, but I wish he'd accept more personal counseling."

"He's on probation?" Indie did a terrible job at keeping the surprise out of her voice. Why hadn't the sheriff or Eli mentioned it when she'd asked about formally questioning him?

Still holding her gaze, Dr. Strickland nodded.

Indie felt her pen almost bending as she wrote down this new information, annoyed that she hadn't checked Logan Nagle's record herself.

Questions for Eli and the sheriff bubbled up in her like rising magma. She wanted to charge out of the hospital, throw herself into her Explorer, and race to the station with lights and sirens on.

She glanced at the TV. A familiar face on the screen, now front and center, made her reach for the remote and jam her thumb on the volume button. Jennifer Blake's voice filled the room, making Dr. Strickland groan.

Jennifer looked down the camera with the poise of someone used to public speaking. *"I'm sure you've all seen the news about the rise of teenage deaths in our community, but how many of you are really concerned about it? How many of you are actively taking steps to make sure your child isn't next?"*

Her huge ring caught a light from one of the cameras recording her, igniting the flare of a prism on the wall as she made a chopping motion on the lectern behind which she stood.

"You would all be out on the streets protesting if you knew an individual was responsible for these deaths. Yes. But you've allowed this culprit right into your home. Worse than that, you've welcomed it in."

Her gaze hardened, becoming colder, even as her tone heated up and her words tumbled out faster.

"How many of you are guilty of making your smartphone your child's babysitter? How many of you put a phone or tablet in front of them as soon as they're old enough to hold them? A sing-along game when they're babies might seem innocent, but it leads to video games by the time they're six, where they see violence akin to being on a battlefield."

"Jennifer—"

Jennifer held up her hand as though the reporter were a car that needed stopping and talked all over his question.

"Enter social media, and now we have young girls sexualizing themselves in their bid for likes. A whole generation is lusting after uninspiring and empty lives for clicks, and worse, they're bullying others because they think that will make them more popular."

She gripped the lectern with both hands, knuckles whitening.

"This is neglect, pure and simple. Parents should be arrested for allowing their children to access these devil's playgrounds."

Straightening the lapels of her red suit jacket, she glared harder at the cameras in front of her.

"You had time to act, but you squandered it for convenience. And your children are paying the price. If you want to put that right, I'm holding a town hall meeting where we can discuss what we can do. We're not powerless, but you need to step up for your children."

A riot of questions assaulted her as she left the platform and marched off camera.

Indie muted the TV.

Dr. Strickland's eyebrows had reached her hairline. "Does

that woman think her rants will influence parents? Change the laws?" She shook her head and tutted.

The professional in the room did not seem impressed.

"What's your take on her?" Indie kept her question open-ended.

"I haven't seen her in a clinical setting, but from what I understand of her family history, I see why she's taken this radical line against our digital world."

That was well put, and Jennifer Blake's stand was certainly radical. "Is there anything else you can share with me?"

Dr. Strickland looked at the floor as if asking it for permission. A tiny nod signaled her decision. "Well, it's nothing you can't find anywhere else if you were to look. She lost her oldest son, Derek, to cancer when he was fourteen. That's terrible enough, but her grief was compounded by the bullying he experienced on social media while he was undergoing treatment."

Shock rippled through Indie. Bullying while dying from cancer? How could anyone be so cruel?

"Kids mocked his bald head, his wasting body. That experience left Jennifer deeply scarred and triggered her disdain for social media. Every time I see or hear her, she's more hostile about it."

"So that's why she doesn't allow Dylan anywhere near it."

Dr. Strickland nodded and smoothed her skirt. "This fierce protectiveness is a form of complicated grief. Where she felt powerless to stop what happened to Derek, being such a strict gatekeeper over Dylan's exposure to technology gives her back some control. Her actions are rooted in grief, but they've manifested in extreme and unhealthy ways."

Again, Indie was impressed at Dr. Strickland's grasp on human behavior. She could be a useful sounding board in other investigations, since that understanding lay at the heart of everything.

Indie held her pen and notebook ready. "Can you give me some examples of these ways?"

"Take what we've just seen." Dr. Strickland waved her hand at the TV. "That level of aggression, where she's calling for parents to be arrested, indicates a deeper, more dangerous shift in her mindset, where her need to protect Dylan has become all-consuming. This intense protectiveness, this unresolved grief and trauma, could lead her to take drastic and perhaps destructive measures."

Indie scribbled down everything the doctor said. Even without Dr. Strickland's insights, Jennifer Blake was already in the top two of formal interviews Indie needed to undertake.

"What do you make of Tom Mitcham?" She added his name to the page.

Dr. Strickland frowned, staring at her for a long moment. "He appears to be a well-meaning man, and obviously, even as a volunteer, he was subject to a stringent vetting procedure before we let him through the center doors."

Indie could hear Dr. Strickland's silent "but" at the end of that sentence. "But?"

The doctor rubbed the back of her left hand, then her right. Her nails were neatly trimmed, and she had a French manicure. She wore no rings. "I'm starting to be concerned that he sometimes crosses boundaries with them. He's a little too eager to be their friend, and when they aren't keen to befriend him back, he seems to feel rejected."

Indie kept her face blank while her thoughts raced. Being rejected by the kids…was that enough to give him motive? He was rocketing up her list of potential suspects. "Crosses boundaries in what ways?"

The door opened, and Hen stepped into the room. She froze and half stepped out again.

Dr. Strickland squeezed Jayleen's hand before standing. "Can you tell her when she wakes up that I wish her a swift recovery? And that I'm looking forward to welcoming her back to therapy?"

Indie nodded.

The doctor gathered up her purse and smiled at Hen. "I understand Jayleen owes you her life."

"It's nothing anyone else wouldn't have done." Hen stepped stiffly around the door frame, keeping her distance as if Dr. Strickland were contagious.

"Well, I, for one, am grateful. Our children are precious." She smiled at them both before leaving the room.

Hen pressed the door closed against the frame.

Indie put her notebook away. "Everything okay? You seem a bit ruffled."

"It's just something about that woman. I feel like a bug under a microscope when she looks at me. I can't help feeling she's scrutinizing and categorizing me, and I don't like it." Hen blew out her cheeks. "I mean, it's probably as hard for her to turn off being a psychologist as it is for us to turn off being cops. We're never off duty, are we?" She handed Indie a paper bag spotted with grease. "Three cheese. Hope it's still hot enough."

Indie looked inside. The pizza did smell good. "Thanks."

Hen nodded at Jayleen. "Any change?"

"Not yet. You want to sit?" Indie stepped back from the chair.

Hen shook her head. She walked around the bed and back to the door in a U-shaped pattern.

The pizza was good, the herbs and garlic on the melted, stringy cheese perfect. "You were right about this." Indie chewed another bite, watching Hen. "What else is bothering you?"

"Her aura looks muddy. The colors aren't as bright or distinct as they should be." She gave an exaggerated shrug, throwing her arms up into the air. "But you know the things she must hear, must see in her job. She's bound to be carrying that around with her. And I bet she doesn't know about energy work, about how she needs to cleanse herself after seeing each kid."

"Maybe you could teach her." Indie picked a straggle of cheese off her chin. "What?"

Hen was looking at her as though cheese covered her from head to foot.

"What is it?"

Hen paced another pattern. "Your aura's not looking too healthy right now either."

44

Indie didn't know what to do with Hen's pronouncement about her aura, so she ignored it. She finished the last mouthful of pizza and stood. "I'm going to do what I can to progress this case."

Hen placed the chair closer to the bed. "I'm staying."

"Good. When she wakes up, can you find out everything Jayleen knows about Ascension?"

"Sure. I'll be in touch."

"Thanks." Indie walked back to her SUV. She didn't usually trust her own reading of social cues, but Hen felt a bit off, too, after coming back into Jayleen's room. Maybe something had happened in the cafeteria that had her on edge.

Broc's nose was right up against the rear window guard as she approached the Explorer.

"Heard me coming, huh?"

"Smelled you. You got me cheese?"

He looked so hopeful, Indie felt like a cat caught stealing cream. She should've saved him the crust. "Not today. It's human food, for humans, not really for doggos." She walked around to the other side to check his water bowl. "You need to be quick?"

He put his paw on the door.

"Come on, then." Indie clipped him on the short leash and walked him over to the closest grassy area. While he sniffed around searching for that most elusive thing—the perfect spot to do his business—she pulled out her phone and called one of her recent numbers.

Jennifer Blake surprised Indie by answering.

"Mrs. Blake, I wonder if I might speak with you again. I could use your help to clarify some details at our end. It's just a routine part of our investigation. And after your press conference, it's clear you have a better handle on these risks than most people. I'd like to use that knowledge to help us."

"I'd be delighted to put my feelings about these teen deaths on the record. That's the first stage in change, after all, and that's what I'm fighting for. I can come to the station at two."

That was a surprise. If Jennifer was as guilty as Indie was coming to believe, she'd have run a mile from Indie's sorry explanation.

Indie's mouth worked for a second before she got words out. "That would be perfect."

After thanking her and hanging up, she checked the time before pocketing the device.

"Everything okay?" Broc had finished his business but continued to sniff every object in his path.

"I thought I'd have to fight to get her to agree." She headed to the cruiser. "Ready?"

He jumped into the back. *"We going to the park?"*

"Not now, bud. We're working."

He got into the SUV but threw her a look. She knew he was still holding the cheese incident over her head.

Indie started the engine. "Fine. We'll go to the park." He

grinned, his tongue lolling out several inches. "You don't play fair."

He was still grinning when she let him out of the SUV a few minutes later.

She ruffled his head. "Next time, I'll save you the crust."

"Yeah, you will."

He swished his tail as he bounded in the direction of her hand gesture. She wished she could run off her troubles as easily.

"Halt." Broc stopped at her call, waiting for his next instruction. *"Komm."* Come.

Backward and forward. She sent him away and called him back, running through instructions for him to sit partway, to lie down, to turn and go as far away from her as she was comfortable with.

"Good job." She patted him when he came back, tongue lolling out, panting. "Special treat for you. *Warte.*" Wait. She walked behind him to a stand of bushes, into which she threw a handful of kibble. Returning to him, she gave him a piece. "Find the rest."

While he sniffed out and gobbled down the treats, she made another phone call. The man who answered sounded hesitant, as though he knew it would be her.

"Mr. Nagle, I'm K-9 Detective Indira Re—"

"Logan's here. And before you go accusing him of something, he's been here all night and morning."

Indie lowered her voice, keeping it extra calm to counter his bluster. "I'm not accusing him of anything. All I wanted was to ask if he could help us with some inquiries—"

"That's the thing. Now that he's in your system, you'll be hauling him in whenever there's anything going on."

"This isn't that. I can assure you."

"You can assure me whatever you like, but because he's on probation, he's got no choice but to jump when you say so."

Broc sat looking at her, treats all found, waiting for more.

"You can sit in with Logan, and as this is only routine questioning, you're free to leave at any time."

"He don't need a lawyer?"

"That's your choice, of course, but I only have a few background questions."

Carl Nagle's tone had become less belligerent. "My wife's not here. She's not off work 'til four."

"Would coming in at five work for y'all?"

He took so much time thinking about it, Indie checked her screen to make sure the call was still active.

"I guess so." The words dragged out of him as if she was asking him to attend his own funeral.

"I'll see you then." She hung up and looked at Broc. "Two for two. Let's get back to the station and see what else we can clear up while we're on this run of luck."

※

Jennifer Blake arrived at two on the dot. Indie couldn't help feeling the outfit she'd worn for the press conference was her suit of armor and that she counted on it being as provocative as the red cape a matador flapped in front of a bull.

When Indie opened the interview room door, Jennifer wrinkled her nose.

"We're in here because it's a little more private." Indie made her voice reassuring, but that didn't smooth the woman's reaction when she noticed Broc sitting near the back wall.

"Him again? Do you have assistance needs?"

"Broc's a working dog, so he has to be in here with us. He won't bother you."

"Unless she bothers you."

Indie pressed her lips together so they wouldn't curve into a smile.

Jennifer muttered something about it smelling bad enough in there already.

Indie took the seat next to her pup, holding a hand out for him to be steady as she looked at Jennifer.

You should be thankful he hasn't eaten any squid since breakfast.

Jennifer pulled out the chair opposite Indie and swept it with her palm before sitting down. Taking a bottle of hand sanitizer out of her purse, she slathered it over her palms, placing it on the table between them. She went to put her purse on the floor but decided against it, placing it on the end of the table.

"Mrs. Blake, is there any reason I can't record this interview?"

Jennifer shook her head as Indie had expected, but then she surprised her. "As long as I can." She withdrew a large smartphone in a pink case from her purse, tapped the screen, and placed it in the middle of the table.

Indie hit the record button on the camera fob and introduced them and Broc for the benefit of the recording, giving the time and date.

"May I call you Jennifer?"

She nodded stiffly.

"Thank you. I want to begin by reminding you that you're not under arrest and that you may leave at any time."

"I understand."

"As you know, I've asked you here today as an information-gathering exercise. I'm talking to everyone who had connections to the teens who recently died. Your press conference this morning seems a good place to start. Your passion for protecting children from the dangers of social media and technology is very evident."

Jennifer bowed her head slightly, acknowledging the compliment. "I'm glad that came across. I've unfortunately witnessed firsthand the devastating effect keyboard warriors can have on vulnerable teens."

"Your son, Derek?"

Jennifer crossed her arms over her stomach. His loss still hurt her deeply.

Indie needed to get her back into the overconfidence that had her spreading her resources all over the table—because that was where she'd likely trip up. "After his passing, was that when you first got involved with this fight?"

As Jennifer gave Indie a rerun of the speech she'd delivered at her home, her arms uncrossed, and her hands relaxed onto the table.

Indie watched her, listening closely for any signs of guilt or defensiveness. When Jennifer fell silent, Indie wasn't sure what she'd seen cloaked within her rage. The recording would help her untangle it.

"I'm going to give you some dates, and I'd like to know your whereabouts for each of them."

"These would be the days the kids died?" Jennifer's face remained impassive, but she reached for the hand sanitizer and applied another liberal dose. "Why do you need to know that?"

The sharp smell of the alcohol in the gel made Indie's eyes water. Poor Broc's nose must've been going wild. "I'm trying to build a picture, and in order to do that, I'm asking everyone these questions."

"Don't I need a lawyer if you're asking about alibis?"

"It's your right to retain one, but I'd reiterate I'm asking everyone these questions." Indie studied the woman opposite her. Her body language had become more controlled and tighter.

Jennifer snapped the lid shut and placed the sanitizer back into the middle of the table. "I have nothing to hide. Ask away. When do you want to know about?"

"The first date is last Sunday, August eleventh, at around eleven in the evening."

"I was at home with Dylan. He was in bed, as obviously he had school the next morning. He has a curfew on school nights."

"Can anyone verify that?"

Jennifer shook her head. "My husband, Dominic, was in New York. We spoke on the phone, but that was earlier in the evening. At around eleven, I was probably preparing to go to bed myself."

Indie looked at Broc, but his face didn't show any sign that Jennifer was being deceitful.

"Thank you for that. The next is Wednesday, August fourteenth, at around five in the morning."

"I was where every right-minded person would be, in bed, asleep. My phone's GPS will prove it."

Indie ignored what could be perceived as a slight, given that she and Hen had been up and about then. "Can anyone corroborate that?"

"Dominic was in bed beside me, but we were both asleep."

"How about yesterday, Friday, August fifteenth, at around nine in the evening?"

Jennifer's gaze flicked up to her left, and she nodded as she recalled the answer. "Yesterday, I was writing a chapter of my new book called *Viral Decay: The Hidden Epidemic Targeting Our Youth*. I was in my home office, hard at work on my laptop for a couple of hours. And before you ask, Dominic and Dylan were also home, watching a PG movie for a little father-and-son time."

"Thank you. And the last time I need to know about is

this morning at around eight." Was it really only this morning that Ava Johnson shot herself? So much had happened since that Indie had to double-check her notes.

"I take a walk every morning at seven, so I was out."

"Did you pass by any places where you might've been seen by others?"

Jennifer thought again, then went to purse her lips but ran a finger over them instead. "It's impossible to say. I mean, I could've been seen by any number of dash cams, camera doorbells, street cameras, but I wouldn't know. I had my phone with me, playing a podcast while I walked. So again, GPS will confirm my statement is true and accurate."

"What was the podcast about?"

Jennifer's face flushed with resentment or anger. Possibly both. "The evils of social media. Look, I can even take you on the route I walked."

"And your family?"

"Dylan's a teenager. He was in bed asleep. Dominic had already left for an early flight to California."

"How do your husband and son feel about your stance on social media?"

"Dominic sells software called SafeGuard Pro, which exists to protect children from online predators. Once you know that, I shouldn't have to spell out that he supports me one-hundred-percent. He wants to protect children. Derek was his son too."

"His loss must be very hard on everyone." Indie could understand the need to blame someone or something for his death. "What does Dylan think about your stance?"

"He's a child. He doesn't get to have a say in what I do."

Indie knew what it was like to be treated like a kid when your world was falling apart. And she knew how fast that kind of silence turned into resentment.

"Do any of his friends' parents share your beliefs?"

Jennifer pressed the lid of the sanitizer. Still closed. "As I believe I told you the first time we met, I'm a lone voice in the digital wilderness. I'm afraid my words will have to get much more shocking to make people listen."

"More shocking than your comment that you were glad the teens had died so there was less competition for Dylan?"

"I thought you understood that those words were taken out of context. I don't like to repeat myself, but it seems I'm fated to do so. It's a hard truth that actions speak louder than words."

Indie tensed. She held her body still so she didn't betray how significant what Jennifer had just said could be.

Broc also became more alert at her heightened state. His ears pricked up higher, and he watched Jennifer as if he expected her to magic a ball out of the air.

"What kind of actions do you think need to happen to ensure children's safety?"

"Whatever it takes. Our laws are hopelessly outdated, and as the pace of technology speeds up, our lawmakers will need to become more agile just to keep up. Our judiciary system needs to become more robust, and we need to keep accountability at the forefront of everything."

No wonder Jennifer had been so comfortable in front of the cameras. She sounded like a politician.

She straightened her purse along the edge of the table and reached up to her hair. But she hesitated before touching the perfectly aligned strands. "The context in which I said those words *you keep bringing up* was that while these deaths are tragic, what if they spotlight what needs to be done?" She tapped the table with her palms. "I'm on this planet to protect children, not harm them. Even the evilest of all the little shits. Because I know the pain of losing a child."

Her gaze dropped to her hands, and she snatched up the hand sanitizer, squeezing yet more onto her poor skin.

"I understand. Did you know any of the deceased teens?"

"I help out on various school committees. I see a lot of the students, but I wouldn't say that means I *know* them."

Indie knew not to sigh out her frustration, but Jennifer wasn't so guarded, huffing as though Indie were an annoying child shredding her last nerve.

"One final question." Indie gave her the out she was looking for. "Did you ever have any confrontations with any of them?"

"Of course not." She pinched her lips together.

That was all Indie was going to get today. "Thank you for your candor, Jennifer, and for coming in. If you think of anything that might help, please call me." She pushed a business card across the table. "Just in case you misplaced the first one."

Jennifer snatched it up, gathered her things in silence, and left without a farewell.

Indie stared at the closed door after her departure for such a long time that Broc put a paw on her leg.

"Did we do a good job?"

Indie smoothed his fur. "We did, but there's something that's poking at me. I need some paper."

On the way back to her desk, she took a skinny handful of paper out of the printer.

Indie caught Broc's hopeful look. "It's not for you to shred."

Once she'd settled him with a toy, she filled the first sheet with circles containing the keywords of everything Jennifer told her.

Indie's pen drifted to the one at the top right, *software*.

Jennifer Blake's husband sold software to protect children on electronic devices. Arun Chang's mom had said her husband had installed software to protect theirs. There was generally never such a thing as coincidence in an investigation. Indie had more background work to do before the Nagles arrived at five, but Jennifer Blake was still high on her list of suspects.

45

Logan Nagle's parents couldn't have been more different from Jennifer Blake.

Indie showed them into the interview room. "If you'd like to take the seats on this side…" She indicated the two with their backs to the door.

Sherry Nagle tucked herself into the first chair without a word, legs underneath her, hands folded in her lap. Carl Nagle pulled the chair out and away from the table and sat down, legs spread.

"Logan, why don't you take the seat at the end of the table?" Indie gestured to where she'd placed it for him before they arrived. Then she settled herself and Broc so she was at a right angle to Logan, with Broc on her far side.

The young man wasn't as carefree as he'd been at school. He glanced at Broc before dropping onto the chair.

Broc looked from him to Indie. *"No drug smell today, but he needs a bath."*

Indie thought the kid had already taken one in a tub full of body spray or cologne. She hoped it didn't asphyxiate them all before they finished.

She introduced herself and Broc and explained why he was in the room. "It's procedure to record the interview. Is that all right?"

Sherry looked at her husband, and when he nodded, she did the same. Indie aimed a fob at the camera, and the red recording light blinked on.

"I just want to reiterate that while this is a formal interview, you are free to leave at any time. The reason I wanted to speak with you, Logan," Indie turned her attention to him, "is that your name came up in an investigation, and I need to clarify a few details with you. Your parents are here while I talk to you because you're a minor. That being said, it's still necessary for you to tell me the truth. Is there anything you're not clear about?"

"I'm not stupid."

His father shot him a look that Logan challenged with a glare of his own.

Indie had a feeling that happened often.

"What?" He scowled. "I'm not gonna sit here and pretend to be something I'm not."

"There's being stupid and being smart. Right now, I see you being only one of those, and it's not the one you think." Carl delivered his rebuke in slow, measured words.

Indie tried to defuse the tension in the room. "Logan, it's my duty to get one-hundred-percent clarification for the legal side of the interview. Now, I'd like to start by asking about your relationship with Jayleen Levin."

His face crinkled in a combination of confusion and distaste. "Relationship? Nah, we're not together."

"You've been texting her."

He shifted in his seat. "Not against the law."

Indie looked at Broc, but he wasn't showing any warning signs other than what she already knew—that Logan was way out of his comfort zone talking about girls in front of his parents.

"So what? I texted her." He finally filled the silence. "I text a lot of people. She gave me her number. I was just hitting her up."

"Jayleen took an overdose of pills yesterday."

His jaw dropped. "You're shitting me."

"Logan." His mother's rebuke sounded well-worn.

"Sorry, Mom. I mean, why? She was real mad at group, but that's nothing new. I thought she had her shit together." He held a hand out, rebutting his mom's next reminder.

"I know you and Elliott Greene didn't get along. Tell me about your relationship with Ava Johnson." Indie worked down her list of teens.

"Don't know where you're getting your intel from, but again, no relationship."

"Even as friends?"

"Ava didn't have guy friends. She only had fuck buddies." He looked at his mom. "Sorry. That's the only word for it, and I'm not a fuck boy." Logan's reaction seemed real, not just him wanting to come across better in his parents' eyes.

"Tell me about you and Zach Mitchell. You and he didn't get along, either, correct?"

Logan crossed his arms. "Your intel sucks."

Indie mirrored him, keeping her hands relaxed. "In what way?"

"Why don't you ask them?"

"Them?"

"Zach's football buddies. They have a problem with everyone not on their team. Like they're gods and the rest of us are losers." Logan's hands tightened around his arms.

"So you didn't get along with them, but Zach was okay?"

"That ain't it, boss."

"Logan!" Sherry sounded mortified. "Behave yourself. You

heard Detective Reign introduce herself, so have some respect."

Logan rolled his eyes. "Mom, I'm not being disrespectful. It's a saying."

"Well, use sayings we can all understand."

Indie gave Sherry a sympathetic look. Language changed so fast now. Yet another facet of their children's lives that must've sometimes felt impossible to navigate.

She brought the questioning back to Zach Mitchell. "You were telling me about Zach."

"He could be as bad. Everyone's making him out to be a saint just because he's dead."

"Logan, really?" Sherry's rebuke had gone up a few octaves.

"What? It's true. All the jocks, Zach Mitchell included, flex every chance they get, think it's their right to be dicks to people, and are always messing with me. In the halls, after class, wherever. Wait 'til they find themselves working for me and other nerds ten years down the road. I'll be laughing all the way to the fucking bank."

Sherry just shook her head that time. She'd all but given up.

"What did you do to the bullies?" Indie lowered her arms slowly.

"Messed with their socials." Logan copied her this time. "Stuff like that."

"What other stuff?"

When he didn't immediately respond, Indie waited for his clarification while his parents fidgeted in their seats with increasing discomfort.

"It's not like them tanking in class means anything. Coach just bulldozes over everything that interferes with practice or a game."

So he'd changed their grades. He was lucky that wasn't her concern today.

Indie glanced at Broc, but his face still wasn't showing anything she needed to act on. Nor did he react when she asked where Logan was at the times of the teens' deaths.

"Wednesday morning, when Elliott blew himself up, I was asleep. I don't do early mornings."

"I can confirm that." Sherry looked at her son with affection. "He's a nightmare to wake up."

"And the other times, in the evenings?"

"Online." His parents both looked at him as if he'd said he'd been robbing a bank. "Not building an app. Jeez."

That gave Indie the perfect entry to her next question. "Tell me about that, Logan. The app that put you on probation."

"What's to tell? It kind of got away from me."

"Explain it like I'm five. I'm not very good at tech." Indie gave him the same excuse she'd given Tom Mitcham, and like him, Logan jumped at the chance to school her.

"The app was a joke. How was I to know it would go viral? Even I didn't think I was that fire, but you live and learn."

Carl shook his head all through Logan speaking, while his mom pulled herself tighter into herself.

Logan leaned forward, and his words tumbled out. "The app allowed users to send fake emergency alerts to other people's phones. Harmless things like fake weather warnings or jokes about local events. It was dope, indistinguishable from real government notifications. But I didn't account for the boneheads."

"The boneheads?"

"Yeah, the morons who sent more alarming messages. One of them sent out the fake school lockdown alert that got everyone in a panic. They should be on probation, not me."

"And since then?"

"Got my head down, staying out of trouble." He sat back in his chair, put one ankle on the other knee.

Carl nodded. "I can confirm that. He's been home all the time apart from going to class."

Indie scanned her page of notes. "Tell me why you used the word 'ascend' when we talked at school."

"It's just a word. What's the deal?"

Indie mirrored his body language again, leaning back in her chair as she organized her thoughts in the most logical way. "It's the name of an app that urges kids to ascend and leap into their futures."

Carl's face had creased into deep worry lines. "Logan hasn't broken his probation by doing something as stupid as another app."

"Do you give Logan an allowance?"

Indie asked Carl the question, but Sherry answered for him. "He gets a small one, but he's good at finding sales for his computer parts and such."

She glanced at his feet. "And your sneakers?"

Again, Sherry jumped in. "His friend at school did them for an art project. They're good, aren't they?"

"Your friend's really gifted. You'd pay nearly four figures for similar sneakers online." Indie looked at Logan. "Why're you lying to your parents about your money? We looked at your financials, but your bank account seems legit. Do you have income in crypto? Is that why we can't find it?"

"Logan?" His mom looked ready to cry.

"Now's the time to be honest with me, Logan." Indie pulled his attention away from the tabletop. "If you lie on this next question, there will be terrible consequences for you. Did you build the Ascension app?"

"No. Straight up, I've got nothing to do with the back end."

"What about the front end?"

He looked at her like she was nuts. "Not that either."

"Where did the money come from?"

Logan traced one of the symbols on the sneaker resting on his knee. "I wasn't quite honest what I said last time. One of the companies I hacked did pay me to plug their security gaps. It's legit, and yeah," he half shrugged as he looked up at Indie, "it's in crypto."

While Indie let his parents vent their disappointment—their "What were you thinking?" and "Why would you lie to us?" recriminations—she ran through what he'd just said. And her heart rate picked up.

"Logan, you said you had nothing to do with the back end of Ascension. But do you have the app?"

"Why're you so hung up on this app thing?" Carl interrupted her. "He said he had nothing to do with it."

"Because 'ascension' is one of the last words those kids ever spoke or wrote. Zach Mitchell, Nila Radler, Elliott Greene, Ava Johnson, and Jayleen Levin."

"What?" Logan pulled his phone out of his jeans and pressed the power button.

"Stop!" Indie reached out toward him. "You have the app, don't you?"

He nodded, shooting his parents a guilty look.

"Don't turn your phone on. I've seen it disappear right in front of me."

"It's listening or watching?" Sherry looked from her son to Indie.

"Could be," Logan confirmed.

"Even when it's powered off?"

At Logan's nod, Indie held her hand out. "Can I put it in a safe place so it can do neither? You'll get it back."

"Don't we need to sign something, like a receipt?" Carl half stood. "I'm still paying for it."

"Chill, Dad." Logan handed Indie his phone.

She considered running to tech for a Faraday cage, but didn't want to risk making the Nagles wait too long. Instead, she took it to her desk and locked it in a drawer, her head a whirl of questions. This could be a real lead.

"Okay, Logan," she started before she'd taken her seat again. "Tell me about the challenges you were invited to complete using Ascension."

He put his interlaced hands on the table. "First was to spend a night sneaking around the school campus without being caught."

"Why in the world would you do that?" his father blurted.

Logan lifted one shoulder. "No cap. It was a test of stealth and courage. I had to find hidden clues to start with, but then the Guide told me to avoid security cameras and hide from the night janitors. I thought it was lame 'til then, but then it was bussin'. Nearly getting caught pushed me to carry on."

"You were nearly caught?" Sherry's voice was high and squeaky again.

"No one saw me." Logan's casual assertion didn't do anything to reassure her.

Indie wanted to get as much information as she could without having Logan sidelined by explaining himself to his parents' shock. She also didn't want him to clam up, so she went straight to the most important question. "Who's the Guide?"

"The dude who's in charge, I guess. He issues all the challenges. It all happens on his timeline."

The mastermind felt closer than before…and further from her reach than ever. "Did you ever see his name or any identifying clues?"

"Don't think so, but I haven't paid that much attention."

"Tell me about your next challenge."

"Second one, I had to blindfold myself to get through a

crowded area. The Guide said it would improve my instincts and force me to rely on other senses. At first, I ignored it, but after a few days, I got a message, like the Guide really got me. So I did it."

"How did it make you feel?" Indie kept her tone even and light. No censure here.

"Truth, I was low-key rattled to start with. The Guide was upping the challenge even during the challenge. But that was exciting, like a game IRL. Then," he licked his lips, drilled the table with his gaze, "the app told me to hack into a local government database."

"While you're on probation?" Sherry and Carl shouted the same words as though they'd rehearsed them.

"Let Logan tell us." Indie tried to soothe them, but she didn't need the look on Broc's face to tell her she wasn't succeeding. "Right at this moment, Mr. and Mrs. Nagle, I'm more concerned with this app and any vulnerable child about to take their final leap than about what Logan may or may not have done."

Logan nodded and took a couple of seconds to find his voice again. "It's no big deal. All I had to do was retrieve some nonsensitive info as proof of my hacking skills. It felt great to start with. I'd missed the thrill of it. But," he finally looked at his parents, "I realized how dangerous it was, so I shut the hack down."

"But not the app?" Indie held herself rigid against his answer.

He shook his head. "Not the app."

Her shoulders dropped. "Did you have any other challenges after that?"

"Two more. The next one, I almost got rid of it. I had to climb to the top of something high and sit on the edge for thirty minutes."

"And you did that?" his dad asked. "What the hell did you climb?"

"I know it was stupid, and I was terrified, but the Guide told me it was a way to overcome fear. I only climbed up to the high school roof. The building's all brick. It was easy to scale. I knew if I didn't do it, I wouldn't reach the ascension stage."

"You scaled the outside of the...but what if you fell?" His mother's voice was hushed. "What if you were seen? You'd have been arrested again."

"It's okay, Mom. It was all good. I knew I wasn't gonna crash out. But the next one was easy. All I had to do was delete all my socials and stuff."

"And the tech forums like Starscrew?" Indie knew he was going to nod before he did.

"The Guide said cutting ties to my former self was the only way to ascend to a new level of awareness."

"When you completed that, did you get any more information about ascending?"

"The Guide's been talking about a final leap, but I haven't been challenged to do it yet."

"I can't believe this." Carl was shaking his head as though he could jog the words right out of his brain and that would make them untrue.

"What were you thinking?" Sherry's voice was high enough to make Broc wince. "You could've been hurt. You could've ended up like the others." She pressed her hand over her mouth as she realized what she'd said.

Indie shared their anger and shock, but her gaze was on the closed interview room door.

On the other side was her desk, with Logan's phone in a drawer. Their best shot at the break they needed to catch the person tormenting and murdering the kids of Sherwood County.

46

"I just need to step out for a moment. Will you be all right waiting in here?" Indie looked from Logan Nagle to his mom and dad. They all nodded. "I appreciate that."

Indie tapped her leg for Broc to follow.

Please still be here.

She sent the silent prayer to the sheriff as she raced to his office, with Broc on her heels.

"Eli," she called as she shot past him, "you need to hear this."

When Indie barged into his office, the sheriff was standing behind his desk, staring at his computer monitor. He put a hand on his chest. "Hold the reins there, Reign. That was some entrance. I'm just leaving."

"You need to hear this. I've just been talking with Logan Nagle. I think we have a way to break this case."

She'd gotten as far as Logan's involvement with the Ascension app and the shocking revelation that the entire operation was bigger than she'd thought when Hen rushed in.

"I've just come from the hospital. Jayleen woke up enough

that I could question her, and she told me this Guide gave her the challenge to take her grandmother's heart medication."

"This is bigger than us." The sheriff picked up his phone and dialed.

Indie heard the efficient voice on the other end before he put the handset to his ear.

"Federal Bureau of Investigation. How may I direct your call?"

"We have a situation here in Sherwood County that requires FBI expertise. Cybercrime is probably a good place to start."

Indie mentally checked off the list of things Sheriff Sammy ran through as he detailed what they had and what was happening. He didn't miss anything when he told the man on the other end that he was giving the green light for them to step in.

So he *had* been listening each time she'd told him something. And more than that, he'd taken it all on board. She'd do well not to underestimate him in the future.

"There's the very real possibility that more lives are at risk. How soon can you get here?" He nodded at the response. "I'll see you then." After hanging up, he looked at Indie and Hen. "Good work, but you're in over your heads. We all are. You'd best stick around to liaise with the Feds over what's happened so far."

Indie nodded. "Whatever they need. I'll let the Nagles go."

When she returned to the interview room, the family looked at her expectantly. "Thank you for your patience. The sheriff's called the FBI in to assist us. We'll need to keep your phone for a while, Logan, for their tech experts to examine." She handed him the form she'd brought in with her. "If you could put your passcode on there, and Mr. Nagle, if you could sign it, as the phone's on your account. I'll let you know when it's been cleared for you to pick up."

Once the form was completed, she let them go.

"But please, don't speak to anyone about any of this. It could jeopardize other lives."

"Of course not." Sherry answered gravely as if it was the last thing she'd ever do.

"We'll be keeping Logan on a tight leash, hog-tying him to his bed, if that's what it takes," Carl reassured her.

Logan took his time following his parents out. He stopped in front of Indie. "You know, for over a year now, I've wanted to make up for what I did. It's part of the reason I got suckered over that Ascension app." He seemed altogether different from the couldn't-care-less ego he'd been projecting. "Guess I was trying to be a better me, like it said I could be. But maybe this, helping you stop it…this is what I can do to be better."

Indie's eyes filled as he held her gaze.

He shuffled awkwardly. "You know, if you need my help…"

She nodded back, blinking hard. "I respect that, Logan. You've got it in you to change your narrative and right your wrongs. I can see that."

He gave her a crooked smile. "There is one thing, though. Can I go to visit Jayleen in the hospital?" He looked from Indie to his parents.

Carl checked in with his wife, and some nonverbal communication passed between them. "We'll take him."

Sherry glanced at Indie. "If that's okay with you."

"I'm sure Jayleen would enjoy seeing you." Indie lifted a finger. "But remember, not a word about any of this, especially to her. She's going to be fragile for a while."

Logan made a zipping motion across his lips with one hand. "You got it."

"We'll show ourselves out." Sherry laid a hand on Indie's arm. "Thank you."

"Anytime."

"And you too, Officer Broc." Sherry patted him on the head, and he gave her his silly grin. She smiled, and the family left.

Indie knew they were close to unraveling the mystery and, with the FBI's help, there was nowhere the Guide could hide that they wouldn't find them.

"You're on borrowed time," she promised the mastermind. "We're coming."

47

After only twenty-four hours of working with the FBI, Indie's overriding impression was that they made things move fast. The Feds had gotten them all ready with cutting-edge tech support for the evening's operation in record time. The other thing she'd learned, as if there'd been any doubt, was that Broc was much better than her at climbing trees, especially in the dark.

And he wasn't going to let her forget it. *"You okay there?"*

She would've been a lot better if the treehouse they were perched in still had a complete floor. But their vantage point gave them a full view of the back of Jennifer Blake's house. "I'm good. You mind you."

Indie raised her binoculars and zoomed in on Jennifer Blake. The woman hadn't moved from where Indie had first seen her, sitting at the island in the middle of the kitchen, one hand on the pages of a glossy magazine that apparently had her whole attention. The resolution was so good, Indie could see a drip of red wine rolling down the glass—puddling on the white marble countertop—and the striations in the pale-pink lipstick mark on the rim.

Still no electronic devices on show. Not even a phone.

She looked so normal. She was someone's mom. Could she really be the mastermind who had orchestrated the deaths of thirty-one teenagers? At the briefing before the stakeout, Special Agent Michael Danner had shocked them all with that number.

"I have to stress these are our preliminary findings. We'll be taking a deep dive into each case, but these deaths fit the pattern of what's been happening here in Sherwood County. If they're all connected, this makes for a prolific and dangerous killer."

A prolific and dangerous killer. Indie repeated Danner's words to herself as she watched Jennifer Blake in her kitchen, as she knew Hen was watching Tom Mitcham across town.

How could either one of them do this when they both knew the pain of losing a child? Though Tom Mitcham's son was alive and well and living with his mom in another state, his ex-wife's reaction to the FBI's phone call for information about Tom left them all with no doubt that he would never be seeing his son again.

Indie and Broc had thought he was shifty. The more she'd looked into him, the more she'd discovered he'd behaved borderline illegally when he thought he was being judged for being such a poor parent. Which could feed his motive.

"Satellite Three." Hen's voice came through Indie's earpiece. "Target has been joined at the restaurant by an unidentified female. Still no use of a phone."

Indie tapped the binoculars with her index fingers. That didn't mean Tom Mitcham wasn't the Guide. It just meant he wasn't online at that moment. Another check, and neither was Jennifer Blake.

"Satellite Two." Indie gave her update. "Still no use of any electronic devices by target."

"Satellite One is going live." Someone should tell Sheriff Sammy he didn't need to shout to be heard through the comms. "Okay, son, you can log in on the app."

"Okay." Logan's voice came through clearly, even though he wasn't hooked up to the surveillance team.

"Satellites Two and Three, you have visual of these messages?" Eli's question was a good one.

"Satellite Three. Clear visual," Hen confirmed immediately. She was playing a lone diner scrolling her phone at the restaurant where Tom Mitcham was on his date.

Indie should be safe to look too. The glare of the kitchen ceiling lights blazing down on Jennifer would turn her French doors to mirrors. If she did look out, she wasn't likely to search high in the trees, but still, Indie turned the brightness down on her phone.

"Satellite Two. Good visual of the messages." Indie lined her phone up with the edge of the board, pushing it closer to the next one.

She stretched her legs out in front of her, arching her back. The floorboards creaked, making her grab the edge of the platform. The neighbor had assured her the treehouse was probably sound. A loud creak reminded her that "probably" could go either way.

It helped that Broc jumped onto the closest horizontal bough to her position. *"Better?"*

Better? Just as she was thinking about that, movement on her phone grabbed her attention. A message on Logan's mirrored screen popped up.

Hey, WhiteHat. Nice to see you back.

RisingStar77's words were echoed by a whole stream of welcome-back messages. The users on the app sure were active.

"This is Mothership. They're looking like bots to me." A

man's voice Indie didn't recognize came through her earpiece. He must have been the tech analyst leading the effort to pinpoint the Guide. "Pretty sophisticated, though. The syntax is spot-on. Satellite One, respond how you normally would."

Logan—aka Satellite One, aka WhiteHat—did as instructed and answered each message in turn. The back-and-forth felt warm and friendly. No wonder the teens got sucked into this make-believe nightmare.

When a new user joined the chat, their username jabbed at Indie's insides. The Guide.

WhiteHat, I've been waiting to give you your final challenge. Are you ready?

Indie trained the binocs on the French doors. Jennifer sipped her wine and turned a page of her magazine with her free hand. The messages could be part of an automated sequence, but she seemed very calm for someone about to give a teenager instructions on how to kill themselves.

Logan responded, *I was born ready*.

Furious typing filled Indie's ear. "Mothership, we're trying to track the Guide's IP address. We need you, Satellite One, to keep them engaged long enough for us to lock onto the source."

"Understood." Sheriff Sammy's voice came over the earpiece. "You got that, son?"

"Yeah." Logan's confidence made Indie proud. He really was trying.

She looked back at Jennifer. The stool Jennifer had been sitting on was empty. When Indie scanned the house, she wasn't in the kitchen breakfast nook or the living room. The next window over was in complete darkness, not even the localized light from a laptop or phone screen showing.

"Where are you?" Indie swung the binoculars from room to room across the back of the house.

Jennifer was walking into the kitchen with a full bottle of wine in her hand. She retrieved a kitchen towel to mop up the spill from her last glass and poured herself a new one.

"Satellite Two. Confirm target is accounted for, no device in sight. Still drinking wine with a magazine."

"Satellite Three. Confirm target is still at dinner. He and mystery female are just starting their main meals. Still no interaction with any device." Hen's confirmation added to Indie's doubts.

Were they wrong about the suspects?

Logan's mirrored phone screen showed a whole page of messages between him and the Guide.

Indie scanned them to catch up. He was doing a great job. And the Guide was reeling him in and getting him to agree with their twisted agenda effectively. Logan's responses were so convincing, if he wasn't under the supervision of the sheriff and Eli and half a dozen FBI techs, Indie would've rushed to his location to make sure he wasn't going to do what he said he was.

I knew you would understand, Logan, that it is most fitting that your ascension takes a radical line against our digital world. You're the only one with the necessary skills to do that.

Indie froze. She reread the last message. Her body was ahead of her mind, which scrambled to play catch-up. Broc matched her sudden tension, watching her closely.

Something in the words. Indie seemed to have heard everyone ranting about the evils of the digital world lately. But, no, that wasn't what had her hackles up, had her scarcely breathing. She scrolled up, and her eyes widened. It seemed so innocuous, and buried in the middle of everything else, it would've been easy to overlook.

"There's nothing we can't deal with."

The tech had summed it up. The syntax. The syntax was

everything, because the average person would say, "We can deal with anything." But "there's nothing we can't deal with?"

Indie had heard someone say that double negative recently.

She looked at the back of the Blake house. She and Hen were wasting precious time watching Jennifer Blake and Tom Mitcham.

Because Indie knew the identity of the Guide.

48

The keys of my laptop clicked quietly, almost reverently, in the silence of my office as I typed. This evening, I would add at least one more Pathfinder to my Pantheon. Things could only go better if Hex Spectre would answer my last message. Giving me a backdoor to reinstall the app once I'd deleted it from a device couldn't be so hard.

While I waited for the two Ascension users I was actively engaging to respond, I realized I felt lighter than I had in a while. And for that, I had Jennifer Blake to thank.

Reactive, emotional, and as ineffective as her methods might be, she was a very convenient megaphone. She'd looked so sure of herself in her press conference, but hot air and bluster was the wrong way to drive lasting change. And the detective at the hospital knew that, given how unimpressed she'd been with Blake's performance.

I focused back at my screens. Logan had responded to my last message. Emma, my other target tonight, hadn't. I typed a reply to WhiteHat.

I've been saving a special challenge for someone intelligent and fast thinking. Is that you, Logan?

Very soon now, the time would be right for me to make my own ascent. My rise to Congress would surprise no one once these teen deaths tipped over into national and international news. And I was certain that would happen soon, thanks to Detective Reign. I could almost hear her saying the encouraging words to the public. *"Listen to Dr. Strickland. She's an expert in this field."*

I was becoming more used to the idea of sitting behind the Resolute Desk in the Oval Office. In fact, it felt like a perfect symmetry of all that had happened before in my life. Even when my laws had come into force, I would still owe it to the lost generation of children out there to continue the fight. And from a political platform, it would be easy to lobby for additional laws to protect them.

I would have to retire Ascension, but by then, it would have more than served its purpose. And it would always be there if I ever needed to resurrect it.

My gaze drifted to the photo of my son beside me. "If only you could be here to see it, Miles."

I set my shoulders and pressed my lips together. Understanding now that he was lonely and lost when he took his own life didn't make his choice to leave me easier to endure.

"I wish you were here to see me fighting for the kids who're hurting as you were."

Though it had been just a little under four years since I'd lost him, the prevalence and influence of social media had intensified so much, he'd barely have recognized today's online landscape. And that pace was only accelerating.

I needed the hammer of a high position to bring tech companies to heel, because new laws might not be enough. They needed to be hit where it hurt the most—their bottom line.

A ping brought my attention back to the app. Logan had responded. Excellent.

Tell me what I have to do.

Finally.

No response yet from Emma. But I'd talk her through her final leap tonight too. I had all the time they needed.

This, Logan, is your challenge to take your final leap and ascend with your friends.

I hit the command to fire the bots, and they populated his screen with *I'm so excited for you to join us* message variations.

The knock at the interior door of my office jolted me. It was eight in the evening, and with group sessions concluded, the center had long been locked up. I flicked to the view of the security cameras, scrolling to the one showing the hall. Rolling my shoulders, I quieted my breathing. Nothing to worry about.

I looked back at the screen. This was such a pivotal moment. But it would perhaps make Logan braver if I kept him waiting for his instructions. The knock came again, more insistent this time.

Muting and closing my laptop, I opened the door.

The girl on the other side threw herself into my arms, tears pouring down her face. "Dr. Josie."

Emma, my other target, had come to me.

"What's the matter? How did you get in?"

"I hid in the bathroom when everyone went home." Emma's slight body shuddered against mine as she broke into a fresh round of sobbing.

Smoothing her hair, I closed the door behind us. "Come on in and tell me what's happened. Remember, there's nothing we can't deal with."

49

SWAT team vehicles pulled up behind Indie's Explorer, staying beyond the range of the cameras mounted on the exterior of the Evergreen Counseling and Wellness Center. Indie read one last paragraph about Dr. Josephine Strickland, then shoved her phone into her pants pocket and pressed the flap closed.

She slipped Broc's safety goggles over his ears and lined them up so they sat right on his face.

"I look scary?"

"You sure do." She checked his Kevlar harness. "I know that's heavy, but does it feel okay?"

He nodded.

"We don't know what we're going to find in there. She might not resist, or she might put up a fight."

Dr. Strickland had appeared graceful, empathetic, and sensitive to Indie, which made it hard to imagine that she'd brawl and physically fight her way out of this situation. But meeting a person on a regular day was a lot different than cornering them with the threat of deadly force and imprisonment. And the doctor was mentally ill, possibly psychotic, so there was that too.

Broc's bulletproof vest was as much for Indie's peace of mind as for his protection. She tightened one of the straps on her own vest before tapping her leg and joining the SWAT team assembling and checking gear.

"Reign." The tactical team leader didn't waste time with greetings or intros. "Who's the K-9?"

"Broc."

"Roger that. Broc and Reign on the team."

Nods all around, and the team leader signaled for them to move as per their plan.

Streetlights picked up the reflective K-9 patches on Broc's harness as they double-timed it across the parking lot toward the rear entrance. They moved past the only vehicle in the lot, registered to Dr. Strickland.

The team formed behind the breacher, who stooped on one knee and, gloves off, inserted picks into the lock. He unlocked it as fast as if he'd had a key. With well-practiced fluidity, he stepped back into formation as he put the picks away and his gloves back on.

Inside the building, their plan was the same—stealth for surprise. Heavy boots made hardly any sound as the people wearing them lined up on either side of Strickland's office door. The breacher repeated what he'd done outside, but this time, when he stepped back into formation, the team leader crashed the door open, and the space erupted in shouts of, "Police! Put your hands where we can see them," as the team piled into the room.

Drawing her weapon and holding it at low ready, Indie commanded Broc, *"Zugriff." Seize.*

He rushed ahead but slid to a stop a second later. Inside the door, Indie immediately understood why he hadn't already seized their target.

Standing behind her desk, Dr. Strickland held the shoulder of a girl in front of her as a human shield. The gun she pressed to the teen's temple made the girl shake so hard, her teeth rattled, and her fast breathing shuddered in and out in sobs and gulps.

Indie's gaze whipped to Broc, who'd dropped in a half crouch, sizing up the situation, calculating points of entrance and risks to rewards. He slowly stood upright, and she huffed out her relief that he'd understood that even with his speed and agility, he couldn't get at their target faster than the doctor could shoot the girl.

"Good boy." Her words were softer than a whisper.

He didn't break eye contact with the doctor. *"Waiting."*

"Put the weapon down." The tactical team leader spoke with authority.

Indie could tell from the close lines of sight in the room that none of his team could take a shot without hitting the girl. She stepped forward so the doctor could see her. "Hello, Dr. Josie."

The doctor stood as still as Broc as she assessed the situation, but nothing else in her behavior suggested she was as intimidated as she should've been by all the people with guns aimed at her. Her grip on her own gun was steady, the muzzle solid against her hostage's head.

"Detective." Even her voice was steady and firm, as though she were the one in charge. "What did I do wrong? How did you know?"

Indie swallowed so her words would also come out cool and confident. She was the only person in the room who'd met the doctor. If this was to be a successful outcome, Indie was responsible. Even if she was terrified she might say the wrong thing, they couldn't stay locked in this awful checkmate.

"We found out about the Ascension app. I recognized your phraseology."

"My phraseology?" Dr. Strickland laughed at the words. "That's unexpected. I should've given you more credit."

Indie wished she'd been wrong. Somehow, it felt worse, more obscene, that the Guide who'd been steering teens to their deaths from behind the anonymity of a screen had offered them tissues and hugs and calming, healing words to their faces.

The photo frame on Dr. Strickland's desk was facing away from Indie, but having read up on the woman's history, she knew there was only one person she'd ever truly cared about.

"Miles was an impressive young man. You must miss him very much."

Dr. Strickland mouth twitched. "What would you know about that?"

Keeping her aim steady, Indie let the pain of her family's loss show on her face for a few moments. "I know more than I wish I did about loss. I lost my family to violence. If there were a way to make my family's deaths make sense, mean something, I'd want to take it too."

"You don't understand."

"What don't I understand? I really want to. Tell me."

The doctor shook her head vigorously.

Indie tried a different tack. "I saw you talk to Ava. You have real empathy and sensitivity. I can see that's because you've dedicated your whole life to helping children. And there are other ways to make a difference, to protect them. That's what you're trying to do, correct?"

She seemed shocked that Indie understood so well. "No one else will step up and do what's necessary. The world isn't listening."

"Tell us what we need to listen to. Tell us about your noble mission."

"Jennifer Blake's not wrong. We have to stop the social media machine. It's used up too many kids already."

"Like Miles."

Tears gleamed in her eyes. "Like Miles."

"I know…we know…that you're trying to make things better." Indie spoke slowly and clearly, urging the SWAT members with fingers beside their triggers to give her the time to try to talk the woman down. "We know this comes from your sense of duty. It's brave to be willing to take on tech giants and make this stand."

Dr. Strickland's face twisted briefly with grief, but she shook it off and pulled the girl tighter against her chest.

Broc tensed beside Indie, and she desperately wished he could read her mind as easily as she read his. She offered a hand signal instead. *Wait.*

There were far too many guns trained on where he was about to leap. His sudden movement could set off a cascade of gunfire. And he'd be right in the path of the bullets.

Broc's weight shifted very slightly to his back legs. *"I know when."*

She knew he did. Even though she wanted to send him out, away from the danger, this was what they trained for. He'd save the child. Indie couldn't think past that. They were professionals, and they'd do their jobs, both of them.

"We understand what you're trying to achieve." Indie swallowed her disgust and anger at what the woman had done and tried to sound encouraging and understanding. "Your mission…it matters. It's bold. But if you pull that trigger…" She took a careful step forward. "You're smart enough to know what happens next. You die. Maybe by our hand, maybe by your own. Either way, your voice is gone.

Your message will forever be buried under headlines about murder and madness."

Josie's finger twitched, and her chin trembled, but she said nothing.

Indie pressed on.

"But if she lives…" She nodded to the girl. "If you live, there's a trial. Media coverage. Hundreds of interviews. Books. Your story. Your reasons. Your *truth*…heard by thousands. Maybe more. The world would still listen." She took another small step forward, and Broc moved with her. "Isn't that what you wanted from the start? To be heard?"

Indie didn't need the silence in her earpiece to tell her the team still had no clear shot. Or the silence from the doctor to know she wasn't completely getting through to her.

"Dr. Josie, I know you're not a heartless murderer." She pulled on every sentence from her training not to scream the truth at the woman. She poured out the lies, tried to keep her tone warm and reassuring, tried to hold an *I understand* expression on her face.

"If she lowers her weapon, lethal force authorized." The SWAT leader's voice in her ear nearly made Indie jump, but she managed to stay still.

"You didn't come this far to be remembered as just another tragedy. Or worse, a killer who used a child as a shield. That's not your story. That's not Miles's story." Indie took a breath, slow and steady. "You care about these kids. That's the part people will remember…*if* you let them."

A single tear slid down Dr. Strickland's cheek, but the gun didn't lower. "Miles will be remembered by the laws bearing his name to make it criminal for children to use social media. The laws I'll get enacted."

That was it. The mission. In her mind, this wasn't madness. It was martyrdom. A twisted reign, born of grief, cloaked in righteousness, and paid for in blood.

Villains always think they're the hero.

"I want that for him, too, and for you. If you cooperate with us here, now, we can make that happen. You can be remembered for your intelligence and efforts to make the world listen. That can be your legacy. All you have to do is put the gun down."

The teenage girl drew in a huge, shuddering breath, her plea barely more than a squeak. "Please let me go, Dr. Josie. I haven't done anything wrong."

"Put the gun down."

Finally, the deranged doctor seemed to understand Indie's repeated request. Her shoulders slumped, and her expression softened. Indie was getting through to her.

"Give it to me." She took another step, Broc by her side. "Live to tell the world your story."

Voices through Indie's earpiece told her that SWAT was gearing up for a shot as soon as the doctor moved her finger from the trigger.

To Indie's enormous relief, Dr. Strickland did just that. She lifted her finger and rested her manicured nail on the trigger guard, but only for a heartbeat. As if the tiny act had stirred a sea of rage, her expression twisted, and empathy drowned in a surge of cold, calculated resolve. Her jaw clenched. The finger began to move again.

"Dr. Josie, no!" But even as Indie shouted the words, she knew it was too late.

The psychologist turned the gun, clearing the girl with a sweep and tracking it toward Indie like a guided missile. She ducked her head behind the sobbing teenager.

As Indie looked for a clear shot, Broc's dark form filled her line of sight, his black harness gleaming as he leaped over the desk and twisted in midair. His teeth flashed white, and light caught the curve of his safety goggles just before he clamped down hard on his target.

Dr. Strickland let out a wild, savage scream.

Broc's weight and his steel-trap grip yanked her arm sideways, sending the gun arcing away from Indie and the young hostage. The teen dove for cover.

A single shot cracked through the room

Dr. Strickland's chest exploded, and she collapsed like her strings had been cut, taking Broc with her.

No, no, no!

Indie shot forward, scrambling around the big wooden desk, her heart pounding louder and more urgently than the shot.

Broc had her. His jaws were still locked around the doctor's right arm. A growing red in her center mass bloomed through her rose-pink blouse.

He growled. *"Stay down."*

Indie grabbed the corner of the desk to stay upright. He was okay. *"Aus."* Let go.

Broc did and turned with a grin. *"Got her."*

Indie nodded, sinking her fingers into his fur. "Good waiting. Good job."

From where she'd crouched behind the desk, the teenager peered up at Indie from beneath a mass of hair.

"Are you all right?" Indie asked, though of course she wasn't.

The poor girl was wide-eyed, shaking and sobbing. "Dr. Josie, Dr. Josie."

She'd probably need a sane therapist for years to come to get over this.

"Paramedics are on scene." The team leader held his weapon trained on their killer, even though there was no getting up from that fatal wound. "Too late for this one, though."

50

On Monday afternoon, Indie closed a form on her screen. She'd lost count of how many she'd completed that morning and didn't dare add up how many she still had to get through. The morning after the resolution of a case meant lots to close out, lessons to be learned, information to be collated and added to the collective law enforcement knowledge pool.

She still found it shocking that Dr. Strickland had been able to control and coerce thirty-one teenagers to their deaths. Though it was early in this larger investigation, already the FBI had found evidence tying the deaths together —coincidences that weren't coincidences and a pattern of damning behavior.

A squeak made her glance at Broc lying beside her, happily chewing on his new rubber chicken. She resisted the urge to crouch and check him out again just in case an injury had snuck up while she wasn't paying attention. His leap over the desk had been the talk of the SWAT team as they'd parted company. And, of course, he'd lapped up the accolades.

He waggled an eyebrow at her while chewing the tip of the chicken's wing with his back teeth.

"Hey, Reign." Special Agent Michael Danner strode over to her desk.

Indie hopped to her feet, not just because of etiquette, but to save her neck from strain. The man was seriously tall.

Danner beckoned the sheriff and Eli, who were just coming into the bullpen. "Just wanted to say to you all, job well done."

"Sure was." The sheriff hooked his thumbs in his belt and smiled broadly.

"First rate work, Reign. Not just how you handled things in the perpetrator's office. And things were real tense in there for a while." He glanced at the sheriff, then back at Indie. "But you managed to find the thread that unraveled the whole case."

Eli cut Indie off before she could answer. "She'll be even better once I've fully trained her."

Danner looked surprised. "You're not a full detective?"

"Trainee K-9 detective." She lifted her shoulders in a minuscule shrug. "Today starts my second week on the job."

"You did all that in a week? Well, count me even more impressed. Those're some fine instincts you have." He turned back to the sheriff and Eli. "You're mighty lucky to have her on your team. She's a fine officer."

Broc stood, chicken clamped tightly between his jaws in case anyone got any ideas about taking it away. He stepped closer to Indie.

He was probably wondering why she was blushing, why she was feeling uncomfortable. Praise was nice and all, but in front of everyone and making such a thing of it?

"The FBI could always use a sharp investigator like you."

Indie flashed Danner a quick smile and patted Broc on the head. A sharp investigating team like her *and* Broc?

"You couldn't keep him with you working for us, though."

And just like that, she had no problem telling him she was happy right where she was.

"We're about all tied up here now, so we'll get going," Danner told the sheriff.

"Hope not to see you again." Sammy nodded.

"I get that a lot," Danner said with a smile. "Until the next time."

The sheriff turned to Indie after they'd watched Danner leave. "Like he said, good job."

Eli slid the silver clasp of his shoestring tie down and back up. "Great start for sure."

"Well, I can't stand here yakking all day. I've got another media interview to get to." Sammy patted his hair. "Everyone wants a piece of me after we cracked this."

"We." Broc sounded incredulous.

Sammy looked away from her at the deputies milling around the station, at the empty desks where their occupants were out on patrol, on calls, off the clock. "Excellent chance for me to talk up what we do here and how I lead such good people."

Broc knocked gently into Indie's leg. *"You letting that go?"*

She'd have to have a conversation with the dog about her desire to avoid attention later.

Indie knew she'd done her job well and how important her input to the case had been. But now she was carrying the guilt at not having been able to talk Dr. Strickland down. The sheriff was very welcome to the airtime in front of cameras. She didn't want any part of that.

She sat down and rubbed Broc's head. "This is where I'm happy."

He put a paw on her leg. *"With the smartest dog in the world?"*

Indie's heart pinged in delight. "With the smartest dog in the world."

※

That evening, the smartest dog in the world was still in fine form when Indie parked in their driveway and let him out of her Jeep.

Aunt Edith walked off her porch toward them.

"Dinner at Aunt Edith's." Broc threw his prediction out before the older woman could speak a single word.

"You think? That would be lovely." So lovely, just the thought made Indie's fatigue vanish. She hoped he was right.

"Indie, dear, how are you feeling after everything?" Aunt Edith hugged her, a long and firm hold, the familiar welcome she needed while she processed the case's emotional toll.

"It's a lot, but I'm okay."

"Why don't y'all come join us for dinner?"

"We'd love to."

"But don't give me that green stuff." Broc's reminder came with an emphatic tap of his paw.

Hen stepped out of the house dressed in turquoise flowing pants and a purple cami. "Congratulations. You did it."

"We did. It was a team effort."

Hen stepped toward her as Indie stepped back. Indie stepped forward as Hen stepped back. Hen stuck her hand out, and Indie reached for it to stop the awkward dance. They grasped left hand to right hand—a strange clasp that had them both letting go instantly as the awkwardness bloomed. "Anyway, well done."

"You remember Cash?" Aunt Edith smiled at the man stepping out of the house onto the porch.

Indie blinked. She definitely would have remembered him if she'd seen him before.

Cash grinned, and her face heated. Tall with messy blond hair and a scruffy beard, the man was sexy as all hell.

Her face burned hotter. He tipped his head to one side, his grin widening as though he knew exactly what she was thinking.

She fought to get her brain back under control. *No more random thoughts about this Cash guy being sexy, thank you.* That word wasn't even part of her vernacular…usually.

"You look like we woke you up." Not so under control. Couldn't she have said something normal like "hi?"

"Are you okay?" Broc's question only highlighted her nerves. She clearly wasn't.

"He always looks like that." Hen rolled her eyes. "Probably spends hours trying to look like that."

"Is that any way to introduce your uncle?" Cash teased her before turning that million-dollar smile back on Indie. "Nice to meet you. Last time I saw you, you were about here." He held his hand out just above his waist.

"She was older than that." Hen lifted his hand up about a foot and a half.

"Well, she grew up good."

Great, now even her ears were burning, while her stomach did slow backflips, one after another.

Hen's uncle? That made him Aunt Edith's son. He hadn't looked like that when she was younger. "You're Obadiah?"

He winced. "Kind of dropped that. Just Cash these days."

Satch came out of the front door and headed straight to Indie. If a dog could frown, he would have. *"You're all sweaty. Did you go on a run?"*

Oh, boy, being caught in the middle of whatever this was made it so much worse. Indie looked at the ground. She didn't need to be a detective to notice how solid it was, what little chance a gravel pathway had of opening up to swallow and save her from further embarrassment.

Her hand slipped to the seam of her pants pocket as she risked a glance back at Cash.

"Come on in," Aunt Edith flapped her arms at them all, "'fore dinner gets cold."

"Tell Broc that heroes get extra broccoli." Satch bumped shoulders with Broc as they walked behind her. *"All the broccoli."*

Broc whined.

"Cut it out," Indie told them, sure that talking to her dogs would only cement Cash's opinion of her—that she was beyond awkward.

With bright-green florets only in Satch's bowl and nowhere near Broc's, dinner progressed smoothly. Mostly.

Except Indie actually found it harder to look away from Cash, as if he were north, and her eyes a compass. Embarrassing, especially given the dogs were both in tune. And after they'd cleaned their bowls, they'd come over and flanked her.

"They always like that?" Cash nodded at them, tearing a bread roll in half.

"Only with criminals." Hen waggled the tip of her knife at him. "Anything you want to share?"

He held his hands up as though surrendering to the dogs, looking from one to the other. "No criminal here, guys. And though I'm sure you can tell, I'll spell it out. I'm definitely team dog."

His gaze turned to Indie, because, of course, she was staring at him again.

"I'm team animal," she blurted and stared at the tablecloth. Why did she say that? What did that even mean?

Satch tilted his head. *"You like him. That why you're not eating?"*

Indie ignored him and picked up her fork.

"I can eat your dinner for you." Broc nonchalantly looked over the table to see what was left on Indie's plate.

She scooped up a forkful of mac and cheese and rammed it into her mouth.

Broc cocked his head. *"I thought you liked the V-E-T. You smelled like you'd been running lots then too."*

If it wouldn't have drawn more attention to her awkwardness, Indie would have covered her ears.

Satch seemed surprised. *"You don't normally like people at all, especially men."*

Indie tapped his shoulder twice, signaling him to hush. She couldn't handle a conversation regarding the state—or lack thereof—of her love life. When the dogs ambled away, Indie chewed, shoveling more pasta into her mouth.

When she'd cleared her plate, Indie put her knife and fork down. "Aunt Edith, that was lovely. Thank you. Really welcome, every day. I mean, I don't expect you to have us over for dinner every day." What was she saying? "I mean, I don't—"

Her phone usually annoyed her when it rang. Not now.

"Excuse me." She scrambled to her feet, tripping over the chair as she disentangled herself from her seat. "K-9 Detective Indira Reign."

The caller's frantic words blasted into Indie's ear, so loud she had to jerk the phone away. "Are you the detective who solved the Ascension case?"

How had a reporter gotten her number? "Ma'am, can I suggest you call the PR department in the morning? Or the sheriff—"

"Please, no, no, you have to listen to me. You're the one with the K-9, right?"

She glanced back at the table where every set of eyes was watching her closely. "Yes."

"I know you'll help me. You have to. Please…" Her voice cracked. "Say you and your dog'll find him. Please. I don't know where else to turn to find my husband."

The End
To be continued…

Thank you for reading.

All of the *Indie Reign* series books
can be found on Amazon.

ACKNOWLEDGMENTS

How does one adequately express gratitude to all those who have transformed a shared dream into a stunning reality? Let us attempt to do just that.

First and foremost, our families deserve our deepest thanks. Their unwavering support and encouragement have been our bedrock, allowing us the time and energy to translate our collective imagination into the words that fill these pages. Their belief in our vision has been a constant source of strength and inspiration.

As coauthors, our journey has been uniquely collaborative and rewarding. Now, with Mary also embracing the additional role of publisher, our adventure has taken on an exciting new dimension. This transition from solely writing to also publishing has been both a challenge and a joy, opening doors to share our work more directly with you, our readers.

We are immensely grateful to the entire team at Mary Stone Publishing — a group who believed in our potential from the very beginning. Their commitment extends beyond editing our words; it encompasses the tireless efforts of designers, marketers, and support staff, all dedicated to bringing our stories to life. Their expertise, creativity, and passion have been vital in capturing the essence of our tales and sharing them with the world.

However, our greatest appreciation is reserved for you, our beloved readers. You took a chance on our book, generously sharing your most precious asset—your time. It is our fervent hope that the pages of this book have rewarded that generosity, offering you a journey worth taking and memories that linger.

With all our love and heartfelt appreciation,

Mary & Karen

ABOUT THE AUTHOR

MARY STONE

Nestled in the tranquil Blue Ridge Mountains of East Tennessee, Mary Stone has transformed her peaceful home, once bustling with her sons, into a creative haven. As her family grew, so did her writing career, evolving from childhood fears to a deep understanding of real-life villains. Her stories, centered around strong, unconventional heroines, weave themes of courage and intrigue.

Mary's journey from a solitary writer to establishing her own publishing house marks a significant evolution, showcasing her commitment to the literary world. Through her writing and publishing endeavors, she continues to captivate and inspire, honoring her lifelong fascination with the mysterious and the courageous.

Connect with Mary online

facebook.com/authormarystone
x.com/MaryStoneAuthor
goodreads.com/AuthorMaryStone
bookbub.com/authors/mary-stone
instagram.com/marystoneauthor

Discover more about Mary Stone on her website.
www.authormarystone.com

❄

KAREN GUYLER

Always being the new girl at nine schools on two continents was no fun at all so books became the only constant in Karen Guyler's life. It's a shame they couldn't help her get out of sports days. Now settled in Milton Keynes, England—Britain's best kept secret—she juggles reading with writing, her husband, their children and their partners and two grand-dogs, a much nicer mix. Karen is a Reiki Master and rolls out her yoga mat as often as she can in between swimming, trekking, cycling and trying to remember to lift weights. If she were ever bored, she could tackle her growing "it's gone wrong" pile of ambitious knitting and crocheting projects.

Connect with Karen online

facebook.com/karenguylerauthor
instagram.com/karen_guyler_author
x.com/originalkaren
tiktok.com/@thrillerbooks
uk.linkedin.com/in/karenguyler

Discover more about Karen Guyler on her website.
www.karenguyler.com

Printed in Dunstable, United Kingdom